DON'T BELIEVE HER

JANE HEAFIELD

BLOODHOUND
— BOOKS —

Print ISBN 978-1-913942-23-6

ALSO BY JANE HEAFIELD

Dead Cold

PART I

1

LUCY

You'll get two versions of this story. But Mary is a liar. Don't believe her. Not one word. What I'm about to tell you is the truth. And it all started with a terrible accusation...

We weren't expecting visitors at The Cascade, so it was a shock to get a rap on the door. I opened it to see two of my husband's male friends, and his sister.

I'd been with Tom for eight years, married for five, and in all that time Mary and I had never seen eye to eye. We have nothing in common except being roughly the same age: we don't like the same music, or hobbies, or food; we're even opposites in appearance, with Mary six inches shorter at barely five-and-a-half feet, skin pale, hair long and black. About the only thing we did agree on was a love of apple juice. And, of course, that the other woman in Tom's life was a pain in the backside.

I didn't even know why we had this enemy status. I didn't take Tom away from his family, because they lived near us, and I don't stop him seeing his friends or indulging his hobby. I always wondered if it was because we didn't have children. Mary was infertile, so maybe it was a sore point that she hadn't been gifted a niece or nephew.

Or perhaps it was because, at forty-three, I was an eyebrow-raising eighteen years his senior. But I was guessing. In eight years of antagonising me, she'd never provided an answer or even a clue as to why I rubbed her up the wrong way.

Anyway, here she was, wearing a face I suspect she'd honed and reserved solely for me: obvious distaste at sharing the same air.

'Are you here for Tom?' I said. The door was only halfway open and I partially hid behind it, with a foot pressed against the wood as a stopper in case Mary tried to barge inside. I saw Tom's rusty spare key in her hand; if not for my own on the inside of the locked door, she would have walked straight in.

'Who else? He's missed my calls today.' For a petite girl as pale as a vampire, Mary had a potent anger. She was an assistant amateur football coach and Tom had told me he'd seen lads bigger than him cow before her.

One of his friends said, 'It's trucker night.'

Tom and his friends love monster trucks. Four of them – including this pair – own and operate one called Animal, and on this Sunday night it was on show at an event in Manchester, some thirty miles from The Cascade.

The Cascade, by the way, was the name of the getaway cottage Tom and I were staying at. Cullerton, in the constituency of Chorley, Lancashire, is a tiny village off the A675, about half a mile east of Abbey Village and a few hundred metres north of Rake Brook Reservoir. Tom and I liked to rent the place a couple of times a year to unwind and usually picked rainy weekends.

It was summer, but we'd been blessed with a very wet pair of days. When the skies soaked the land, the brook right outside the cottage turned from idyllic to manic and the noise was song-like. There was a very picturesque waterfall, hence the name Cascade.

'But you weren't supposed to come here,' I told them, which was true. The plan had been for Tom to leave the cottage in the early evening and meet his friends at the event, since there was no point in his travelling back to Sheffield, where we, his friends and sister lived.

'Well he wasn't answering my calls, so I came to make sure he was coming,' Mary bellowed. 'So where is he?'

'He's...' A loose grip of my mobile phone caused it to slip out of my hand. I bent to pick it up. 'Tom is not available.'

'What's that mean?' Mary jerked a thumb over her shoulder, to where Tom's BMW 3 Series was parked on the dirt track running past the cottage. Mary's sports utility vehicle and another car are parked near it. 'He's not out at all. His car's here. Why hasn't he been answering my calls?'

'No, he actually is out. He stayed on the walk.'

I explained. Earlier, Tom and I had crossed a makeshift bridge over Low Man Brook, a tributary of the River Darwen, and taken a stroll along a hiker's path through the woodland, heading for a pub/restaurant called the Fox and Hound a couple of miles away. Shortly thereafter I got tired and wanted to return home, but didn't want to ruin Tom's hike so convinced him to go on. I said I would take the car and meet him later. I returned to the cottage without him.

Mary took out her mobile phone and made a call. I said, 'Don't bother phoning Tom. He left his mobile phone here.'

She called anyway. My uninvited guests raised their eyes skyward as we all heard the faint ringing of a mobile from the bedroom upstairs.

Mary snorted like a bull about to charge. 'This is the tenth time he's not answered. I called him about midday to remind him what time we'd be here. It isn't like him to not answer all day. I don't like this. Is this because of the argument?'

'What argument?'

She gave another snort, but this time one of derision. 'Don't act all innocent. Tom told me all about it. He said you were shouting at him in the pub last night. Is this because you haven't had your tablets?'

Embarrassed, I glanced at Tom's two male friends and noticed they had taken a couple of steps back, obviously perturbed at watching Tom's sister and wife argue. 'I wasn't shouting at him. We had a falling out because he was smoking his vape and getting a funny look. He ignored me when I told him to put it away. It had nothing to do with my medication. Then we left, and we were fine. If we had fallen out, we wouldn't have taken that walk this morning, would we? Couples fight, not that you'd know.'

That barb at the end stung, I could see, but she ignored it. 'So where is he? Did something happen at the pub to cause another falling out?'

'I just told you—'

'Not last night, you fool. Today. At the Fox and Hound, where you said you were going. You drove to meet him. Was there another so-called falling out there?'

'I didn't meet him. I got sidetracked. He'd already texted that if I changed my mind about meeting him, he'd see me back here later.'

'Texted?' She loaded the word with mockery. 'His phone is right here.'

'I meant he said it. On the walk, when I was about to head back. He said it to me then.'

I could tell she didn't like this answer, given the imperceptible shake of her head. Even Tom's two friends looked at each other suspiciously. Mentioning a text had been a silly slip, but I knew my error now gave the impression I was lying, although why she'd assumed that was beyond me. What could I possibly be hiding?

So I got defensive. 'Look, why is this so hard to understand? Tom and I went for a walk this morning. I got tired and hurt my foot. I told Tom to go on without me, and he said if he didn't see me at the Fox later, he'd see me back home.'

'Okay, nice and clear, thank you,' Mary said with sarcasm. 'Except he went out this morning and it's nearly eight at night. I must have misunderstood something, because I know you can't be claiming he's still out on that same walk.'

'No, he hasn't come back yet.'

Tom's two friends pulled puzzled faces and checked their watches. I knew what Mary was going to say next. 'Tom never misses appointments, and he knew we were coming. And you say he's still out from this morning? Are you sure something else didn't happen?'

'Like what? Yes, I'm sure. Maybe he forgot about the truck event.'

That claim raised eyebrows – three sets. 'He never misses a truck show,' one of his friends said. Now, clearly, they were all doubting me.

'Look, ask Tom when he comes back. I don't know the answers. Maybe he's on his way to the event right now. Maybe he was still a little annoyed at me so didn't mention it. Which brings up a point, actually. Why did you all come here? You should be down at the event, wondering where he is. Turning up here like this you would have missed him.'

'We decided to come pick him up, that's all,' Mary answered. 'Good job we did, or we wouldn't have found out something dodgy is going on.'

'Nothing dodgy is going on.' Five seconds ago I felt weighed down by their eyes, but now I only feel rising annoyance. I shouldn't have to accept being interrogated on my own doorstep. 'Look, Tom's not here, so you have no reason to be. Go to the truck show and maybe you'll find him. I'm closing the door now. Goodbye.'

I tried to shut the door, but she stepped forward and put a hand on it. 'Calm down. We'll go in a minute. I need Tom's mobile phone. There's a number I need out of it. So you're going to have to let me in.'

I told her I'd go and fetch it instead. I didn't really want to let them in, because the house was a little messy, but I made the mistake of leaving it open.

The mobile was on the vanity desk in our bedroom. As I picked it up, I heard:

'I need to use your toilet.'

I nearly jumped out of my skin. Mary was in the doorway, having crept upstairs right behind me. She had clearly taken the open front door as an invitation to enter. I clutched the phone to my chest. 'It's rude to sneak behind me like that. What exactly do you need from Tom's phone? I don't think he'd like you snooping in his private property.'

She almost spat at me. 'I'm his sister. What secrets would he keep from me?'

'Then I don't want you seeing text messages between us. For all I know he's taken sneaky pictures of me getting undressed. Tell me what you need from it and I'll find it.'

'He took a photo of an internet voucher.'

Standing there, with the double bed between us like a barrier, I accessed his photos, and sure enough what she wanted was there. I held the device out and showed her, but kept a tight grip in case she tried to reach over the bed and snatch it. Also leaning and reaching out her arm, she took a photo of the photo with her own device.

'Now I need that toilet.'

Before I could object, she zipped into the bathroom and slammed the door. Suspicious that she might try to look around the bedroom if I left, I stayed put. Not that I had a chance to move – within a second of entry, she yanked the door open.

'What's this mess? What's happened in here?'

She returned inside. I moved into the doorway so I could see. She was pointing at blood. A spattering of it in a series of thin lines across the sink and the floor. She was aghast.

'I thought it had been cleaned up,' I said.

'You thought you'd cleaned it up? Is this Tom's blood? What the hell happened?'

I moved past her so I could grab toilet paper with which to remove the mess. 'Tom cut himself. I thought he'd cleaned it up. He said he would. I was downstairs, so I didn't see what happened.'

'So how do you know what happened?'

I was squatting down in order to mop up the mess and she stepped closer, to tower right over me. I didn't like my vulnerable position so stood. The top of her head didn't even reach my nose, yet I felt trapped. I tried to step back, but the toilet was right there.

'Tom cut himself on one of the taps. He came downstairs with a bandaged finger. I thought he'd cleaned it up. He said he had.'

Mary grabbed my arm with the speed of a striking cobra. The shock caused me to drop the balled, red-stained toilet paper.

'And what's this?' she said, lifting my arm so I could see. Right below where her stick-like fingers barely encircled half my biceps, my yellow blouse had a thin streak of blood. I stared at it in horror. 'Is this Tom's blood? How can it be if you were downstairs? And if he'd bandaged it already? How could it get on you?'

I avoided her intense green eyes. I focused on the ragged bloodstain below my elbow, amazed that I had missed it all day. 'No, that's my blood. I had a nosebleed. That's where I wiped it.'

I tried to pull my arm free, but Mary had a firm grip. 'You had a nosebleed?' she said, mocking my claim. 'That's stupid. This isn't a nose-wipe stain, it's more like from flying blood. And no way would prim you go out in this blouse if it was stained.'

Mary let go of my arm – more of a push away, actually – and pulled out her handkerchief and dabbed at the sink, and scrutinised the blood staining the white material. I used that moment of distraction to slip by her, to stand outside the bathroom. 'The taps are clean,' she said. 'What, he cleaned the taps and left this mess on the sink and floor?' She balled up the handkerchief and put it in her pocket.

'Maybe he didn't see the...' I stopped, very aware how silly my answer was going to sound.

Mary slapped at both of the taps, hard, five, six times, and even scraped the back of her hands all over them. It was a maniacal gesture. 'And how can a tap cut you? They're rounded and smooth. They're not cutting me, look. You better tell me what really happened.'

I remember thinking the same thing about the taps, so her doubt had a strong foundation. But I'd had enough of her attitude, here in my own place. 'Well I don't know how he cut himself, if it couldn't have been the taps, like you so professionally demonstrated. Look, I need to tidy. Tom's not here and you got what you wanted, so I'd like you to leave.'

I didn't even get time to clear the doorway. She pushed past me and headed out. I followed at a careful distance. She said nothing until she was outside, where she turned towards me as I stopped in the doorway. Tom's friends had waited exactly where they stood. 'Something's not right here. Tom wouldn't miss the truck show. You're lying about something.'

Time seemed to have looped. Again she stood slightly in front of her comrades, while I half-hid behind the oak front door with a foot braced to prevent it from being pushed open. I told her to go try to find Tom at the event.

'Oh I will. I'll scan every face in there. And if I don't see him, I'm coming right back here, Lucy. And I'm bringing the police.'

I almost dropped to my knees. 'Why would you want the police?'

She jerked her head as a way of telling Tom's friends it was time to leave. 'Come on, I'll explain in the car.'

As they walked away, the friends looking thoroughly confused, I called out, 'What are you talking about, Mary? What do you mean, bring the police?'

She didn't answer, but I heard her say something to the pair of friends about a 'tap'. I stayed by the door until their car had turned on the dirt road and gone. As it pulled away, all three occupants glared.

I didn't like that look. I didn't like the horrible feeling I was getting. The blood and Tom's not being here appeared a little suspicious, I had to admit, but surely they couldn't think I'd done something to him? That I'd hurt Tom so bad he was going to miss the truck show. He was twice my size, which made the idea preposterous.

But I had seen that look on their faces as they left. That was exactly what they thought.

MARY

Everything spat out of Lucy's foul mouth is a lie. Take that bullshit, burn it, and bury the ashes. Don't believe her, not back then, not now, not in the future. I'll tell you the truth – not a *version* – of what happened. And it all starts with a nasty feeling that something is wrong...

'Is something up with Tom?'

That question comes from Fat Pete, my brother's estate agency business partner, who calls me while I'm making Dad his breakfast. I grip the mobile hard because I've got a pretty good idea what's coming next out of the guy's trap.

'Mary? You there? Is Tom okay? He's not at work. He didn't call in. His mobile is dead.'

And there we go. Every time Tom's missed some appointment, meeting, party or whatever, he's called ahead to explain why. He missed the truck show last night and now he's missed work on Monday morning, and in both cases there's been no contact. Not right.

'Mary? Can you hear me?'

'I'll go find out.' I hang up. I rush through finishing Dad's breakfast, change into cleaner jeans and a shirt, then grab my car keys. I tell him I'm going to the shops. Sorry for the lie, Dad.

Tom's house is only a ten-minute drive from where I live. I make it in five, sure I've been caught by one red light and one speed camera, but so what? Points on my licence and a fine: the last things on my mind. With Tom's no-show at the truck event last night, I should have kicked in that cottage door and throttled answers out of his damn wife, and I should have kept my promise to get the cops involved.

Like I said, this all started with the feeling something was out of whack, and I shouldn't have ignored it. I'm angry that Lucy managed to trick me into giving her the benefit of the doubt. Maybe those damn incense sticks she fills the cottage with clouded my mind. I chose to wait and see if the new day brought a smile, and the new day kicked me in the teeth. I'm just as angry at myself for being so blind and ready to do some kicking of my own.

With time to spare on that short drive, I think about calling Tom's pals. His two partners who accompanied me to The Cascade last night must have gossiped like old women when they got home, because late into the night I had missed calls from three of Tom's circle. They were worried about him because they got no reply to their calls to his mobile. Or to Lucy's. The bitch must have ignored them, knowing she'd have no good answers.

This morning I sent two of his buddies a text message each saying I'd get back to them. And I made a call to someone called Jen, because the lass and her hubby are Tom's oldest pals. All three had been close since primary school and Jen and her man had been school sweethearts, although she'd got bored of him recently, because he was a fat slob, and had started cheating on him.

It's early in the United States, but Jen was up. She hadn't been contacted by Tom's gossiping partners, so knew sod all about Tom's disappearance until I mentioned it. Lucy hadn't called or texted to ask if she'd heard from him. Calling pals is the first thing anyone would do if a loved one was missing, yet I'd bet money Lucy hadn't rung a soul.

I had told Jen I didn't like Lucy's tale about Tom's vanishing, but made sure I hid the worry from my voice. Jen might live thousands of miles away, but she'd have hopped right on a jet if she thought Tom was in trouble. I'd told her I'd call back when I knew more.

Well, after the call from Fat Pete, I now know more. Like an idiot, and in the face of what I'd learned on my visit to The Cascade, I chose to believe that Tom might be back in the morning. Wish I hadn't. Foolish. And now the horror can't be ignored, so I pull my phone to ring Jen again.

But she doesn't answer and there's no time to try again. I've arrived. Tom's home is semi-detached with gravel out front to make a driveway. As I pull up at the kerb, I see something worrying. Lucy's crappy Ford Focus sits before the front window. The space where Tom lays up his BMW is empty.

I slam my car door hard, because I want some of her neighbours to see this. Then I rap on the front door loudly. When Lucy answers, it's at the bedroom window. She opens it and sticks her head out. Lit from behind by the sky, and with her cheap blonde bob creating an alcove for her face, I can't really see her eyes, but they look sleepy. Tom's cat is there, too, both of them peering down at me.

I named the cat when he bought it – Zuzu – but I don't like the thing because it always gives me a look like it would bite my head off if I was its size. It's lightly raining and looking up at Lucy means squinting, but I can see the same look on her ugly face.

'Tom didn't go to work,' I yell. That seems to wake her up. I don't take up much space in the world, but I've got a deep, operatic voice. 'And his phone is dead.'

'He's ill in bed,' Lucy replies after a pause I don't like. I tell her he also didn't call in sick, and her reply begins with a slapped forehead, totally contrived. 'I was supposed to call in for him. I got sidetracked. He lost his phone.'

'His car's not here.'

She pauses and stares at the empty spot in the driveway. 'I think he said something about lending it to a friend.'

Tom's prized BMW? He'd sooner let a pal bang his wife than drive his car. Even I got a big fat no when I asked one time. I try the handle, but the front door is locked. 'Let me in. I want to see him. Is this something to do with yesterday and your silly tap story?'

'What do you mean? Tom cutting himself? No, that was just a finger cut. He's got stomach problems today.' Her eyes go up, across the road. I look back and see some nosey bint in the house opposite has stuck herself to her living room window to see what all the commotion is about. Good.

'Well, that might be because of his insulin,' I call up to Lucy. Then, louder, 'Let me in. I need to see if his blood sugar is okay.' After that I call for Tom, even louder. No answer, and Lucy just keeps her bleary eyes on me instead of looking back into the bedroom, to see if he heard. Which she would have if he'd been in bed.

'Why are you yelling for him? He's asleep. You'll have to see him later. He told me not to wake him for anything.'

I'm seething. 'Is he hurt, Lucifer?' It's my secret nickname for her, although I've never before used it to her face. 'Did you have a fight or something, like before? I know he didn't cut his hand on a damn tap. What the hell is going on? Why do you look like a zombie? Have you been up all night? Are you on drugs?'

She's very calm when she answers with a repeat of the same dross: Tom's ill, doesn't want to be interrupted, she'll get him to call me and call work later. And what she did overnight is none of my business, apparently. As for the drugs, the bitch thinks she's got a smart comeback:

'Why, do you want some for your death-row friend?'

I have a pen pal in America who's on death row. So what? If she thinks an unimaginative crack like that will upset me, she's a whole level more stupid than I thought. I don't rise to it. 'Tom sent me a text about your argument in the pub on Saturday night and I've forwarded it to other people. So a lot of people know you had a falling out. Wake him up. Let me in. I want to see my brother.'

She flicks her dodgy gaze up and down the street, worried about onlookers. Good. I want her neighbours to hear. I want them to gossip about her. I want them to shun her like a leper. Then she shakes her head. 'No, Tom gave me instructions not to wake him. Now go home and I'll get him to call you later. And work.'

There's no silly incense to hypnotise me here, so I'm going nowhere. 'I need something from his backpack. My batteries are in it.'

This stuns her. I can almost hear her rotten brain whirring as it scrabbles for an answer. It's obvious she's thinking hard, and I can't help but say it.

'That's the same look you had last night, Lucy. You were trying to buy time and you're doing it now. I want his bag, right now.'

Tom's backpack is his version of a lady's handbag. He takes it to work, to the shops, and every time he goes on walks up in Cullerton. If she can't produce it, right now, then that's concrete proof Tom didn't come home last night. Which means something bad definitely happened up at that cottage in Lancashire.

Lucy vanishes from the window, leaving Zuzu and me to glare at each other, and for a moment I wonder what the hell I'll say if she hangs Tom's backpack out the window. Doesn't happen. She's back a few seconds later and she's got her purse in her hand. A five-pound note see-saws and somersaults its way down to me.

'You'll have to buy some new batteries. Tom lost his bag while in the woods.'

Right in the middle of summer, and I feel a cold shiver. I hadn't noticed that I'd left my fist wrapped around the front door handle, which I now need to keep me from faceplanting on the doorstep. Concrete proof.

Numb, I head back to my car. I can see that a couple of neighbours' faces are at windows. I slump behind the wheel, mind cycling through the gut-churning evidence from this morning and last night. The raging barney, which I know is just one of many Tom and Lucy have had over the last few months. The domestic violence Tom has told me he'd suffered. His dead mobile. The missed truck event and now a missed work day.

The blood in the bathroom, and Lucy's bizarre explanation for it.

I pull out my mobile and call the cops. The nightmare is real. Lucy has killed her own hubby, my brother, and is trying to cover her tracks.

2

LUCY

When Mary sat in her flash Range Rover, watching my house, I knew that she was waiting for the police. Every few minutes, I joined my cat, Zuzu, at the bedroom window. Zuzu was probably watching the birds that alighted in gardens and atop lamp posts, but I watched Mary's car.

I had expected the police to visit me last night, back at the cottage. Deep into the dead hours, with sleep denied to me, I watched my phone buzz with calls from Tom's friends. Mary must have eagerly called them to spread this vicious rumour that I've hurt Tom. I ignored the calls because I hoped Tom would be back home in the morning, thus negating the need for an explanation. The whole thing would be forgotten. If asked why I hadn't answered the phone, I'd say it had been late and I'd fallen asleep.

I saw a patrol car turn onto my street fifty metres up the road, so that gave me time to plough my fingers through my hair, although it was knotty and tangled and I didn't use a mirror, so I probably made it worse. I smoothed my right eyebrow to try to hide the four thin diagonal slits as best I could. The baggy eyes I could do nothing about. I'd had a sleepless night.

When I rushed to the window again, the car was stopped outside and two officers got out. A young man and a woman in sleeveless high-vis jackets and short-sleeved shirts, both tall and imposing. The woman looked a little like me, and I could see the shock on her face, which matched my own surprise, when I answered the door. Mary was beside them, a good foot shorter. Beyond them were faces at windows. This little urban street was as uneventful as hundreds of others in Sheffield and today's activity would be talked about.

Unlike Mary, the police weren't likely to push their way inside, so I didn't need to hide behind the door. I threw it wide open and didn't give them a chance to speak: I knew why they were here. 'I'm Lucy Packham, Tom's wife. He's not here. He stayed in Cullerton. Nothing's wrong.'

'That's a lie,' Mary barked. That big voice of hers, on a body tiny and insignificant next to the tall officers. 'She said he was ill and couldn't come down.'

'He was ill when I left him, but I didn't say he was here. I left him up there in Cullerton. That's why his car's not here. Or his bag. I don't know why she thought I said he was here.'

'You left him up there all right, probably dead. Look at the state of her. Have you been up all night, worrying about what you did?'

In part I could understand her shock. Embarrassed because Tom had abandoned me in Cullerton and hadn't come back to the cottage last night, I had foolishly pretended that he was ill in bed this morning. I did this to make Mary think all was okay between us, because nobody wants to admit they fell out with a spouse, do they?

Her question about Tom's BMW and his backpack threw me off and I gave an impromptu answer, which I shouldn't have done. I know it reinforced her belief that I was lying, but the damage was done. But that didn't excuse her wild accusation.

But before I could object to this foolishness, the female police officer took Mary aside for a chat. Or a telling off, hopefully. The male said to me, 'Your husband's sister called us because she's not happy with your story of why your husband isn't here. Can you tell me that story? Inside?'

I nodded and turned away. The officer followed me down the hallway and into the living room. Through the bay window, I saw Mary and the female officer get into the patrol car. The woman officer was probably going to get an outrageous tale, and it made me want to get mine out first. So I immediately launched into it without even sitting down.

I'd known Tom for eight years. We'd met when I returned from Germany, where I'd been sent on a work placement after school. Germany was nice, so after the six-month placement I decided to stay a little longer. I was there for seventeen years. 'But then I chose to come back.'

'Why was that?'

I paused. 'Personal reasons. Anyway, that was how I met Tom. He was only eighteen, but he owned an estate agent's, and I needed somewhere to rent.'

I saw the surprise in the policeman's eyes. It often shocked people to hear that a teenager had bought and operated a successful business. Or maybe he'd worked out that, at eighteen, Tom would have been half my age when we met.

MARY

As I talk to the female officer in her car, I can't help glancing at Tom's house. The morning sunlight glares off the living room window, so I can't see beyond, but I can easily imagine the pantomime playing out inside. Lucy will be sitting down, probably with her dowdy knee-length skirt hiked up a little to show some patchy thigh; she'll have a childishly pouted face of sadness and an emotion-cracked voice; and she will be lying through her back teeth.

I must have been a bit hypnotised by that window because the female copper has to re-ask her question: 'Mary? You said Tom owns an estate agent's?'

I drag my eyes from the house. 'Yes. Since he was eighteen.' In my purse is a picture of Tom and me, arm in arm, snapped at a monster truck event ten days ago in Manchester. At over six feet tall, Tom literally casts a shadow across me. He's in a T-shirt that shows his toned arms. His hair is slicked back and he's got a thick beard, which I've often said makes him look like a castaway. The officer keeps the photo in her hand as I continue.

'Our parents had a construction company which they sold when Mum got ill, about ten years ago. She died two years ago. They bought two houses, one for each of us. I got given mine immediately, but Tom was only thirteen at that time and had to wait until he was eighteen. Tom sold his and used the money to buy an office and set up an estate agency. He wanted to get into property development eventually, but the agency stuff stuck. That's how he met Lucy. She was living in Germany, forced over there by her parents–'

'Forced?'

'Oh, sure. She'd probably say her parents gave her a choice, but that's not what she told Tom. What Tom told me. They wanted rid of her, so they sent her off to work overseas. She got married over there like six months after meeting some idiot. After she was fired from the job her parents set up, she was teaching English, but she messed that up, too. She even spent time in a mental hospital over there. She's supposed to be on antidepressants now, but she's not been taking them for a couple of weeks. I bet she won't tell you about the mental home or being abusive to her hubby back then. You should look into that. Anyway, after her life over there fell apart, Tom helped her find a place when she ran away–'

'Ran away?'

'Oh, sure! She fled back here with her tail between her legs. That's when she ensnared Tom. Tom's agency only deals with commercial properties and offices and stuff now, but it used to be flats as well. So he was showing her around a place one day and they hit it off. She wooed him because he was only young and she was already in her thirties. That's all it was. He was a kid mesmerised by the trickery of an older woman. She knew he had money, being only eighteen and owning his own business. Bet you didn't know that he has a contract with his partner that neither man can sell their share of the business unless both agree to sell? Yep. Tom set that up so Lucy couldn't force him to sell and then take his money. She tries to act all young and hip, especially around Tom. You've seen those four eyebrow slits she has. Stupid, she's not a teenager. But she likes the younger men, used to flirt all the time with Tom's male buddies. They were engaged within nine months. She's a cradle-snatcher...'

3

LUCY

'...grave-robber, that's what some people think of Tom,' I told the male officer, with no hidden disgust. He was sitting on the other armchair with a notepad he hadn't yet used. 'That he wanted an older woman. But we got on well. Age didn't matter. His sister hates it. Tom and Mary were given houses by their parents and when they sold them, Mary blew the money on the high-life, parties and holidays and such, until it was all gone, and now she's living with her father in the hopes of getting his house when he dies, and she's in love with a prisoner in America who's a lot younger, so she's not one to talk.'

'Can I ask about your relationship now? Do you argue?'

I became a little unstuck here. I'd always thought Tom and I had a good marriage. Not perfect, but whose is after so many years? I didn't think we were in danger of splitting up, let's put it that way. However, he'd left me without notice, apparently without cause, and it was hard to still think of our bond as strong.

As for arguing: 'Of course we argue. All couples do. But we make up. Most couples do.'

'How about on the weekend? On Sunday, the day Tom disappeared? Or Saturday? Mary said there was an argument on the Saturday evening.'

'Of course she did. Look, we had a little fall out on Saturday night, at a pub, and a little argument Sunday morning, and that's when he walked away. But it wasn't as bad as Mary makes out. She's never liked me because I'm the only thing that ever bypassed her force field.'

'What do you mean?'

'Mary is very controlling of her brother, has been forever, because she's older. I respect that, as a young teenager, she took care of him when he was a toddler. But it's continued into adult life. She started looking after his money, telling him what to spend, what he couldn't have. She tells him how to style his hair, what kind of clothes to wear, even though I'm his wife. I have to watch his money for him or she'll spend it for him. And girls, she always vetted the girls he wanted to date. But not me. The only thing he ever got to choose was me. She never liked me, and she wanted him to end the relationship. It was the only thing he ever said no to her about. She hates me because of it.'

The male officer moved on: 'So what happened over the weekend?'

I recounted the story. Tom and I had arrived in Cullerton on Saturday morning, spent the afternoon unpacking at the cottage, and in the evening visited the local pub, the Serengeti, for a meal – free due to the fact that Tom and the landlord are friends because of their love of monster machines. The next morning, we got dressed for a hike in the rain and crossed the brook and went into the woods.

There, we had another slight argument, nothing serious, but when I hurt my foot and wanted to return, Tom insisted on going on ahead. We split up and I went back to the cottage. He didn't return that evening. I stayed up most of the night, waiting for him, but must have drifted off at some point. Early the next morning, when he still wasn't back, I drove home alone.

During the relationship backstory, the officer hadn't jotted a word in his pad. But when it came to my story of what happened on Sunday, he started scribbling. 'Is that common? For Tom to stay out overnight?'

'Oh yes. Tom likes to visit his friends. At my age they're all married off, but his friends are young and still like to hang out. So he sees them a lot. And sometimes he stays out because of monster machine shows – you know, if they're far away and it's easier to get a hotel. That's why I'm not worried that he's not back. He will be.'

'And you've contacted his friends? To see if anyone has heard from him?'

'Well, no, not yet. If he needs space, I thought it best not to.'

'Okay. Well, we can do that. I'll need a list of friends and family, if you can get me that. So, Tom is known to stay out overnight without contacting you?'

'Oh yes...'

MARY

'...No way,' I almost spit, with probably my thousandth glance out the passenger window at Tom's house. 'Without word? No, no way. Sometimes my brother will stay out overnight because he's away at an event – he watches monster machine shows around the country. He and some friends own one that performs in the shows. But he will always text me or call his business partner, or someone. Or post something on Facebook. He'll never not contact someone.'

The female officer raises a finger to slow me, like a matronly teacher. 'But you did say he left his phone behind.'

'Yes, but that's also suspicious. Tom wouldn't plan to be away overnight without his phone. He's never gone off on a jaunt while he's staying at the cottage. And he wouldn't ever miss a truck show. Never has, until now. His wife's story is a blatant lie, I tell you.'

The female officer gives a slight nod that I can't read. 'So, bottom line is that this is out of character for him?'

'Yes. That's what I've been trying to tell you.'

In a rush when I called the police, I blurted all the evidence down the phone to the operator, so maybe she was doing that day's shopping list in her head and didn't catch it all. Now, nice and slow, I list everything that doesn't gel with Lucy's little fantasy tale. 'So that's why you have to search the house, and you have to go up to Cullerton to search the cottage. They had a big falling out at the pub on Saturday. Big, and that's not usual.'

'So it's not a volatile relationship?'

'No, no way. Tom loved her. And he's the most easy-going man in the world, so he was not one for starting arguments. Which is a good thing, because she's violent.'

'Violent?'

'Yes. The last time they had a big argument, she hit him. And that's why I know she's done something to Tom. If they had a big argument, I doubt she can control her anger. Here, let me show you a text message he sent me...'

4

LUCY

…Sorry for falling out lets take a make-up walk through woods
tomorrow.

The male officer took a long look at the text message, but I
pulled my phone back when he raised a finger to the screen.
Although I would happily show him other texts if he asked, I
would have to sift through them first. Some were personal ones
from Tom. Sexy, even.

'What was the argument in the woods about?'

'Nothing, really. We were both in a bad mood, I think. He
stormed off and I guess I was happy to let him.'

'Why didn't you call the police when he didn't return that
evening?'

'I know the woods can be dangerous, but Tom's a well-built
young man and only a fool would try to harm him.'

'It didn't have to be an attack. Were you not worried he
might have fallen or injured himself in some way? He didn't take
his mobile phone.'

'No. I mean, the woodland trail is popular with hikers. If he'd gotten hurt, someone would have found him. You can check hospitals if you like.' I added the last bit out of irritation because of his tone, as if he thought I was silly. I often spoke to Zuzu like that.

'We'll do that. Now, his sister mentioned he's diabetic. That's a worry if he's out there and something goes wrong–'

I cut in here with, 'No, Tom always has his insulin. He's type-one and insulin-dependent, so always carries it around with him. Always.'

The officer nodded and then looked out of the window at the sound of a car door slamming shut. 'My partner and your husband's sister are coming back. We'll have a little group chat and then I'd like to search the house.'

I watched the two women walk towards my house, seeking a sign that the interview hadn't gone Mary's way. But she had a contented swagger, and I knew she'd had a good old time ripping me to shreds in front of the police officer. It annoyed me so much that the male officer got an abrupt answer. 'Why search the house? He's not hiding under the bed.'

He took it well enough. 'You'd be surprised how many missing people we find hidden in their own homes. Even adults.'

MARY

After a half-arsed peek around the house, the two coppers chatter out by their car, leaving me and Lucy alone. I'm on the armchair, she's on the sofa. She won't look at me, but my eyes are nailed to her.

She's hugging herself and slightly rocking, and I've read somewhere that this is a subconscious signal of deception, to put it nicely. She's closing up because her lies are being challenged. In that tacky quarter-zip fleece, she certainly isn't cold. She even licks her over-glossed lips, which some say is a way of wiping away spoken untruths. How the cops didn't notice her guilty-as-hell body language is beyond me. Or maybe this is exactly what they're jabbering about outside.

I realise it's been over a year since I was last in this living room, and back then most of the furniture was in the kitchen because the place was being decorated. Tom knows sister and wife are enemies and tries to keep us apart. When he meets me for a catch-up, it's usually outside or at his office, but almost never here. And when Lucy visits my dad, which she tries to do once a week to watch their special TV programme, it's always when I'm out.

So on the day I helped with decorating, Lucy wasn't around. I helped Tom with the wallpapering, but now wish I hadn't. The clock on the wall, the pictures, and a crappy little floating shelf are all Lucy's additions, but she would have probably vetoed the wallpaper if it wasn't to her taste. I chose it and put effort into hanging it for my brother, yet she enjoys it, and I don't like that. Is that petty? Can't help it.

But I smile when my eyes go to a spot above the fireplace. In a childish moment, I scribbled LUCY SMELLS on the wall before plastering flowery paper over it. I want to be right there in that room on the day she tears the paper down to put a new roll up and spots my sweet little message.

I'm surprised she hasn't changed the wallpaper already. This is Tom's house, but it wears a mask applied by Lucy. All around I see evidence of her foul touch. He put the fireplace in, but she's painted it demonic altar black. Tom bought the three-piece suite, yet the slate-grey fabric hides beneath tacky purple throws. On an alcove shelf is a monster truck trophy, but you can hardly see it behind a trio of ugly snow globes. The full-length curtains are a gruesome bright blue – Lucy's favourite colour.

And where's the large monster truck print I bought him? No doubt demoted to the bathroom like some thrift shop piece of junk. How dare he act like it's his home too?

The uncomfortable silence I force on Lucy begins to wear on her more and more. She's fidgeting and casting her eyes everywhere but at me. I could watch her squirm all day, but the two coppers come plodding in. The male sits near Lucy on the sofa, but the female stands between us, as if ready to break up a catfight.

I had insisted that the officers force Lucy to explain the text message Tom sent me from the Serengeti pub on Saturday, the day before he vanished, and now it's the first thing they bring up. They've got a copy of the text and the male shows Lucy, while reading it aloud for her from memory.

God why did i marry this crazy woman she pulled a knife on me.

Lucy looks like she just saw a ghost, and it's no act. She had no idea Tom had sent me that text.

'That's not true,' Lucy blurts, hugging herself again for comfort. She even pulls her hands inside the fleece's long sleeves, trying to insulate herself, like a hedgehog. Her eyes slam to the carpet. 'I never threatened him with a knife. It wasn't a major argument.'

I know what's coming next, because I've unloaded this, too.

'Apparently, there was blood in the bathroom sink. Tom's blood,' the male says.

I can't not jump in here. 'She says he cut his hand on a tap, but it's a lie. The taps aren't sharp and he would have cleaned it up immediately. Tom wouldn't leave a mess like that.'

The officers don't seem to mind my outburst, probably because they want to get a read on Lucy's reaction. Which is just more histrionics.

'I don't know why he didn't clean it up. And he did cut himself on the tap, but I don't know how. He was flicking the blood on the floor. But we went out after that. He was fine. *We* were fine. You think I did something to my husband, but that's preposterous. He's much bigger and stronger. I couldn't possibly...'

'But he couldn't defend himself against a knife in the back while he's standing in the bathroom.' Now the female warns me about shouting out, politely. But I'll have my say. 'Tom's not coming back because this evil bitch has killed him out in those woods.'

Lucy's response: a tapping foot. That's another sign of deception. Her fully-zipped fleece collar is over her chin, and she probably wishes she could climb right inside that cheap garment and wink out of existence. The guilt pulsing off her is flagrant and now, come on, these two officers have to realise she's playing a game and arrest this pathetic excuse for a human being.

5

LUCY

I could not believe it. I didn't know if Tom sent Mary that horrible text message, but if he did he overplayed the intensity of the pub argument on Saturday night. Yes, there was a knife, but it wasn't as bad as it sounded. And, like I'd said before, it was nothing to do with missed medication. But I could prove neither, unfortunately.

And now I had to endure further embarrassment. At Mary's insistence, the police had had a cursory nosey around the house, but now they wanted to search The Cascade, our summer cottage we rented in Cullerton. Nothing of worth had been found in the house, and they would find nothing incriminating at the cottage.

Or would they? Incriminating evidence could be a matter of opinion. The blood in the bathroom, from Tom cutting himself on a tap, meant nothing until Mary gave it weight and substance. The police might accord it the same importance. What else might they find that painted me in a bad light? I had to admit I was a little bit worried, even though I had done nothing wrong. I couldn't help but be annoyed at Tom for running away and dumping me in this mess.

But that's a little unfair. I never imagined I'd be in this position, so Tom couldn't possibly have envisioned it, either. And I couldn't blame him for his paranoid sister, whose antagonism towards me had jumped up a level. I'd need more than two hands to count how many times she'd tried to phone her brother, or popped round unannounced to see him, and been denied contact. On none of those occasions had she suspected foul play, so why now? It made no sense.

The police told me that they could not yet list Tom as an at-risk missing person because he was an adult and he had a history of staying away overnight. I'd provided the names, phone numbers and what addresses I knew of his friends; the police would contact them, as well as Tom's wider family, and would even search properties his agency was in charge of.

These actions suggested the police believed my story that he had left me, especially when added to the fact that they hadn't taken anything away as evidence or asked me to repeat my version of events at a police station. But I still got a vibe from them that wasn't wholly positive. Hopefully, their search of the cottage would extinguish niggling doubts and I could put this mess behind me.

But I couldn't put Mary behind me. Clearly sensing the animosity between us, they'd suggested she should go home. She'd made a song and dance about getting ready to drive off, allowing the police officers to depart first. Then she went nowhere. She'd moved her car across the road and a little way up, partially hidden behind a car on my side of the road. But from my living room window I could see the nose of her car and the driver's half of the windscreen, which meant she could see me.

I pulled the curtains to thwart her, but couldn't help having a peek every now and then. I burned my dinner because I was at the window, and I couldn't concentrate on a TV programme I was watching. I was wary of her presence out there, like a predator waiting to pounce.

In Stuttgart I had taught English, and my years over there had given me a good enough grasp of the German language to try my hand at teaching here in England. I had a course registered with Udemy, an online school, and about fifteen current students who paid a small amount to access my coursework. If there was one thing always guaranteed to keep me zoned in, it was posting a new video or lecture or test, so off I went to do it.

I was in no physical state to appear on camera, so I sat in our upstairs office with the computer's voice recorder software loaded and a classic short story in my lap. The next piece of work I was due to post was a full translation of Charles Dickens' ghost tale *The Signal-Man*, to give my students something cool to recite. But I couldn't get into that, either.

After saying 'Halloa! Unten dort!' – a translation of the story's first line, *Halloa! Below there!* – I went blank. My mind wouldn't shift Mary aside in order to allow concentration.

Because by then I had figured out Mary's plan. She didn't really believe I killed Tom, because that sort of thing just didn't happen, couldn't happen. No, instead, she was leaping upon an opportunity to create tension, to use Tom's abandonment of me to chisel away at our marriage. She was trying to make me angry at Tom for running away.

When Tom returned, she would tell him about how she had called the police, not me, and emphasise the fear I'd put upon her by my lack of care that he'd left me. Her mission was to stress our relationship. Her ultimate goal was our divorce. Always had been.

Eventually, I couldn't think straight having her out there,

lurking like a vulture, so I grabbed my car keys. As I walked to my car, her engine started up. I pretended not to notice. I put my fingers to my temple, pretending to scratch so I could block her from sight.

But I couldn't resist a look once I was in my vehicle. She was on her mobile, animated, staring at me. I had no doubt she was calling Tom's friends again, trying to poison them against me. Or calling a newspaper. Something to embarrass me. Well, she would be the red-faced one when Tom returned.

MARY

Now it's time to spread the word. I send a text to various pals of Tom's, which says:

TOM IS MISSING LUCY HAS DONE SOMETHING TO HIM WILL CALL WHEN I KNOW MORE.

This'll give Lucy a headache because Tom's people won't sit back and wait for me. They'll call her. They'll knock on her door. She'll probably try to ignore them, but that will make her look worse and up everyone's determination to find answers. They'll tell the cops what they know, all the juicy bad stuff about her, and that'll make the police finally see past her fake sugar and spice mask.

Tom's old schoolpal, Jen, answers her phone this time and I jump straight in: 'Lucy has hurt Tom. No one can find him. I just spoke to the police with Lucy and she's acting suspicious.'

She's heard the rumour already, so this isn't a massive shock to her. She takes her time answering. 'You need to contact all his friends, see if—'

'Done that. No one knows anything. She's killed him.'

Still no shock. 'Something else is going on. She wouldn't kill him. That only happens in films. You need to give it time. It's only been one night.'

I see Lucy coming out of her house, trying to ignore me as she goes to her car. She has the gall to put her hand to her face and pretend to scratch, but she extends a sneaky middle finger right at me. I want to slap her.

'No, you don't understand, Jen. I know what's going on. I know Tom and I know his bitch wife.'

'Calm down. Don't shout at me. And don't say that word, Mary. It's too early to know anything. So calm down and let me call some of his old friends and see what they know.'

'They won't know anything,' I snap, and hang up on her. I'm worked up even more now. How can she ignore my worries like this? She must have her mind on whatever man she's having an affair with.

Lucy gets into her car. I don't know where she's going, but I suspect she's up to something that will help hide her crime. I'll be damned if she's going to ride off as if nothing has happened.

LUCY

When I pulled away from the kerb, she followed. Every so often I checked the rear-view mirror, and there she was. She made no effort to hang back, but instead stayed right on my tail. Either she wasn't particularly good at this spy-like tradecraft, or she wanted to unnerve me. I hate to admit it, but the game made me giggle.

My phone rang three times during the first few minutes of this journey. I ignored two of Tom's friends, but when I saw Jennifer's number on screen, I picked up.

Although she lived in America and hadn't seen Tom in the

flesh since a few Christmases ago, he'd known her since they were six years old. Jennifer was a former model and married to another of their old friends, although the marriage was strained because her husband had problems with his feet and couldn't work or take her out, and he'd put a lot of weight on. He permitted her to see other men, strangely. I knew Jennifer liked me and I hoped she, if only her, would not judge me without all the facts.

I was right. As soon as I answered, she said, 'I've heard some silliness about Tom going missing. Did he leave you, sweetheart?'

'Yes.' I ran through my story, which she accepted without scorn.

'His sister sees it another way. But she's never been your fan. I just got off the phone with her.'

This annoyed me – so it was Mary after all who'd spread gossip, not one of the friends who'd accompanied her to The Cascade last night. 'She already called the police. I just had to tell them what happened. I don't know if they believe me.'

'He'll be back. You just keep your chin up and continue to try calling around friends and places he likes to go.'

'I will, I will. Look, let me call you later. I'm driving.'

Actually, I ended the call because I was stopped, not driving. I'd hit red traffic lights and the urge to vent my anger at Mary for spreading vile gossip took over. I got out of my car and stood by the open door. At the last turn I'd made, Mary had had to wait for another car and it now sat between us. I yelled past it.

'Are you lost, Mary? Do you need me to drive to your house to help you out?'

Mary's head came out the driver's window. 'No, Lucifer, I'm following you, as you well know. So bang goes your plan to flee the country.'

Did she really believe that was my plan? Without a bag of clothing and in my old trainers?

'Are you driving to where you buried his body, then?' she added.

'If I was, do you think The Count of Mont Clare would give me tips?'

I saw her face darken at that joke. I knew that she was aware of my disdain for her stupid hobby of writing to death-row inmates in the United States of America and, according to Tom, she particularly hated my nickname for the criminal she was currently obsessed with. As proven when she said, 'No, but when you're in prison, his contacts will bury you.'

Surprisingly, she seemed a little shocked at her own words, as if she'd overstepped a line. I couldn't help myself: 'Are you upset because he's getting the needle soon?'

And now, in a stark turnaround, she just grinned at me. 'You'll wish we had a death penalty after you've done thirty years locked away.'

In the car between us, two baseball-cap-wearing teenagers were watching with glee, their eyes alternatively ahead and behind as we argued. I could see some pedestrians were also captivated. Someone more concerned with the hold-up honked his horn, which was when I realised the light was green.

'Why don't you just piss off and get a life, Mary?'

'Who's going to be the one with a life when you're locked in a cell? Did you know, Lucifer, that six or seven hundred years ago, you would have been broken on the Catherine wheel for what you've done? You know what that is?'

I did, but I couldn't prevent Mary from giving me a lesson on this ancient torture device. Broken bones, crucifixion, a protracted, painful death, all very terrifying. For criminals way back, that was. My response was a grin and a history lesson of my own:

'Did you know that those accused of murder could opt for trial by combat? Against the accuser?'

'Oh, you want to fight me? You're an idiot.'

Of course not, and I didn't want to continue this public dispute any longer, so got back in my car. Angry and confused, I hadn't noticed that the light had turned red again and found myself crossing traffic, with lights flashing and horns blaring. I had to stamp the accelerator to get across the junction as fast as possible, my hands shaking. I knew I must have come across like a madwoman in the last thirty seconds.

But after just a few more, I didn't care. I was beyond the junction, safe, and in my rear-view saw that Mary's Range Rover had zipped past the car between us, intent on following, but had been caught at the lights. I turned a quick left, into an estate, and found a way out of it at the other end. After two more turns, I parked. And waited. Ten minutes later, Mary's car still hadn't made an appearance.

I had lost her. The relief was nice, but I couldn't fool myself. She knew where I lived and for sure I would see her again, and soon.

MARY

'Tom's here!'

My father struggles out of his armchair and reaches for his wheeled walker. I jump up and take his arm before he goes down on his face.

'It's a delivery, Dad, that's all. Stay here.'

'But Tom's coming.'

I help him back into his chair. Despite hardly going out, Dad likes to wear trousers, shirt and blazer, and today's are the same blue as his chair, making him almost invisible when he's swallowed by its long back and high arms. At the door, I sign for a box. The package contains a large print book my father ordered about the Central China floods. He snatches it like a spoilt child, but soon has to thrust it right back at me because his frail hands can't get it open.

'The three biggest natural disasters in history were all in China, you know.' He's happy as Larry, but soon puts the book aside. 'Tom's not here, then?'

I've been dreading this conversation. On Mondays Tom normally takes Dad to the park in his wheelchair while his silly wife farts around at a yoga class. I don't have the courage to mention that Tom won't be coming tonight, but I have to say something.

'Tom can't make it today.'

That isn't a lie, but it doesn't fix the problem. Tom could get away with no Monday visit for maybe a few weeks, but I can't fob Dad off forever. His memory is shot to hell, but he never forgets how much he loves quiet time amongst the trees and hills with Tom. At some point I'll have to mention that Tom's dead.

'Work?' he says.

It almost breaks my heart to lie again. 'Not work, no. Something important came up. Hopefully Tom will be able to take you to the park next week.'

I hope I've got it wrong about what Lucy did to Tom and that he'll pop up with a mad story of getting lost for two days down a well or something. But if he's not around next Monday when Dad thinks about the park, I might have to tell the truth. His son's dead.

As Dad turns his attention to the TV, blinking in that slow, wide way of his, as if he's just woken up, I wonder about the weeks following that. Lately he's stopped mentioning Tom between their park visits, as if he forgets he's got a son until

Monday rolls around and sunken memories bubble up. It's almost Pavlovian, and it gives me a nasty feeling that I'll tell him Tom's dead and he'll forget. That I'll have to repeat the shitty news come park day again. And again, and again.

'Will he bring Lucy for the *Towers*?'

I alluded to this a while back. I can quite easily avoid Lucy for the rest of my life, but she's Tom's wife and it's not the done thing to keep Dad and his daughter-in-law apart. So once a week Tom brings her round to meet him. I'd usually be out or in another room. Dad's a big *Fawlty Towers* fan and watches the classic sitcom about an obnoxious hotel owner every day.

Thinking about this kicks my anger up a gear. The *Towers* visit was always a special thing for my dad, but now she's dive-bombed that, killed his son, and forced me to shatter his world over and over. No one's ever wanted another so dead.

With no park on the cards, I take Dad into the backyard to get him some sun. Then I make a quick call to Tom's business partner. Fat Pete's been awaiting word from me on why Tom missed work. I itch to tell him the truth and dig at Lucy, but he likes the woman and it might turn him against me if she's already hypnotised him with her lies.

But he's still clueless about everything and asks me if Tom's in bed with a hangover because he got drunk at the monster truck event last night. Lucy hasn't even returned his calls.

I can't be bothered with a drawn-out conversation, so I tell Fat Pete that Tom's gone away somewhere and told no one, and didn't take his phone. He asks if Tom's okay and right here it's hard not to just blurt the truth. It would be nice to take a dump on his rosy opinion of Lucy. Again, though, I don't want to get into it. He's not a priority, so he can wait.

I head to my bedroom, sit at the desk and stare at the wall. Seeing a picture of Richard there, smiling at me, makes me dwell on Lucy's smart remarks about him earlier. I'm broad-shouldered usually, but this time her words really got to me. Tom usually likes to tell me things Lucy's said about Richard, because he also finds it a little strange that I exchange letters with a death-row inmate, and I normally just laugh it off. Today I can't.

Richard Chester's fifty-two and was convicted in 1999 of two murders, and he's at State Correctional Institute, Greene County in Pennsylvania. He was born in Mont Clare, hence Lucy's nickname for him based on the classic novel, *The Count of Monte Cristo*. A drug dealer robbed his girlfriend, so Richard, thirty years old at the time, confronted the man at a house. There was a fight and in self-defence Richard killed the man, plus a second person who tried to help his drug-dealer pal.

The court stupidly didn't accept the self-defence aspect and Richard was convicted of first-degree murder. He appealed it based on ineffectiveness of trial counsel, because his lawyers didn't apply for a change of venue. The murders received massive coverage in newspapers in Philadelphia, where the trial was held, and Richard felt he'd never get a fair jury. It forced him to opt for what they call a bench trial, meaning his fate was in the hands of a single judge. But the bastard had it in for Richard. Result: death penalty.

Richard doesn't deny he killed two men, but they were bad guys and it was in self-defence. But now his appeals have run dry and there's nothing he can do. But Pennsylvania hasn't carried out an execution since the year Richard was convicted, which is good news.

It was while reading about the case on the internet one day that I got intrigued enough to send Richard a letter, and we've been in contact ever since. It was right after Tom met Lucy, and he's often ribbed me that I was jealous and desperate for a man, but Richard's case really interested me. Yes, he's officially a criminal, but his crime was a sole event, many years ago, and he was defending his girlfriend – who dumped him the moment he got his collar felt, by the way. Richard's a good man, full of remorse. I plan to visit him one day.

I know people think having a relationship with a convicted man is bizarre. I've heard all the jokes from Tom: Richard's the perfect boyfriend because I know where he is at all times; there's no laundry to do for him, or meals to cook, and he won't ever cheat unless he 'bends down to pick up the soap'. Ha ha.

Dad knows little about Richard, and his only ever remark was that I 'can't make a leopard change its spots'. A pal once told me to take up singing if I wanted the limelight. Just jokes and I can laugh them off. The more serious might reckon I see a little boy turned bad and hope to change him. Perhaps I'm love-avoidant. Or that I feel powerful because a man depends on me. No, wait, it's an innate female attraction to aggressive men.

All bullshit. I'm simply helping Richard. I see my relationship with him as giving a man locked up and abandoned by his family something to attach to on the outside world. Plus, he's innocent of murder, guilty only of protecting his woman.

And Lucy's insults make me want to strangle her.

In the afternoon, I get a call from Lancashire Constabulary. It seems, as promised, some copper down here had a word with his comrades in the north-west and now they want to meet me. Officers have already told Lucy they want to search the cottage in Cullerton for clues as to where Tom might have gone, and she's agreed. The shocker is that they asked her if I could come along and she didn't object.

This is good news. I think they want me there to shoot down any answers Lucy gives them. That means they don't fully buy her story and the search is probably to snoop for evidence of foul play. I rustle up an early dinner for my Dad and hit the road.

6

LUCY

Because Cullerton was little more than commercial buildings arranged along the main road, with residential places behind those on the western side and the woods to the east, there was a prime spot for taking in the whole village at once. It was the church grounds at the south end, where I sat on a bench on the sloping front graveyard.

The last time I'd sat here, I'd been in a wedding dress. I'd had to come away from the photoshoots after the service, because I was having stomach pains and had already thrown up once. I was nervous about beginning my new life with Tom, which I knew was silly – the only thing that had changed was the ring on my finger. I sat for a few moments, my head in my hands, and the bellyache soon cleared up.

I thought about the mass of real people back at the church, probably wondering where the bride was. Before heading back, I had to scrape mud off the end of my dress's fishtail which had slipped through the slats of the bench and onto the grass.

Now I felt my stomach playing up again, but for an entirely different reason. Instead of worries that I wouldn't be the perfect wife for Tom, it was the fear of a future without Tom that debilitated me. But I would endure a lifetime of sickness if I could have him back.

I watched the main road. I saw shoppers walking to and fro. About two hundred metres away was the Serengeti, the blue-painted pub marking the start of the village. This was where Tom and I had had our argument on Saturday night. About fifty metres away, on the opposite side of the road from the pub and the church, was the Kwaint Cottage Gift & Tea Room. It used to be a pub, which explained why the car park was so big.

At the back of that car park, out of my sight beyond the building, was a track that curved downhill through the woods to The Cascade, in a circular clearing split in half by Low Man Brook. There was a rumour that the previous owners of the pub and the cottage had been killed on holiday in Africa. Now The Cascade was the property of an Australian businessman who'd apparently never visited it, or Cullerton. Tom and I had found it by stumbling across his website, where the cottage advertisement sat incongruously amongst the stock of his maritime business.

I sipped my apple juice, bought from the newsagent's on the main road. Six years ago, when we'd learned about this place and had first visited, Tom had dragged me into every shop to say hello – an investment, he'd said. Get to know the locals and they'd do us favours, especially at our wedding. The tactic had paid off because a local baker had supplied a buffet for free at the Serengeti, whose conference room for our reception had also been gratis. Shame I hadn't been able to eat or drink.

And the locals remembered us. The apple juice I had had been a freebie because the newsagent, a fat chap who laughably claimed he'd once been a champion bodybuilder, had remembered me from last summer.

Thinking about Tom, his smiling face as he pulled me by the arm from shop to shop all those years ago, brought a tear to my eye. There had been arguments, especially over the last six months, when a change seemed to have come across him, but my most vivid memories all had him smiling. Selective memory, or maybe the good stuff gets tattooed deeper in the mind.

But I didn't have time to dwell on my own sadness because my phone rang. It was the police. Somewhere behind the church a lawnmower was buzzing, so I put my empty apple juice bottle by my feet to allow me to block one ear with a finger while I took the call.

Lancashire police had called me early that afternoon because they wanted to search the cottage for clues regarding Tom. This was good news, because last night I had worried that I'd get arrested. But that had been down to Mary's vehement, but foolish insistence that I had killed my husband. If the police even half-suspected this was true, they would have escorted me to Cullerton.

Instead, they'd given me a meeting time and let me make my own journey. But they had insisted that I didn't go in the cottage until they arrived, hence why I was awaiting them at the church. I had set off early in order to have some thinking time here.

Now, one of the same officers told me they were running late. 'Event on the motorway,' was all he gave by way of explanation. I reckoned it was the same poor soul whose crashed green Audi I had been a little delayed by. I hoped no one was hurt.

After the call, I decided I didn't want to sit in the graveyard any longer, so I headed for my car. I was eager to tell the police about some good news I'd received an hour earlier.

MARY

I hoped to arrive at the cottage earlier than the cops and Lucy, but some selfish bastard in a green Audi crashed and blocked a motorway lane, tossing a spanner into the plans of a thousand others who managed to drive nice and safe. A short way down the road on my left is the Kwaint Cottage Gift & Tea Room and I turn into the car park.

At the back, just before the woods, is a wooden fence with a gap: this is how to access the dirt track cut through the trees. It's like a tunnel because it's so dim even in bright summer and curves downhill for about fifty metres, to the treeless area where The Cascade is. At the end, as I exit the trees, I spot Lucy's crappy Ford outside the cottage, about thirty metres away. Only hers. Where are the cops? And where's Tom's BMW?

I cruise slowly alongside her passenger side and stop. She's behind the wheel, head back, eyes on the ceiling. Praying for a miracle she won't get, I reckon. I buzz my window down, but still she doesn't notice me. It takes a thrown penny from cash in my centre console to get her attention. One second, and then she looks down at her phone. I get out, go around and rap on her window.

'Where's Tom's car? You said he left it here.'

When that gets no response, I try the door. Locked, of course.

'Answer me, Lucifer. You lied about Tom's car. He didn't stay here at all. Actually, no, he did. Because you've chucked him into the ravine or something. Open this door. I want the truth.'

But the truth isn't coming, is it? She still ignores me. I sweep my eyes for a rock, and there's lots scattered around here, because the dirt track's much wider out front of the cottage. But I toss this idea because I don't want to get in trouble.

She still won't look at me. Eventually, I drive a short way on, turn, and park with my car's nose an inch from hers. My Range Rover's taller, so I've got a good view of her. She's got her hands in her lap, playing on her phone. I just stare. I want her to feel uncomfortable. The sun is on my windscreen and I hope the glare won't prevent her seeing my angry eyes.

But I'm also uncomfortable. I must have misread today's plan. The cops allowed Lucy to drive here alone, so they don't think she'd try something sly like faking a breakdown. It means they don't suspect anything sinister with Tom's disappearance. They trust her. Not a good sign. Hopefully, I'll prove them wrong by the time we're done here.

I can see her staring at me, even though she's pretending to read from her phone. Every now and then I honk my horn, just to make her jump, but mostly the wait is without incident.

Eventually, a cop car comes ambling down the dirt path, into the open area. It parks behind Lucy's car. I'm at their door before the vehicle even stops. As one door starts to open, I say, 'She's lying. Tom's car isn't here.'

Two young, tall, handsome male officers in uniform exit. Lucy doesn't step out until they're both clear of their vehicle, in a position to get between us if something happens. She keeps a wary eye on me.

'Ask her why Tom's car isn't here,' I demand.

'Tom must have come back and took his car and his things.'

'Bullshit, she…' I start to recount events and expose her lies, fast, angry, but one of the officers tells me to stop before I'm ten words in.

'Okay, both of you, just hold on a second. Let me ask some questions based on what I've already been told by officers from South Yorkshire, and we'll get the story that way. But let's do it inside, please.'

That's when Lucy drops her bombshell news. Not half an hour ago, when I arrived, and not five minutes ago when the cops turned up. No, apparently now is the correct time to unload this gem.

'I got a text from Tom.'

My jaw drops. 'What? How? No, bullshit. He left his phone behind.'

She waves her mobile. 'It's off a new number. He must have bought one.'

For just a second I wonder if this is true. But only one second. 'No way. Why would he contact just you? I've had no contact, nor anyone else. They would have told me. Let me see that.'

I try to step forward, to take the phone, but a meaty law enforcement arm blocks my way. The other officer takes the phone from Lucy and reads. It gets passed to his colleague, who shows me a text on the screen, from an unknown number.

Its tom new phone dont contact me might be in touch in the future.

'This is bullshit,' I snap. 'Tom's phone is expensive, and it's on contract. He'd come back for it if he needed a phone. He wouldn't just buy a new one. She's lying.'

I snatch the phone and step back, away from everyone. 'I'll ring it.'

'I tried calling it, but it won't work,' Lucy says. I sense the desperation in her voice and hope the officers see it, too. She tries to step forward to get the phone, but the officer by her gives her the barrier arm treatment.

'Let's just see if he answers,' he says.

'He won't,' I announce as I hit redial. 'I bet this rings in her pocket. Watch this.'

'That's my phone,' Lucy yells. 'I want it back. That's theft.'

The officer guarding me actually steps over to Lucy's car and opens the door. I know why and it pleases me: they want to see if the phone Tom apparently texted from is actually in Lucy's possession. We all fall quiet and wait.

'It's turned off,' I eventually say, disheartened. How bloody convenient for her story.

And she knows it, given the satisfaction on that bitch's face.

7

LUCY

On Sunday morning, when Tom and I left the cottage, we walked across the dirt road and into the still-wet grass by the brook. In the dry season, which is normally now, the brook was barely there and with careful steps you could make your way across the exposed rocks without soaking your shoes.

But, even hours after the rain had stopped, the draining surface water across the surrounding land had kept the brook deep and fast, like rapids, and crossing anywhere inside the clearing was risky. After the water vanished into the woods it slowed, but here passage from one side to the other was even more dangerous: the brook bored downwards into the land and the banks were steep and treacherous.

The safest bet was the waterfall. Its lip rested upon a flat shelf with steep sides some fifteen feet high, almost like a promontory, and just before the drop was where the brook was thinnest. This was where the owner of the cottage had placed a large square stone at each bank and bolted a ten-foot aluminium perforated metal walkway to create a bridge. But reaching it meant scaling a steep grassy bank.

Sometimes Tom would go behind me and hold my bum in case I slipped, and sometimes he led with my hand grabbing his coat for stability. Today it was the latter. At one point I slipped onto my knees, muddying my jeans, and expected him to help me up. But he gave me no arm, didn't even turn his head. So, no help, and sympathy wasn't on the rota either:

'Can't you climb one little hill?'

He'd been funny with me all morning. I made no reply, not wanting another argument. I got up and continued. The walkway is three feet above the water, so even if someone fell on the good side, they'd be swept under and over the edge. There is an initial drop of about four feet, then the bedrock slopes steeply down about ten feet before the final drop of another few feet.

Tom had climbed up and down the waterfall in the dry season, and once he even sat on a flat rock on the edge with his feet dangling, water cascading all around him. But in wet times, like today, the water was far more violent and anyone plunging in would tumble all the way down, crashing against rocks, and be carried away into the woods, and eventually down into a ravine.

Our habit was to hold hands to make the crossing: I would grab one of Tom's in both of mine and follow him, clutching so hard I almost broke his bones. But...

'This, babe, is where things transmogrify.'

Tom liked to use big words to make powerful statements, and this one I knew from previous use. He meant things were going to change. And when he scooted across the walkway without me, I knew how this day was going to play out. He only called me babe when he was annoyed at me. I would get no help. Some romantic weekend away.

I'd walked across the walkway numerous times and never fallen, but now, without his help, I got on my hands and knees to crawl across. It was less than three feet wide, but the perforations gave good grip. Water splashing off rocks below the walkway soaked my jeans at the knees and calves and the lower arms of my jacket. Tom watched with a stony expression until I was almost safe, then – no hand to help me up – turned and went down the slope towards the woods.

It was at this point that I considered abandoning our day out – making a transmogrification of my own – because it was going to be no fun with him in this mood. But I decided to press on, figuring his attitude might brighten once we got to the Fox and Hound, a beautiful public house at the far end of the woods. Our getaway Sunday tradition of lamb dinner there always put a smile on Tom's face.

But we'd never get there.

We crossed the clearing and met a dirt path through the slanted woodland. The ground sloped upwards to the right, meeting the brook behind the waterfall. Fifty metres to the left the trees ended at a ravine with Low Man Brook continuing far below. The locals called it a ravine, but only the woodland side was a steep edge, with a rocky river three hundred feet below: opposite was hilly, open land. Running along the cliff edge was a less-often-used path that we enjoyed for our return journey because of the view.

Tom walked ahead a few feet and, apart from a glance back here and there, didn't even acknowledge my existence at his rear. He said nothing. I felt like I was there alone. Then, a mile into the three-mile trip, Tom abruptly stopped.

The path is sometimes wide open, with spaces big enough to picnic, and sometimes so thin a couple would have to travel single file. Here upon a tight portion, trees had their roots half-exposed across the path, snaking in and out of the soil like the

Loch Ness monster, so I had my eyes down, watching my step. I bumped into Tom.

Because I'm only five feet six and Tom's six feet two, my lowered head hit his backpack. Surprised, I stepped back; my heel caught a root and I fell. I tried to get a foot under me, but succeeded only in twisting my ankle.

But when I yelled in pain, Tom didn't reach down to help me up. Staring down, taking a puff on his vape, he said, 'Can't you even walk? What's wrong with you?'

I struggled to my feet. My ankle badly hurt and I was unsteady and reached out to grab Tom for balance. But he took a step backwards, out of reach. I tried to take a step, but it hurt. A sprain, I thought.

'My ankle hurts. I need to go back.'

'I'm sure you do,' he said as he slotted his vape in his pocket. 'But I don't. I can walk without falling on my arse. I'm going ahead. Keep up if you can.'

'I don't think I want to be around you in this mood. Best you just go on ahead.'

As he walked on, he said, '*Your* mood, more like. I shouldn't be near you at Sunday lunch in case the roast potatoes aren't crispy.'

This 'insider joke' annoyed me, but I didn't want to give up on the day. I tried a few steps, but it hurt too much. Unwilling to make it worse, I decided to go back. I called after him, telling him we could go to the Fox and Hound later, but he ignored me and shrank into the distance, then around a slight bend and out of sight. I waited still, but he didn't return. I gave him another five minutes to have a change of heart, but it didn't come.

I headed back. I bathed my foot in a bowl of ice, which helped. I tried to call Tom after about an hour, but his phone rang upstairs. After that, I periodically peered out of the window in the hope of seeing him crossing the walkway over the river. A couple of times I ventured outside and yelled his name, hoping he was within earshot and would reply. Nothing. He didn't come back. That evening, Mary and his friends came–

'And that's when you lied to us,' Mary cut in.

We were in the cottage's living room. I was perched on the ottoman, so that no one could sit beside me, and the two officers were standing in the middle of the room so they could watch us both.

Mary had chosen the right-hand seat of the sofa in order to be as close to me as possible. We were just a few feet apart. She had even turned slightly so she could face me, but I ignored her and stared ahead, at the coppers. They were waiting for my response to Mary's outburst at the end of my recap of last Sunday.

I took a few seconds to put her accusation out of my mind. I would not rise to her taunts. 'I was embarrassed. I didn't want anyone to know we'd argued and that he'd stormed off and left me. I wasn't thinking straight. So when Mary and Tom's friends came to the door, I guess I was hoping that they'd just accept my story that Tom had stayed out longer than normal. That nothing was wrong between us.'

Mary tried to interject here again, but was told to wait her turn. Then one of the officers asked me to continue.

'Later that night, when Tom still hadn't returned, I left the door unlocked and slept on the sofa downstairs, so that I'd hear him when he came in. I figured he might wait until I was asleep to avoid a late-night explanation.

'But this morning he wasn't there. I'd packed all our things the night before I got ready to sleep, because we were leaving the next morning. I put my gear in my car, but I left Tom's suitcase in the bedroom. His car was still here, so I knew he still had to come back. And that's the note I left him.'

I pointed to the fireplace. One of the officers lifted a postcard standing on the mantlepiece. On it I had scribbled, SINCE WE HAD SEPARATE CARS, I FIGURED YOU WOULD WANT TO AVOID ME UNTIL WE'RE HOME. I'VE PACKED MY THINGS AND YOURS. BUT YOURS ARE UPSTAIRS. SEE YOU LATER. X

'Why is it you brought separate cars?' one of the officers asked.

Without pause, I said, 'We normally do that. In case Tom gets called to go visit one of his properties or needs to rush into the office. So I'm not stranded. We always do it that way.'

Here Mary said something under her breath, which I thankfully didn't catch.

'I called home before I left, to see if he was already there. But it just rang. I figured he was going to stay here a while longer and would probably wait until I'd gone before he came back into the cottage.'

'Even though he had work today?' Mary spat, with obvious disdain.

'I don't know what I was thinking. I wanted to give him space. We had separate cars, so it wasn't like I was abandoning him.'

Here Mary got up and announced that she needed the toilet. There was one downstairs, but she headed upstairs for some reason. I knew full well that she was going to have a snoop around.

One of the officers said, 'And at some point between when you left, yesterday, and before we all arrived today, you say he came and took his car and his suitcase?'

'He must have. Both were still here when I left.'

'Have you called the Fox and Hound to see if he turned up there?'

I shook my head. 'I didn't, no. He was angry and wouldn't have come to the phone. But I should have, I know that now.'

Just then there was a shout from upstairs. Mary, angry and

bellowing for the police. I was right behind them heading up the stairs. I couldn't imagine what had freaked her out so. But I knew as soon as we found her in the bathroom. She was enraged, words tumbling out of her so fast I barely caught what she was saying. Something about *bleach*, and *varnish*, and *overkill*.

Everyone was watching me. I stammered through my words. 'I couldn't just leave it there. It was a mess.'

She pointed at the taps. 'She says Tom cut himself on the tap. Have a feel. You can't cut yourself on one of those. Look at it.'

One of the officers stepped up for a look. He didn't touch the tap, but bent and leaned this way and that, staring intently.

'How much blood was it? Just a little, we heard.'

Mary was here forced to admit, yes, it was just a little blood. She didn't like that. But then she perked up and pointed at me. 'She got some on her blouse. Where is it? She reckons Tom brushed past her while bleeding, but you'll see it's not a smear. It looks like blood sprayed on her. Where's the blouse?'

'It was only a little bit on the arm,' I countered, upset by her depiction of a jet of blood fountaining across the room.

'Get the blouse. Show them. Or did you bleach that, as well?'

The officers were watching me and I saw something I didn't like in their eyes when I said, 'The blood wouldn't come out. So I threw it away.'

Mary made a hand gesture at the officers that I could best describe as, *You need more proof? Listen to this crap!*

'Where's the blouse?' Mary demanded. 'I know they can do tests to see if blood dripped or was smeared or was thrown. In the bin? Where's the bin?'

I still couldn't believe what was happening here. My sister-in-law accusing me of... well, I think I'd tried to ignore it before, but absolutely had to accept it now. She was accusing me of murdering Tom and disposing of his body. Preposterous, I know, but when I gave my answer to her question, even though it was the absolute truth, even I had to admit it sounded a little suspicious.

And the looks all three gave me said they didn't believe a word of it.

MARY

I'm amazed that these two cops don't immediately arrest her. She's clearly acting suspiciously. After she shows a nicely convenient note she claims to have left for Tom, she's asked why they brought separate cars for a trip away together.

She gives a long pause, obviously feeling trapped by the hole in her story behaviour. Her answer is: 'We normally do that. In case Tom gets called to go visit one of his properties or needs to rush into the office. So I'm not stranded. We always do it that way.'

I've known this to happen, but only on a couple of rare occasions when Tom had already planned to shoot off before his wife. And I know there was no such plan this time. I can't let such bullshit hang in the air, but keep my anger in check, and my voice low enough so that only the target hears: 'You're so full of shit your eyes are brown.'

Lucy ignores the insult. 'I called home before I left, to see if he was already there. But it just rang. I figured he was going to stay here a while longer and would probably wait until I'd gone before he came back into the cottage.'

'Even though he had work today?'

She spouts more bullshit, but I've heard enough. Pretending to need the toilet, I go upstairs to see if the blood is still in the bathroom. And sure enough she's cleaned it up. The floor and sink are spotless. I'm in the middle of telling myself it was silly to expect to find the blood, because nobody would just leave it splashed there, when a familiar reek hits me.

Bleach. A lot of it.

I scream for the officers to come look. This wasn't just a little spot of housework: the bitch has scrubbed this room with bleach in the hope that a forensics team won't find the blood with their fancy chemicals or special lights. The teeny amount I saw on Sunday was probably the remains of her first attempt at cleaning it up. Maybe it was all over the walls and the window and the mirror.

The cops thunder up the stairs and Lucy's right behind them, and they all walk into a barrage from me: 'She's scrubbed with bleach to get rid of the blood. It was on the floor and the sink. Blood will wipe off varnish and ceramic easily, but she's used bleach. That's overkill. Why would you use bleach on blood?'

No elaborate excuse needed here: she simply points out that she cleaned up a mess. When I remind the officers that Tom supposedly cut himself on one of the smooth taps, one of them a takes a long look at the sink. His expression tells me he agrees that the notion of slicing flesh on such smooth, rounded metal is horseshit. But he says nothing. So I bring up the blood on her blouse and demand that she shows us the garment. Hopefully she won't have pre-planned a neat explanation for *that*.

But she has, and it's a corker. She reckons she got rid of the blouse, of course, and that should be bad news for me. But this time she's been too cocky and confident. You see, she didn't toss the garment in the bin downstairs or the wheelie bin out back, where anyone sane would dump a piece of ruined clothing unconnected to a vile murder. Oh no. See if this bit of activity is that of the innocent:

'I burned it in the firepit out back.'

8

LUCY

Mary stormed from the bathroom and clumped down the stairs. We followed and found her in the kitchen, just in time to see her kick the lid off the fifty-litre pedal bin in the corner and bend over it. The bin was half empty and loaded only with food wrappers, clearly with no blouse inside, yet she delved her fingers in, rooting like a tramp.

'It's not here. I told you I burned it,' I said, looking at the police for help. 'What is she doing?'

They ignored me. I turned to see Mary standing with something pinched in two fingers, held up, glaring at it.

'What's that?' one officer asked.

I knew what it was, but couldn't believe it.

'It's Tom's insulin,' Mary said.

It was a half-full bottle, which made no sense. Tom needed his insulin and this was his only supply. It was usually kept in the bathroom medicine cabinet, or in Tom's car if he was out all day, so it couldn't have been accidentally knocked into the bin. He must have thrown it.

But even as I was trying to think why, Mary came up with an alternative.

'This proves Tom didn't go walkabout. She threw this away because he wouldn't need it anymore.'

'What? What are you talking about?'

'He's dead, and that's why you threw this in the bin. Look, it's half-full. It's his only one.'

'I know it is. He must have dropped it in the bin by accident. Maybe when he was clearing out his glovebox.'

'I'm not listening to any more of these lies. You need to arrest her right now for murder.'

An ounce less vehemence in her tone, eyes a little less wide with rage, and I might have laughed at the absurdity of it. But I didn't laugh.

At least the police weren't quite as eager to assume that a dumped half-full insulin bottle was sinister. 'Let's all just calm down,' one said. 'How sure are you Tom doesn't have more insulin somewhere?'

'There's none,' Mary said.

'Maybe he came back and couldn't find it,' I offer, 'because it got knocked in the bin by mistake. He came back for his car and clothes.'

'And when did he last take insulin?'

'Sunday morning.'

Saying it aloud gave rise to a terrible thought. Although Tom usually took his medication before going out for a long period, his blood glucose might have dropped before he could return to the cottage. He might have had an episode out there in the woods and have lain unconscious. He might have died.

And Mary felt the same way. She sat down, right there on the kitchen linoleum, and put her head in her hands. The venom was gone and it was a little girl who fought back tears when she said, 'We need to search. Out there. The woods. The ravine.'

I bent over her, and put a hand on her shoulder. 'Mary, he must have more ins–'

In such a small frame, her power was tremendous. She slapped my arm aside so hard that my wrist stung. I backed away as she jumped to her feet and screamed, 'Get off me, you bitch! You did something to him. And I'll kill you for it.'

The policemen got between us, got us into separate rooms. I sat upstairs in the bedroom with one of them and tried to drown out Mary's voice, but it was audible even through the door. Until she calmed down.

The officer told me the details of Tom's disappearance would be passed to an officer who would assess the risk to him and make enquiries at his work, at places he was known to visit, and at local hospitals in case he had been admitted. They'd also search the area around the cottage, as well as investigating activity on Tom's bank account and social media.

But unless the nominated officer found evidence of a crime or other risk to Tom, nobody was going to call out the cavalry.

'I'm sorry to use such a term, it sounds callous,' the officer said. 'I understand your worry, but your husband is a grown man and adults are basically allowed to do what they want. I see it all the time, Mrs Packham. Husbands and wives suddenly leave the family home. They're allowed to.'

'And how long will it take for this nominated officer to decide Tom warrants the cavalry?'

'It could be days. It could be weeks. Meantime, I suggest you also visit such places and make calls to friends and family again. Someone might have information. He might have contacted someone since you last spoke to them. And if not today, he might do it tomorrow. When you get back to Sheffield, file a missing person's report. That starts the ball rolling officially. That should be done with your local police.'

And then he slipped back into the negative. I was warned

that, even if they found Tom, they had to get his permission to pass his location on to me. And he might not give it. I should prepare myself for that.

I already had, and it was the reason I didn't plan to report Tom as missing. Mary brought the police in, not me. I didn't want them here. But before you condemn me for that, you should know the reason why I was certain Tom was alive. Why he had left me. And why he would not come back to me. It was a reason I hadn't yet told anyone, even though it might have changed Mary's opinion.

Tom was having an affair.

MARY

'We can't deny that something about Lucy's story doesn't add up. The burned, bloodied blouse is especially worrying.'

This line from the copper with me in the kitchen is what finally calms me down. I had freaked out after hearing Lucy's lies about Tom, but his words stop me dead. I listen all wide-eyed, like a captivated child. They're on my side. They know Lucy's a bad woman.

'Unfortunately, we can't just arrest her without proper evidence. Tom is an adult and can come and go when and where and for however long he likes. There's a chance what she's saying about Tom is true, and she could be worried about him, and with that in mind we have to do what's right.'

Despite suddenly popping my bubble, he's leaning close, like we're co-conspirators. Maybe he just needs a little nudge my way. 'But we can do something without her knowing?'

He looks surprised, as if he thinks I hope to be deputised and sent on a secret mission. I realise I've read him wrong.

'There's nothing much I can do right now except report my

misgivings,' he says, quite formal now. 'There's certainly not enough evidence of foul play to warrant an arrest or a search warrant for the cottage. However, my father is a detective inspector and he has a good friend in South Yorkshire who's a DI also, working in major crime. His name is Aaron Reavley. I will pass on my thoughts to my father and see if he'll make his counterpart aware. You'll need to file your own missing person's report, in case Tom's wife delays hers. Now, Mr Reavley won't necessarily be allocated this case, but once he knows about the holes in Tom's wife's story, he might be able to step on board and speed things up.'

'Okay. I'll wait to see if this Reavley contacts me. But what else can I do?'

'I'll give you one more piece of advice. Off the record, and I'll trust you not to get me in trouble by mentioning this. If things seem to be dragging along and you haven't heard anything by tomorrow, suddenly decide that your brother stole your jewellery.'

It seems we might be co-conspirators after all. I'm intrigued, although puzzled. 'What do you mean?'

'It's unfortunate, but missing adults just don't worry the police as much as missing property. If you report that Tom stole from you, there might be a larger effort to find him.'

This is a shock, but something worth thinking about. 'What do I do now?'

'Now you have to leave. Lucy will leave a little after.'

I get it. Knowing of the tension between us, they want to make sure I don't follow her car, maybe ram her off the road. Would be nice to watch her crappy Ford bounce down an embankment, but leaving Cullerton so soon isn't my plan. 'Are you busy right now? We could go walk that route she says they took through the woods. We could go ask for the CCTV at the

Fox and Hound, to see if Tom actually turned up there as he was supposed to. Which I doubt.'

'We can't spare the time for that, I'm afraid. Now–'

'It's just a little look. Just say your time here took longer than you expected.'

'Miss Packham, please listen. A search needs a professional team and–'

I know he's worried about us missing something important, so I cut in with, 'A little look, just on the off-chance. Even if we missed some evidence, no one would know. You wouldn't get in trouble. And they'd find it when you do a proper search. But you never know what we'll find. You could be the man who solves the case.'

Seems he's not a glory-hunter: 'No. By all means take a walk yourself. But I wouldn't advise going alone. And stay away from the ravine. I would also caution you against trying to contact the managers of the Fox and Hound.'

I know I'm attractive and I step a little closer to the man, so he can smell my perfume. 'We could search this cottage properly, right now. And the backyard. For all we know Tom is buried out there, or burned to nothing in the firepit.'

A wasted effort. He shuts me down again and virtually kicks me out of the cottage. At my car, I look up to see Lucy at the bedroom window. Just a vague shape behind the glass, gone the next second.

The cop follows me out to the edge of Cullerton so I can't hide in wait down a side street. Nothing he can do to stop me setting a trap a mile away, except beg. Which he sort of does. By the Serengeti pub, he pulls in front of me and gets out. I drop my window.

'When you get back to the cottage, see if she still wears her wedding ring. It's expensive silver. Tom bought it, obviously. If

Tom is, as she says, just out, then she'll expect him back, won't she? And she'll still have her wedding ring.'

'I'll have a look,' he says, and sounds like he means it. 'Now, don't wait somewhere for her, because we'll escort her partway home. Stay away from her house as well. Please. Please don't contact her. That would be a bad idea and could get you in trouble.'

Warning given, he bids me goodbye and swings his car around to head back to the cottage. He needn't have bothered with his final warning though. And definitely not the word *please*. I've got some plans for Lucy, but they don't involve chasing her vehicle down the motorway for another scrap.

Instead, I'm going to do some detective work of my own.

9

LUCY

Word had clearly spread that there had been a commotion at my house that morning. As I got home in the early evening, I saw a neighbour who was working on his car three doors down give me a long look. Longer than was normal. My next-door neighbour came to her window and stared, then waved when I noticed her. I didn't think it was paranoia. They were eager to know why the police had been to my house.

I checked my mobile for the first time since setting off for home and noticed a missed call from Peter, Tom's business partner. When he'd called that morning because Tom hadn't gone to work, I'd ignored it. Now I realised he was still awaiting word from Tom. I decided to ignore it again. I would talk to him later.

Across the road, the Carter family had a twelve-year-old daughter who sometimes knocked on doors to sell pirated movies. Her parents must have taught her how to illegally download films and burn them onto discs. Only a few days ago I'd bought a pair from her box. There was nothing new in it tonight, but back she came. On my doorstep, she held the shoebox and flipped the lid, just like always.

But here things... transmogrified. Normally she'd talk about school, or tell me which new films were good, but tonight she asked me how 'things' were. A glance across at her house, where her parents were at the living room window, confirmed my suspicions. The little girl had been sent on a mission to find out about the police presence at my house earlier.

'Things are good. Apart from having to report an attempted theft at the garage where Tom keeps his monster truck.'

'Oh, your ring is gone. You didn't give it to someone else, did you?'

I looked at a white band of skin on my finger. The little girl was always impressed by my ring, and even got me to promise it would be hers if Tom and I ever split up. 'I left it at our cottage by accident. I'll get it back another time. I was too busy today.'

'Is that why you haven't had wash time?'

'Do I smell?'

'Oh, it would be rude to say that.'

Yet she just had, basically. I picked up a movie and paid her, and off she scuttled for debriefing. My attempted-theft story wouldn't explain why Tom's sister had been shouting in the street, especially if people had heard some of her threats and claims, but hopefully it would satisfy some. Now I just had to wait for it to spread like a virus.

On the way home, I'd called to cancel my Monday yoga class because I wanted to be at home in case Tom returned, especially if he was planning to sneak indoors to collect more of his belongings. Plus, I was in no kind of mood for company. But once at home, I couldn't bear the sitting around, waiting. I jumped to the window at every slamming car door, every voice I heard, and I knew I had to get out. Besides, it was yoga, and it might help my mental state.

But first, a shower. I hadn't cleaned myself since Saturday afternoon, when Tom and I had prepared for our night out at the pub. There had been no reason to wash on Sunday morning, because we were going for a hike, and, of course, tragedy had allowed no thought or time since. In the bathroom mirror, I noticed baggy eyes and tangled hair right alongside dirt patches, crusty eyes despite the crying, and a thick blob of dirt caught in one of my eyebrow slits.

I'd been going to the yoga class for eight months, while Tom took his father out to the park, but I hadn't bonded with many of the women there. Nothing beyond cursory small talk. That made it easy to tell little lies when questioned about Tom and me and life in general. Only one lady realised there was something up with me, but she asked in such a sideways format that I easily deflected her. I enjoyed my time out of the house, but was happy to get home.

But not for long. There was no sign Tom had been back and I doubted I'd see him that evening. Once darkness arrived, my mood sank and I drank a little vodka to help me sleep. But I didn't have much hope it would work. Without my antidepressants, the last few days had triggered a very strange symptom. It basically returns to me a debilitating childhood fear.

I'd run out of tablets about ten days ago and for the first week or so sleep had been fine, even if my mood wasn't. This was because I had had Tom by my side at night. But on Sunday and Monday night, the loneliness had given rise to what I called the Infinity Dream. I'll get to that.

Still, I lay down and tried. I had an idea that I could sleep in the middle of the bed, so he'd be certain to wake me if he came home in the dead hours. But the middle felt too uncomfortable, was too much of a reminder that I was alone. And the Infinity Dream wouldn't allow it.

As I lay there, with the light on, I accessed our joint bank account to see if there had been any activity. I guess I was hoping I'd see a purchase or cash machine withdrawal with a location, so I'd at least know where Tom was. And that he was alive. But I knew such activity might not show up for a day or two.

I again tried that new phone number he'd texted from, but got the same as before: automated voice telling me I couldn't reach the mobile user. I could only hope the police would trace its location, if they could do that while it was turned off.

Zuzu moaned for food, and I enjoyed the excuse to get out of bed. But when I went down, the bowl was still half-full. He was at the door, wanting out. That upset me a little, because Zuzu usually stayed in at night, curled up on a cushion under Tom's computer desk. He must have sensed Tom's absence. Or also chosen to abandon me.

'Tom has gone,' I told the cat. 'He won't be coming back. It's just you and me.' I doubted there was understanding, but he appeared to watch me with sorrow. 'So, abandon me, too, if you like. I deserve it.' I opened the door and he zipped out in an instant, like a freed prisoner.

After that, I tried to play the film I'd bought off the young neighbour using Tom's Xbox, but it didn't hold my attention. Upstairs, sitting before the office computer, I again failed to record my German translation of Dickens' *The Signal-Man*. As before, I faltered after 'Halloa! Below there!'

But this time it wasn't just because of a lack of concentration. On the software was a list of previous recordings, in time and date order, and I noticed that one had no title, which was strange because I always named them. It also had a date of Thursday 13 June, just a few days ago, and I knew I hadn't made a recording on that day. I clicked on it.

'*Wie viel für einen blasen?*' I heard Tom say. I laughed in shock. The recording was sixty seconds and to boil it down, my husband was educating tourists on how to solicit a prostitute on Berlin street corners. By the end of it, I was in tears of laughter.

Tom had always been a practical joker, and I loved that about him, but thank God he hadn't had my password or this gem would have already been uploaded into my coursework for students to access! I pictured his smiling face as he recorded this after probably hours of research, all to make me laugh.

But those tears became ones of sadness. The sexual aspect turned my mind on to another matter.

I couldn't shake the idea of him with that other woman, whoever and wherever she was. The image of them laying together. Making love. With me non-existent in her mind and dumped in a dark corner of Tom's. Hopefully, he was just letting off some steam and would bore of her soon and come back to me.

I then clicked to continue my recording of the Dickens short story, but instead of reading from the text, I wheezed, 'Bitte nach Hause kommen, Tom.' That caused more tears. I so wanted him back. I was starting to miss him dearly. I wanted him to make me laugh again.

But I also needed him. I didn't want people to think I'd done something to him.

MARY

As early evening rolls in, I decide to go with the tactic a Lancashire copper gave me: report the theft of jewellery because Tom the criminal would be more interesting to the police than Tom the missing person. The idea makes me sick, but I've got to push the action.

Luckily, there's no need. My phone rings while it's in my

hand. Unknown number. 'Hi there. I'm Detective Inspector Reavley, South Yorkshire Police. Are you Mary Packham?'

Ah, so one of them I'm still fuming about today and it filters into my response: 'About time. I hope this is about my missing brother.'

'Yes. I know a little about your complaint and if you've got time, I'd like to talk to you.'

I regret my brash opening line, but can't contain my hunger for answers. 'Do you know anything so far?' I ask, eager. 'You need to find Tom's car.'

'I know little as yet. I need to get some information from you. But not on the phone. Can we meet?'

'Have you not made any enquiries yet? Like about the car?'

'Miss Packham, let's meet up and we'll discuss it. Tonight?'

I force myself to calm down. Happy to meet, I tell him, but not in a cop shop. And I don't want him here, either, because Dad will ask questions. He can't know the truth yet, and certainly not from the cops.

'Oh, I didn't mean at a station. I'm off-duty tonight, if that will do. Outside somewhere. A café?'

'Off-duty? So you're taking this seriously? You believe Tom's wife did something to him?'

'Slow down, please. I was told about Tom's disappearance by a colleague and I asked for my team to take the case on. But I'm just trying to get some background, that's all. A head start. So, a café?'

I have a better idea. 'I'm visiting someone tonight about some business.'

His detective brain can't help but ask who, and what business. I tell him that on Mondays Lucy has some kind of silly class, so that's when Tom takes Dad to the park and then works on his monster truck. On Sunday, at the monster truck show,

Animal lost a tyre, so I'd agreed to go along and help with the repairs.

'Monster trucks are awesome,' Reavley says. 'You know how to fix them up?'

I laugh. 'I make the tea and hand over spanners.'

'I'd love to see that truck up close. I could tag along. We can chat while you hand the spanners over.'

I would have suggested the idea even if he hadn't. It sounds as if Reavley's eager to work Tom's disappearance, which means he doesn't believe my brother just walked out. He might already know something I don't and I want that info. So I give him the postcode and tell him to meet me at seven.

Reavley is already there when I turn up, leaning against his car with his arms folded. He's a middle-aged man with brown hair going grey above the ears, and a fair piece of eye-candy. His build reminds me of Tom. I park and approach and he jabs out a hand to shake. I see him eyeballing my Range Rover Sport. I bite back the urge to blurt a bunch of questions. It's early days and this detective knows nothing yet. I have to be patient.

'I expected a garage. Thought I had the wrong place.'

I get his bafflement. We're on a typical urban street, two rows of terraces. 'Well, as you'll see, it's not really a garage.'

I pull my keys to lock my car. He admires it. 'Range Rover. Very flash. This has got to be fifty grand of car.'

'I got it a little less. I was left a lot of money. I wanted something big and sturdy that I could keep for years. Although young idiots keep pulling up beside me at traffic lights and asking to buy it.'

He faces me. 'I heard about the inheritance. Your parents

had a construction company. You and Tom were given houses, is that right? And you sold yours.'

'Oh, is this my interrogation? Do I need a lawyer?'

I'm smiling, so he grins, too. 'It's not like that. I didn't even bring handcuffs. Just promise to tell me the truth.'

'How about this...' I raise my eyes skyward and put up a hand. 'I do solemnly swear.'

He gives me a funny look, like he thinks I'm weird, and I explain that it was a habit of my brother's to perform the oath when in a joking mood. 'So now you can ask me anything and I can't lie.'

He repeats his question about the houses Tom and I were given by our parents. I didn't mention this to the Lancashire cops, so I'm guessing Lucy blabbed. She knows the full story, courtesy of Tom, but I'm betting the version she spouted was only on nodding terms with the truth – a *transmogrification*, to quote one of Tom's show-off words. So I give him facts, not lies.

I wasn't happy with living in a large home, so I sold it, banked a hundred grand, and decided to play good Samaritan with the remainder. I was in my thirties and a lot of my pals were starting to marry off and settle down, and I helped them out. I paid for all sorts of things: nights out, three honeymoons, one entire wedding, and a life-changing experience for my best pal and her daughter, who's in a wheelchair with a spinal defect. Life has now pushed most of us apart, but I still keep in contact by social media and the odd phone call, and I'm happy to know they're all doing well.

I do admit to the detective that I have sent money to my pen pal, Richard, for food and clothing. He's quite surprised, like most people would be, to hear that I know a man on death row thousands of miles away.

The money I held back was to find a nice little house. But when Mum died, I needed to look after Dad. They'd already sold the construction business and downsized their home to fund Tom and me, so I moved in with Dad. I invested half the money in this Range Rover and I live off the rest, topped up with part-time work every so often.

If I ever get in real trouble, I'll sell the car. And if ever anything happens to me and Dad gets left alone, he'll get my life insurance. Add that to the sale of his house and the Range Rover and he'll get a good care home. Right now I'm caring for my dad, but as for my own future, well, I'll think about that when he's no longer around.

Reavley nods. 'And Tom bought himself a business? An estate agency. How's that doing?'

I can tell from his eyes that this isn't small talk. He's collecting information. So I swing it back to Lucy's black soul, which is the reason this detective is standing here.

'The agency is doing well. He runs it with a partner and they deal in commercial properties. Tom makes a good living. Probably the reason why Lucy married him. She's in control of all his money. She made him give her lasting power of attorney, so she runs everything, his bank account, pension, his bills. But not his business. He's not allowed to sell his share of the estate agency without his partner's permission. That's so Lucy can't force him to sell it. Did you know she made him set up a second bank account that she transfers a small bit of his money to each month, and that's the only account he can spend from?'

'Well, they've been together years. Must be some love involved.'

'Not to watch her on her wedding day. Sour-faced, barely a smile, like she didn't want to be there. She was approaching middle age and already had a failed marriage behind her, so I think she was just desperate to hook up again before it was too late.'

Reavley gives a little nod, which seems to say he's satisfied, at least for now. Proved when he looks around at the street and says, 'So, where's this garage that isn't a garage?'

I lead him down the side of an end terrace. As we dodge overhanging branches of an unkempt hedge, Reavley asks if I have made enquiries with Tom's buddies, colleagues and family.

'Nobody has heard from him. Except for Lucifer–'

'Who?'

'Well, she's the devil, isn't she?' He realises I mean Lucy. 'She reckons she got a text from him. Just her alone in the world who heard from him.'

'I heard about it. No chance that Tom's approached a friend and asked to stay for a while, on the secret?'

'On the secret, as you say, from me? Wouldn't happen. Even if someone did let him stay, they would have told me. On the secret. But that text Lucy reckons she got. Are you going to trace it, see where it was sent from? I think Lucy sent it to herself.'

'We'll get to the bottom of that, no worries. And I'll need a list of all the places Tom is known to visit.'

It sounds a little like he's not bothered about the text Lucy supposedly got from Tom, or at least my claim that it's bullshit. I tell myself he's just doing his job. I know the police can't rely on the word of others, even though I still feel undermined. 'I have your number. I'll text them all to you when I've finished here.'

He gives me a thumbs up for this. We turn onto a path between the high-fenced back gardens and a hedge-bordered farmer's field. The edge of the field parallel to the hedge has been ploughed and in places the earth stacked into man-high berms.

'So, about Tom's estate agency. I'd like to get a list of the properties on their books.'

I know why. 'Tom isn't at any of those places.'

'How do you know?'

'Because he's dead. His evil wife killed him. She's on antidepressants, you know.'

'I know. I have to check those properties. I hope you understand that.'

I apologise and tell him the name and address of the agency. We walk on. The backyard of the middle terrace is the only one not fenced by the field, for good reason. As we walk into it, Reavley whistles in surprise.

Animal's main mechanic, Ian Brandy, lives in the middle terrace and he keeps his pet in the backyard. The truck's fibreglass body is painted green and black to simulate jungle foliage at night and menacing red eyes peek out here and there. On its competition wheels, it's twelve feet high and wide and over half again as long, and weighs over nine thousand pounds. But the machine is too big to transport in a trailer, so the giant wheels have been swapped for much smaller ones. The body sits much higher than the wheels and its innards are exposed.

Brandy's here with three other men, working on one of the giant rims, which was damaged in a jump. The three other competition wheels and the loose tyre are laid around, along with machine parts and tools. The garden is a mess, but that's the least the neighbours care about. The reason for the missing section of fence and ploughed route in the field? Animal practises there. Let's just say the supercharged Big-Block American V8 engine isn't conducive to a tranquil neighbourhood.

Reavley hangs back while I approach the boys to say hello. There's a set of coveralls awaiting me. I'm no mechanic, but I like getting oily and I do what I can to help. I take a heap of questions about Tom, especially from the pair who came with me to Lancashire on Sunday night. Everyone's worried about Tom and they know something's dodgy with him and Lucy, but I have to downplay things. I'd love to tear into Lucy, but I don't want to do that in front of Reavley. I tell them Reavely's a detective and I'm working with him to get some answers, and when I do the boys will hear everything. They know better than to keep hounding me.

When I turn to look at Reavley, I can't help but laugh. He's standing on the loose tyre, a mammoth thing as tall as me and five times as heavy. He gives a childish grin as he does a little bounce, like someone testing a rickety rope bridge. But I'm not fooled: I reckon he heard the boys firing questions at me and he's just trying to lighten the mood. It seems to work.

I'm given the simple job of cleaning and oiling tools, which I do away in a corner so Reavley and me can chat in peace. I tell him about my visit to The Cascade on Sunday and Tom's house this morning. My story matches what he was told by coppers here in Sheffield and up in Lancashire. Even better, he admits the situation is 'a little off'.

I'm not fooled into thinking he's totally in agreement though. I know the cops will look for innocent explanations for suspicious details – like the Saturday night argument in the Serengeti, when Lucy threatened Tom with a knife, and that blood on her blouse, later chucked away. But I make sure he knows that Tom doesn't miss monster machine events. Just doesn't. And if he ever did, he'd let someone know why. Just would. Reavley gives a nod of understanding.

I also know the cops like a motive, and I've got one for him. 'They don't get on these days, haven't for a long time. Lucy has been known to get incredibly angry with him a lot, and the neighbours have seen it. People at the Serengeti pub would have seen it. She pulled a knife on him on Saturday night. There will be CCTV inside that pub. You need to go get it. And you need to find his car.'

'We'll get to all that, don't worry. At the minute I'm just getting a little background. I hear you were very vocal from the outset. Determined right from the off that something had happened to Tom.'

'Yes. Rightly so, it turns out. I dread to think how long she would have lied if I hadn't pressed the point. You have to do something about this.'

'Whatever's happened, I'll get to the bottom of it. Don't worry.'

But I do worry. Lucy's sharp and sly and manipulative, and I have a horrible feeling she's going to get away with my brother's murder.

10

LUCY

I woke up early Tuesday and immediately turned my head in the hope that Tom had returned in the night. But his half of the bed was bare. Again. I touched the sheets in another wild hope: he'd been back but had risen early. But she sheets are stone cold.

The Infinity Dream I mentioned had returned again with a vengeance last night. I need my tablets. I need Tom back.

I call it a dream, but it wasn't anything of the sort because it reared its ugly head while I was awake. As a child, I'd had a fear of water ever since an accident at the Historic Dockyard, a tourist-friendly portion of HM Naval Base, Portsmouth. I'd sneakily gone through the safety ropes, up to the edge, and the next thing I knew I was in the water way below.

It had been sunny, warm, bright, lovely. But down there it was freezing and gloomy. The big hull of the ship and the dock wall seemed to press in on me, casting me into darkness, much like being trapped in a deep water well. But it wasn't a fear of drowning that got to me: it was the thought of that impenetrable blackness below. It was that, rather than the water, that got to me.

I didn't fear dark streets, or dark rooms, and I could quite easily walk into a dark cellar. Streets and rooms had ends, they had substance beyond them. Even the black ocean had a floor. What worried me was the sense of endlessness, and there was no place on earth like that. So my eyes turned to the skies.

And there it was: space, my silly Achilles Hell. Up there, beyond Earth, where the nothingness stretches to infinity. I've seen those videos from rockets launched into space: how the bright day slowly turns darker and seems to pass through a bubble, out, into a nothingness that stretched forever, and they scared me. I am the last person on Earth who'd visit space. I wouldn't go if I was paid. That big emptiness above is to me like a long drop to somewhere else.

Imagine how you'd feel hanging from a ledge fifty stories up, and that was how I sometimes felt when I considered the vastness of space and my tenuous little grip on this speck we called planet Earth. I recalled times when I had woken to find I'd pulled the elastic edge of the bedsheet away from the corner of the mattress and had clutched a big wad of that loose sheet in my fist, as if to anchor myself against being sucked away.

Once, someone had told me that if I drove the distance to Liverpool, but straight up, I'd pass what's called the Kármán line, the generally accepted boundary of space. That was not a good night. When the Infinity Dream wrapped its arms around me late at night, I couldn't sleep in my bed and would have to go downstairs. Just to get an extra few feet away!

The dream consumed me often in my late teens and twenties, but usually when I didn't have my antidepressants. Since I got married for the second time, I'd had that extra barricade. When Tom was away overnight, I had my medication, and if ever my prescription ran out, Tom was there to keep me at ease until I got more tablets. I hadn't had a problem with the dream for years. Until now.

That sleepless night last Sunday after Tom left me? Not, as Mary had said, because I was full of guilt, or because I was out burying his body. No, the dream had come back, boosted by loneliness. Only a heavy dose of alcohol had been able to offer me sleep, if only a little.

Last night hadn't been much better. As I'd mentioned, I'd slept on the sofa in order to better hear if Tom sneaked in late, but that had been only part of it. I had gone downstairs in order to put two ceilings between me and that vastness. Many hours later, as the night had begun to sluice away, I had felt myself slipping into sleep. I didn't remember heading upstairs, but woke in bed.

I felt rested though. My first thought after wondering where Tom could be: the missing person's report I'd been asked to file.

But I was scared to. It was the right thing to do, of course, because once it was official the police could start to trace him, even if he wasn't a vulnerable adult. But something made me pause. Filing that report would be a concrete admission that my marriage was over. I kind of knew it anyway, because of his affair, but I wanted to hold on to hope.

I also had to consider what I'd been told by the police: that Tom might not want to be contacted by me. It was hard to imagine that he wasn't aware I was worried about him, given how he'd simply fled without word, but I decided that I needed to do the missing person's report for those two reasons. Tom needed to know that his actions had been unfair to me and others who cared for him. And I – all of us – needed to know that he was okay.

I opened the back door, expecting Zuzu to shoot in, but the cat wasn't around. I'd mostly been joking when I said the cat could abandon me too, but I wondered if he'd cottoned on to the fact that Tom wasn't going to return. I tipped some cat treats by the step and locked up.

As I was heading to my car, I turned my eyes to the sky. I knew the brilliant blue sky was simply a reaction between sunlight and Earth's atmosphere, but being unable to see beyond it, to the black emptiness beyond, was comforting. It seemed like a barrier. I was able to laugh off the Infinity Dream of last night.

With my head turned back to accept the warmth of the sun, I didn't notice the arrival of a visitor until I heard a voice. There was a car by my gate, a tall man with an army-style flat-top standing beside it. I saw a tie poking out where he hadn't fully zipped up his leather bomber jacket. I instantly wondered if he was a friend of Tom's I didn't know.

'Sorry?' I said.

He approached the gate and plucked a little wallet from a pocket. It had a crest on the front and an ID card inside. I had to step closer to read it. Detective Inspector Aaron Reavley, South Yorkshire Police. He stuck out his hand. We shook across the gate.

'I know why you're here,' I told him. 'The police in Lancashire said they'd pass word on to the police here. So it's about my missing husband. I was just going to the station to file a missing person's report.'

He gave a nod. 'Sure. We've already got a number of details about what happened. And I can get some more from you now. I would have popped by yesterday evening, but I was running late. So can we have a quick chat? Inside?'

Inside for certain, where my neighbours couldn't see. In the living room, I tossed a towel over a pile of washed clothing on the armchair and sat before it. Reavley took the sofa. The first thing he asked me was: 'I was given the list of Tom's friends you supplied. Have you spoken to people he might have contacted?'

'They don't know where he is. Look, before you ask any more questions, I feel I should be open with you. I've been a little bit secretive, a little deceptive with the police.'

He raised his eyebrows and leaned a little closer. I could tell he was intrigued. His piercing eyes unnerved me a little, but I put it down to the ever-analytical brain of a police officer. 'Go ahead.'

'I think Tom is having an affair.'

The look that came across his face was one I didn't like. He was a little disappointed by this revelation, and I couldn't help but assume why. Because he had hoped I was about to confess to something I'd done to Tom.

'Another woman? Someone you know?'

'I don't know her. I don't know who she is.'

'So you've seen her? Seen Tom with her?'

I shook my head. 'I just know.'

'Was Tom secretive with his phone?'

I saw where this was going. 'No, if he was texting her, it was probably off a phone I don't know about. And he never had strange appointments he didn't tell me about, before you ask.'

'So why do you think he's having an affair?'

He was doubtful and I understood why. Tom's actions hadn't been what you would normally expect from a man having an affair. It was just a feeling I got. Little things he'd said. And I explained this to the detective. His reply was that he'd look into it.

Then he said, 'I should start by also being open with you. I am aware that your husband's sister is accusing you of having something to do with his disappearance, but I'm here only to get some background on you and Tom, an overview of his and your movements over the last few weeks. Just to help me understand why he might have suddenly left without word.'

'I'm not surprised by that from her. She's always hated me because I took her brother away.'

'Tell me about that.'

I recapped what I'd told the Lancashire police about Mary and Tom being left houses when their mother got ill, just over a decade ago, and that Tom had wisely used the money from the sale to invest in an estate agency business. Very smart. I wasn't as praising of Mary.

'Credit to her, she spent a lot of her life looking after Tom when he was young because their parents weren't really able to. But when he left home at eighteen, she decided it was time to start spending some money. She travelled, and she bought expensive items, and she splashed out on lavish parties for her friends. Then the money was gone. Her friends abandoned her because they settled down. Mary suddenly had no money and no house and was forced to remain living with her parents. When her mother died and her father got worse, she was forced to become his carer. Tom said his father's got dementia, but Mary doesn't seem to want to get him diagnosed so he can get professional help. She might have to get him moved into a home, and then she'd lose the house. She doesn't care about him.

'I think she still resents that Tom made something of his life and she didn't. She's stuck looking after her father, but she can't blame her brother, so she blames me. If we hadn't got married she would still have her brother and maybe they'd be living together. And she'd have help. It's why she's so eager to read too much into every falling out I have with Tom. That's my theory, anyway. The argument in the Serengeti pub was one such overreaction.'

'That's the night before he disappeared, right? Tell me about that. Is it true you threatened him with a knife?'

I had to shut that word from my mind: disappeared. I kept

using the term *left me*, but nobody else did. They kept saying he'd disappeared, vanished. I didn't like that.

I should have told the police this story earlier and I still didn't know why I hadn't – it had allowed them to believe the worst. Now, finally, I had that chance, and the words tumbled out.

'Yes, I raised a knife at Tom, but it was a butter knife and it was a prop to wave, that was all. We were sitting in the pub, at a dinner table, and there was a fork in my other hand. Yes, I made pointing gestures with it, and yes, my voice was raised. But I would have pointed with my finger if my hand was empty. I remained seated. Tom didn't flinch. Nobody wrestled me to the ground. Nobody called the police. The landlord saw it happen and didn't even mention it when talking to us as we left. It meant nothing. Total overreaction on Mary's part.'

'But she got the story from Tom, right? There was a text message...'

'Then it was a total overreaction on Tom's part. He was smoking his electronic cigarette and getting funny looks. I told him to put it away, but he wouldn't. Said he knew the owner and he wouldn't mind. But we also argued about some furniture I wanted to buy, which Tom said we couldn't afford, although he was happy to spend money on his monster truck obsession. I think he was probably annoyed and, knowing Mary's dislike of me, was aware he'd get a better reaction from her if he overplayed the seriousness of the scene.'

'But why would he do that?'

'Because...' I was aware of what he was getting at: why would Tom 'overplay' the scene if we were a loved-up couple? 'We'd argued. I admit we argue a lot. Tom might have been annoyed with me. But Mary has always hated me and maybe he just wanted a little moan about me to her, to relieve pressure. We all do it, don't we? Exaggerate things a bit.'

'You say the argument was about money? Is money an issue?'

'No more than for any other couple. He didn't like to spend on the house, but he'll spend on his vehicle.'

Was he looking for a motive as to why I'd kill Tom? I'd hoped this detective would be on my side. I had to remind myself that he was simply keeping an open mind. He didn't know me or Tom or Mary, and his was a profession that put him amongst the most bizarre of people and circumstances. But looking at me was just wasting time that could be spent searching for Tom.

'Look, Mr Reavley, do you really need to ask all these questions? Can't you just look for Tom?'

He completely ignored my question. 'He'll spend on his vehicle? The monster machine, Animal? Not many people own monster trucks. How did that come about?'

I explained that Tom had always been a fan of monster trucks and a few years ago he and two old college friends – the same pair who'd accompanied Mary on that fateful visit to the country cottage on Sunday evening – had spotted an advert from a mechanic seeking investment to build a truck. All four of them had a part-share in Animal, which toured the UK performing in shows. Such shows would often keep Tom away overnight, and a lot of his spare time was spent working on the truck. And a lot of our money.

'But none of this is helping to find Tom, detective. Not that I can see. What can you do to find him? You heard that he sent me a text message?'

'I heard. Off a new phone. I'll look into that. First of all, I need his original phone. He didn't take it, I heard. Do you have it?'

I did. Upstairs somewhere. I said I'd fetch it. As I got up, he said, 'We need something that Tom has touched. We need his DNA and fingerprints. They should be on his mobile phone, but

I'd like something else, something more likely to give us those things. A toothbrush would do. Is there one here?'

'No. It was in a bag of toiletries that I packed up. Tom took it when he sneaked back to the cottage in the night. A razor? That's here. He didn't take it. He hasn't shaved in months. He's got a horrible beard.'

He asked for the razor and I led him upstairs, to the bathroom. He put the razor in a plastic bag, careful to pick it up by just two fingers at the end. I said, 'My prints might be on that.'

'We have yours. How about that mobile?'

It was in the bedroom. I handed it over with the same care he'd used with the razor: two fingers. It was put into a separate bag.

'Now, do you mind if I have a little look around the house? For any indication of where Tom might have gone? I saw an office with a computer.'

'Yes. We both use it. We share the office. Until I get my Shangri-La.'

'What's that?'

'I want Tom to build me an office at the bottom of the garden. So we don't get under each other's feet.' I realised that final sentence might give the wrong impression, so quickly edited it. 'When we're working, I mean. We both use the same computer and it will be easier when we have a separate space each.'

He made no reply to this, which I wasn't sure was good or bad or neutral. We went downstairs so he could start his search. I sat on the sofa. After a glance around the living room, he took to the kitchen, where I heard the rustle of papers pinned to our noticeboard. When he returned, he said he'd like to go back upstairs, and would I accompany him?

In the spare bedroom Tom and I used as an office, DI

Reavley sat at the desk and rubbed a finger on the open laptop. He raised his eyebrows at me when a password screen appeared, so I typed it in. Immediately, he saw an icon of a house and hovered the mouse over it.

'Is this what I think it is?'

If he thought it was a folder containing Tom's work, then yes. He clicked on a Word document and was presented with a list of addresses of the properties managed by the agency. I explained that the files on this laptop were backups from the main computer, copied onto a flash drive and transferred.

'This is good. Just what I wanted.'

I was puzzled. 'How can this help... oh. You think Tom might have hidden in one of the offices he has the keys for?'

'Just something we need to check. I assume copies of the keys to all these places are at the agency?'

'Yes.'

He clicked and pointed at the date the document was last edited. 'This list is twelve days old. So this won't have any properties listed on the website since then.'

'Well, it should. Tom makes a copy for home every time they update the website with a new property.'

'But I suppose it's like when you visit a second-hand car showroom, right? Everything clean and good to go is out front with a price tag. But round the back are all the dirty cars they won't want you to see.'

I shrugged. 'You mean there might be some properties that aren't ready for viewing yet? Probably. But if you want a list of those, you need to get that off the main computer, at Tom's office.'

Reavley closed the folder and clicked a Gmail icon to open emails. I decided that he might be here a while, so offered tea, which he accepted.

I took my time with it, to give him chance to read some of

Tom's emails. I had already scanned them and knew there was no blatant clue as to where he'd gone. We had access to each other's emails, so he'd never used his account to contact his other woman.

But when I took the tea upstairs, I noticed a summer field background image on the Gmail. That was mine. The detective was reading through my emails.

'There's an email here from Auto Trader about a valuation on a BMW 3 Series. Tom's car, I assume. Why is this on your email?'

'Tom asked me to value it for him.'

'I understood that Tom treasured his BMW. He wants to sell it?'

'Or to just know what it was worth today. It's five years old.'

'Okay. So he does treasure it? Wouldn't want to get rid of it?'

'Well, maybe at some point. I don't know for sure.'

I thought he was about to ask another question concerning the car, but shifted his eyes to the laptop. 'Do you mind if I take this computer to get it analysed?'

'You won't find anything about his other woman on there. He was careful. Look, I don't have Gmail on my phone, and Tom might send an email. I use the laptop a lot. I do my online tutoring using it. It has my recording software. I use it every day.'

He didn't push it. 'How about if I forward a number of these emails of yours and Tom's to my own account? And a copy of the properties list? Just so I'm not sitting in your house all day?'

I didn't mind that, not if there was a chance that something I'd overlooked or considered insignificant might make the breakthrough in the case. I left his tea and went downstairs. I just sat on the sofa, thinking about places Tom might have gone to.

Reavley joined me about fifteen minutes later. He drank his

tea while standing up in the centre of the room, looking down at me.

'I'd like to visit the estate agency to get an up-to-date copy of that property file, and just to have a look at his workspace. Tonight, when the place is closed. Think you could come with me?'

It was a good idea. There could be a Post-it note or call on the branch phone or whatever that provided a clue. It meant I would have to admit the truth to Peter, but to be honest I welcomed the pressure. Coming clean now beat the idea of a month of sick calls on Tom's behalf. 'I'll call his partner and tell him we're coming. The branch shuts at six.'

'Six it is, then. I'll meet you there.'

Reavley said it was time for him to leave. He thanked me for my co-operation as I followed him to the door. But just before he opened it, he turned to me. We were just a foot apart, in the hallway. It reminded me of seeing Tom out to work on a morning. They were both the same height. I almost told the detective to have a good day and bring me a treat home. Silly.

'I need to just mention something I found on a background check. About six months ago you were arrested for domestic disturbance.'

He gave that prompting raise of the eyebrows again.

'Well, I'm sure you know the reason for that. Tom's a practical joker and he crushed my last two tablets and slipped them into a friend's drink. I'm sure you've been told about my medication, too. It's fluoxetine. Yes, I'm on antidepressants, and yes, I was annoyed at Tom and I struck him out on the street. It was over right then and Tom even made a joke about my punch, but a neighbour called the police.'

'I did know that. But I'm not suggesting–'

'You're not, but his bloody sister is. I've been off my meds for ten days, but that was Tom's fault.'

I explained. I had sent Tom to post my repeat prescription at the doctor's surgery, but three days later when I went to collect the signed form, it wasn't there. Tom admitted he'd forgotten to post it, and had since lost it. I got a new prescription into the surgery, but that was late last Thursday: with the weekend, it meant my medication wouldn't be ready until today.

'I'll be going to collect it shortly. Yes, I have major depressive episodes. Yes, I'm more likely to argue with Tom if I don't have my tablets. No, none of those arguments made me pick up a weapon and kill my husband.'

DI Reavley apologised, then left. I couldn't work out whether he believed my story.

MARY

I'm at the shops when I get a call from Tom's business partner. I realise I forgot that Fat Pete's been waiting for me to call him back with an explanation for Tom missing work. But some other little birdie has already been at his ear.

'Mary. I just heard Tom left his wife and ran off somewhere. What's he playing at? Where is he?'

Suddenly, Tom's the one in the wrong here? Oh, I wonder who that gossiping little birdie could be. I want to tell him that his source actually killed Tom and either buried him out in the middle of nowhere or pushed him into a ravine. But it'll start a long chat I don't want to have.

'That's right. We're calling people. Don't worry about it. You haven't heard from him since we last spoke, have you?'

Unless he held a seance, I know the answer. But for now I'm stuck with telling the same lies as Lucy.

'No, but obviously the cops think I might have.'

'What do you mean?'

What he means is that the gossiping little birdie asked if she could visit the branch at closing time with a detective to have a look at the firm's computer files. 'Why, do they think there's something on the files?'

That bitch. Instead of tying herself up with lies and getting arrested for murder, Lucy has somehow convinced the cops that she's on the level. And I know which one: DI Reavley. I'm sure a flash of thigh was part of the magic trick.

'It's just routine, Pete. They're looking for clues. I'm coming down there.'

'No need. I can sort Lucy out.'

I'm sure the slimy sod would love to try. 'Keep them there till I arrive.'

'No need, Mary, I–'

'One hour.'

I hang up and dump my shopping trolley of goods right in the aisle. Closing time at the branch is 6pm, less than forty minutes from now. I have to be quick if I'm to stop Lucy completely wrapping the detective round her finger.

I'm almost out of petrol, which is annoying. It involves a stop, but after filling up, I find myself at the back of a big queue because the till is knackered. I head outside and round to the night pay window, but before I can say a word the cashier points at the queue, then ignores me. My driver's licence slamming against the glass gets her attention again.

'No cash. I'll be back to pay tomorrow. Remember these details.'

She starts to blab that I can't just take petrol, but I'm already jogging to my car. Seconds later, I'm speeding towards the centre of Sheffield, and cursing the day Lucy was born.

LUCY

Tom's partner, Peter, was lewd, overweight, owner of two divorces, and in the past he'd made no secret of the fact that he liked me. Tom had only been missing a gnat's breath, but Peter greeted me at the door of Packham/Smith Estate Agents like I was a prostitute he'd ordered.

The branch was on East Parade in the city centre, down a little cobbled street between a row of old buildings and Sheffield Cathedral. Because it was the city centre, I expected parking to be horrendous. But Reavley laid up his car on double yellow lines at the Campo Lane end of the street. He didn't leave anything on show that said the owner was a policeman.

The branch was next to the Children's Food Trust, with a big window recessed in an arch and a glass door in the middle. Peter was behind his desk inside, with his feet on the table. Their secretary was gone for the day. As he came to unlock the door, I noticed that he'd already made use of Tom's empty area by dumping files on the desk.

Peter greeted us exactly as I expected. The tall DI got a respectful handshake and not much eye contact, since Peter had been arrested three times for driving offences and had been banned. I got a lascivious look up and down.

He led us inside and over to Tom's desk. Tom's rain jacket, always left here, was still over the back of his chair and an empty teacup was on the mouse mat, as if he'd just popped out. If only. I tried to picture him in the chair, but my imagination was tainted by an old memory: the last time I'd visited had been eight or so months ago, when he didn't have a beard and was fresh off a wrist fracture, so my image had him smooth-faced and sporting a forearm cast.

'So you wanted to take the computer? Any word from him?'

'Not yet. And, yes, I want the computer.'

He and Peter worked at unplugging the machine from all its peripherals and got annoyed at the tangle of knotted cables, all dusty and some of them even stuck together from a long-ago spilled glass of fizzy Coca-Cola. It was almost funny to watch the two men struggle, until Reavley stepped away.

'Bloody twisted mess.'

'This from a man who unravels complex crimes,' I said as I stepped in to help. I felt better suddenly and knew it was because my life at the minute lacked moments of fun. I needed to laugh more. 'A bit of patience and perseverance.'

When the machine was ready to transport, we left it on the table and, over the next half an hour, Peter showed us around the branch and gave details of Tom's role. I was very intrigued because I'd only been to the office a handful of times and usually to drop off or collect something. In fact, as we headed into the back, I realised this was an area I'd never seen.

Reavley was shown the file cabinet in the back where everybody kept personal items, but nothing in there warranted scrutiny. Some kind of detective intuition made him look behind a paper wall planner, where he found the company safe, but his request to see the contents was rebuffed by Peter – 'Some personal items of mine, so I'd rather not open it. I hate to use this TV line, but get a warrant and you can.'

Reavley was then given a rundown of the branch's history and got a negative answer to his question of whether there were any disgruntled clients. He also obtained the details of Joanna, the secretary, and asked a number of questions about her history, personality, and private life. It seemed a little like Reavley was wondering if Joanna might be the woman I suspected Tom of having an affair with, but he denied this when I asked.

Unfortunately, I made the mistake of asking this within earshot of Peter, who perked up. I realised what a horrendous error I'd made. Peter said nothing until it was time to leave. Reavley exited first, with the bulky desktop under his arm, and that was when Peter asked for a quick word. Reavley said he'd meet me at the car, so I was left alone to endure a question I knew was coming.

'If things aren't going well with you two and you're on a break, it's probably okay to go for a drink with other people. How about you and me–'

I didn't let him finish. 'Tom's going to be back soon.'

'Oh, yeah, I know. I just meant if you needed, you know, advice or something.'

I gave a smile, said thanks, and exited.

I had expected this from Peter. The first time I met the guy was actually on my wedding day, when he was a last-minute replacement for Tom's best man due to the other chap busting his knee. He'd been eyeing me up all through the service and chose to make a move within an hour of my finger boasting a shiny diamond ring. I had felt really bad all day with stomach pains, and it had been a chore to try to grin and have fun for the sake of our guests.

I hadn't told Tom about it, not wishing to put a dampener on his day. After the service, when everyone went outside to pose for photos, I had sneaked around to the graveyard to get some air and had started throwing up in a bush. And then Peter had appeared. Pretending to help as I was bent over, vomiting, he'd caressed the back of my neck while remarking how sexy I looked. Bent over, being sick: sexy? I hastily got away from him and found another quiet place. Something else I'd never told Tom.

At the end of the cobbled street, twenty metres away, I saw Reavley just standing there, clearly talking to someone out of sight beyond the corner of the building. I had to move closer before the angle allowed me to see who.

Mary.

She was breathless, as if she'd rushed to meet us. I had no

clue how she'd known we were here, but I knew why she'd come. To make sure I didn't captivate the detective with my so-called lies. I heard Reavley say, 'To check the files on it for information.' She must have asked why he wanted the computer.

When she saw me, stopped about five metres back, she responded to his answer loudly, to make sure I heard.

'I don't agree with all this looking into Tom's files and his friends and stuff. There's no point because Lucifer here killed him. You should be searching the cottage in Cullerton instead of wasting time with computers.'

That got a turn of the head from a guy across the road who was unlocking a pushbike chained to a fence. He didn't try to hide his interest. 'You're the only one who thinks that,' I said. I didn't move closer.

'At the minute. But not for long. I'm going to make everyone aware. This time next week, you'll be in prison.'

'This time next week, Tom will be right here, holding my hand.'

'Oh, did he say that in another phantom text from an untraceable phone?'

'You're just upset that he thought of contacting me first. Where's your text?'

I froze in fear as she moved towards me. But she only went past, with a sneer, and towards the estate agency, doubtless to ask Peter what we'd spoken to him about. Or to pour water on my version of the story.

Reavley said nothing about Mary's turning up. Nothing about her accusation. But after he'd loaded the computer into the boot and we were belted up, he said, 'This is probably going to seem a little awkward in light of what your husband's sister just said. But I promise you I didn't just make this decision and I'm treating Tom as a missing person still.'

I nodded.

'I'd like to get a couple of people to search the cottage in Cullerton, if that's okay? Probably tomorrow morning.'

'Sure. Yes. I mean, it's a good idea, it's just that some officers from up there searched it already.'

'That was just a cursory glance. I'd like to have a proper search. Not like you see on TV, of course.' He gave a smile. 'We won't be lifting floorboards or anything. No damage. No drawers tipped out. Maybe we'll even find your wedding ring.'

I instinctively glance at my finger. Had the Carters' young daughter told him what I'd told her about my ring?

Seeing my puzzlement, he said, 'I noticed you weren't wearing it when I visited earlier. And you didn't have it on when officers spoke to you at the cottage yesterday.'

'Oh, I did leave it at the cottage. You're right. I took it off because I was angry at Tom. Because of the affair. Hopefully you'll find it for me. I'll get you the key when you drop me off.'

'Well, I was hoping you could come with us. Ride there with me. I'll pick you up. You know the cottage, so you really should be there. Being there might make you remember where you left the ring.'

'Sure. Okay,' I answered immediately. It was a good idea. Since Tom had left me while we were having a weekend at the cottage, it made sense as the most likely location to find evidence of where he'd gone. I wasn't too sure about what help I could be though. I'd seen nothing of note during my time alone on Sunday evening. But then, unlike Reavley, I wasn't trained in what to look for.

I tried to relax during the drive home, but I kept glancing at the detective, trying to work out from his demeanour if he trusted or suspected me. If his reason for wanting me to accompany him tomorrow was for assistance, or to keep me under observation. He'd said he wasn't treating Tom's absence as foul play, but... well, also unlike him, I wasn't trained in how to spot a liar.

MARY

I just can't relax this evening. After Dad falls asleep in his armchair, I clean, and I read, and I look for a recipe for cake, and none of it works.

I even try to write to my pen pal, Richard. I want to tell him everything, but putting Lucy's name on paper just makes me annoyed. Besides, he's got his own problems and I don't want to make him worry about me. I try a bath because that can sometimes wipe bad moods away. Not tonight.

For about the millionth time, I try the phone number Tom's evil wife reckoned he texted her from, but again it's a dead line. DI Reavley told me he'd try to trace the phone, which they can do even if it's turned off, but I'm still waiting for him on that. If the cops can do that trace, maybe we'll find out where that phone was when the text was sent.

I know they're hoping to get a location for Tom, but they're blind. Even if Tom had had just one text left in his entire life, it would be to me. The cops might think he'd be more likely to contact Lucy, but they don't know the score. The days of heart-pounding love between Tom and Lucy are long gone, but a brother–sister bond never loses strength. Tom didn't contact me, so Tom didn't contact anyone. He's not able to.

Soon, though, the cops will finally get on my page. I know Lucy sent that text to herself and when it's traced to her bloody bedroom, that will be the proof she's been fobbing everyone off with rancid lies. I can't wait.

I won't sleep tonight, so I jam on my shoes and take a drive, even though it's nearly midnight. When I met DI Reavley the first time, he asked me for a rundown of what Tom, Lucy and I had been doing over the preceding weeks, and I use the drive to think of things I might have missed. I don't think I planned a destination, so maybe I was just taking known streets out of habit or something deep in the back of my mind made a choice. Either way, I end up outside Tom's house.

I park across the road and kill the engine. The street is hushed, dead, just a scattering of lights in a few houses. One of which is Tom's bedroom.

Some killers are bloodthirsty monsters and can't hide it, but others are just typical people. They're not hunchbacks and they don't stroll around covered in blood. They're like me, or you. Invisible because of their normalcy. And they live routine lives on streets like this. Behind closed doors, though, is where the mask slips off. I look at Tom's bedroom window, at the net curtains she put up for privacy, and wonder what Lucy's up to?

What does a killer do at night, when alone? Lay and pray to God for forgiveness? Speak to themselves in the mirror, their mind running through things to do, or mistakes made, or just giving the ego a pep talk? Pace and worry about the door knock that will kick-start a long prison sentence?

That last one gives me an idea, so I head across the road and creep to the front door. At first, I lift the letterbox flap and listen, but that suddenly feels stupid. What am I expecting to hear – Lucy confessing all into that mirror? So I bang on the door, hard. Like the cops.

Once she knows it's me outside, she'll relax, but I like the idea of her spending long seconds collapsed on her knees, heart thudding with utter panic. I want her to open that door with black misery all over her face. But I don't get my wish because thirty seconds after the knock, my phone rings. On the screen it says SUCCUBUS. I wonder what nasty insult I'm listed in her phone as? I open the call but say nothing, waiting.

'What do you want?' Lucy says.

Do killers with rotten minds have a sixth sense for danger? Maybe she just expected a trick like this. More likely she stuck her face against the bedroom window and saw my car. 'I want you to go to prison for my brother's murder.'

'He left me, Mary. Tom's left me and he was your only connection to me, so now why don't you get out of my life?'

She sounds sleepy, as if I woke her. That was something I missed from my list: some killers don't regret their actions, or fear the consequences of them, and can quite easily sleep like babies. It angers me. 'No. I'm here for the long run. You'll see a lot of me. I'll prove you killed Tom.'

'I'm meeting a detective tomorrow to search The Cascade. Soon we'll have all this cleared up. And then you can leave me alone.'

'DI Aaron Reavley,' I say, hoping to alert her that I'm in this deep. I make sure I use his first name. 'Aaron and I had a long chat. Don't start thinking he's on your side. He's looking for that one piece of evidence. And you'll know when he finds it, because he'll snap handcuffs on you. I can't wait to watch it happen.'

'And then what will you do? You have no life. You only had Tom and that was why you always stuck your nose into our marriage. Apart from sit at home, what will you do after I'm in prison and you've got nothing to obsess over except your silly death-row pen pal?'

A weak comeback. She's better at lies than insults. 'You're one to talk. I have friends, Lucy. My own friends. You don't. All the people you and Tom know, they're all Tom's gang, aren't they? You don't know anyone. Have you sent yourself any more texts from that new phone yet?'

'That was Tom. You're just sour he contacted me, not you.'

'You're stupid if you think anyone believes that. Or if you

think the police won't find out you sent that text to yourself. Sleep well knowing that, won't you? I'll see you tomorrow. And the day after. And for as many days as it takes. Oh, and I'll be in court when you get sent down for the rest of your life. Just look for the woman with the big grin.'

I hang up, content with that ending to our little chat. As I walk away, I expect her to be at the window to watch. No. She doesn't appear as I set the car rolling, either. That's a little unnerving. I'm not a worry for her. She thinks she's too clever.

My line about seeing her tomorrow – which is actually today – was meant only to scare her, but it gives me an idea. If she and Reavley are going to the cottage tomorrow, I need to be there. There will be a search of the area, too, and I want to join in. I want her to see me joining in. And I'd love to be the one who finds the piece of evidence that buries her. I'll laugh right in her face as I hold it up for all to see.

I don't like the idea of oversleeping and arriving too late, so I turn the wheel and head for the motorway. I'll go to the cottage right now, so I'm ready and rested when everyone arrives. So what if Cullerton's few crappy bed and breakfasts are shut – I'll sleep in the car, I don't care. I can't wait to see her face tomorrow when she arrives at The Cascade and finds me standing there, waiting for her.

11

LUCY

Four of us rode to Cullerton: me, DI Reavley, and two detectives from his team. Apart from when Tom's obnoxious sister had turned up to feed her bullyish nature, I had had an uneventful evening yesterday. I had stayed indoors and kept away from the windows, unwilling to face stares from my neighbours. I was fearful of another Infinity Dream, so I had stayed up late and spent some time on the internet. Following Mary's appearance at my door and her hint that she was cosy with DI Reavley, I had turned my Google search to the detective.

It had been easy to find reference to him, because only last month his team solved a murder case in which a woman had been missing for seven weeks. It seemed that DI Reavley was a respected, clever policeman with experience investigating missing people who turned up dead. Good.

I realised that Mary hadn't been blowing off steam when she claimed that Reavley was simply pretending to be on my side. A detective like this man didn't chase down adult missing persons unless there was grave concern for their well-being and a criminal to snare. Even then, he could have delegated today's trip to a lowly constable. But he hadn't.

I had to accept the horrible truth that the police suspected Tom had met with foul play and my hand was involved. Reavley appeared to be understanding and sympathetic towards me, but he was analysing me for guilty behaviour, a condemning remark, and enough evidence to arrest me. For murder.

And what better way to do that than by suggesting I ride with him to the cottage?

So there I was, in the passenger seat of his car, while his comrades rode behind us in their own vehicle, and I was terrified. It was a strange feeling, really, because he was on his own in the car with me, just another human being, who was well-spoken, polite, and courteous. Yet it felt like sitting two feet from a bomb, or a sleeping lion. I was completely on edge, fearing that the very next moment he'd suddenly transform and ruin my life.

He'd started asking questions immediately, before the car had even left my street. At first, he wanted to know about Tom – likes, habits, routines – and informed me that knowing all about the missing man might help him 'work out *where* he's gone.' His questions had a light tone, designed to put me at ease. Understanding and sympathetic, right? So, with a thudding heart and a fear that one wrong word could spell disaster, I answered those questions about Tom.

Soon enough, an accusation came: 'We spoke to some of your friends. They'd heard he was missing from another friend, someone who visited you with Mary on Sunday night at the cottage. But they said you never contacted them. You didn't ask around Tom's people if anyone had heard from him. You told me you did.'

'I didn't say that. I said no one had heard from him. They were calling me that night, so I knew they'd been told. Look, Mr

Reavley, they're Tom's friends more than they're mine. He doesn't want me to know where he is, or he would have contacted me. And if he's contacted his friends, you can bet they've been told not to tell me. So I didn't bother.'

DI Reavley turned to another angle. 'You lived in Germany for a while, right?'

He was watching the road for dangers ahead, and I watched him for the same reason. Before his question, he'd said that knowing all about the missing man's wife might help him 'work out *why* he's gone.' But it was hard to avoid thinking that he instead sought to determine *why* I had killed Tom.

'Lucy? You lived in Germany for a while, is that right?'

I broke away from that negative thought, right into another. If Reavley had talked to Mary, he would have already heard a version of this story. And I very much doubted it matched the one I'd told Tom – a *transmogrification*, as Tom himself might have said. I would not lie to a police officer, so Reavley got the same tale. As I recapped my life, I stared out my window at wind turbines on a distant hill and tried to pretend I wasn't being interrogated by a suspicious murder detective.

I had had a work placement in the state of Baden-Württemberg right after school, some twenty-five years ago now. In my final year of school, I had been so finicky about a career path, often obsessing over one before abruptly deciding on another, that my parents had come up with a plan to make sure I stuck at something. As restaurant managers with many contacts in the industry, they got me a job with an old colleague who'd set up three restaurants in Stuttgart. My mum told me the language barrier and distance from schoolfriends would focus my concentration.

So I went over there, worked for their friend and lodged at his house. Six months into it, my dad admitted the truth: their tactic had not been to intensify my learning, but to simply stick me in a place where I couldn't just walk out of a job. And it had been a good call because who would have hired a foreign teenager with no skills and no comprehension of the language?

One of the other two teenagers who worked in the restaurant was Rolf, who I started dating. Towards the end of my eighteen-month placement, we found our own place to live. I quit the restaurant and taught English to a handful of students from home, but Rolf remained in the business. He had been promoted and was earning well. The outlook was good. My parents were happy.

But the marriage crumbled over time and soon became abusive. Rolf drank and it unleashed the devil in him. After one episode, which I didn't elaborate on for the DI and won't go into here, I had a nervous breakdown and spent time in hospital.

I soon came to hate my husband and my surroundings and everything about my life. Slowly, everything tying me to Germany unknotted, until the sole remaining reason to stay was a girl my age called Leona, who lived with her boyfriend and mother in the flat above ours. We'd met after Rolf had thrown me out of the flat and I'd spent most of the evening curled up outside the door.

Finding me asleep in the hallway, Leona had offered her sofa, and from that moment we became the best of friends. A car accident resulting in paraplegia had virtually confined her to her home and I wasn't one for going out, so we spent hours a day together. She would colour and straighten my hair. I would push her around the block in an old shopping trolley someone had left by the communal bins. I helped her develop her English and she boosted my German.

And when her boyfriend suddenly decided he didn't want to be attached to a paraplegic and ended their relationship, our bond strengthened. I would try to convince her that there were beautiful and rich men out there who would look past her disability. And she would insist I'd soon find a man who wouldn't abuse me.

I later found out that when she'd seen me sleeping outside my flat, it hadn't been because the lift opened on the wrong floor, as she'd claimed. Having heard the arguments between Rolf and me, Leona had made a point of travelling down a floor to check up on me. She was also the only person who visited me when I was in a psychiatric hospital.

In short, she was the best thing in my life, a true soulmate, right when I absolutely needed one. Then one day she and her mother moved house, many miles away, and that final bond to the country was suddenly gone. Within a month I had left the country and returned to England. And met Tom. Once my divorce from Rolf was finalised, I married Tom.

When this tale was told, I stared at the detective, hoping to read his analysis of it. All he gave was a little nod, which I couldn't work out. I didn't even try. A couple of miles passed beneath the car before he spoke again.

'Do you miss your life over there?'

A truck trying to undertake us pulled sluggishly alongside, turning my view from green fields to dirty red. It broke my peaceful trance.

The truth was that I was embarrassed by my existence in Germany, and despite having a husband and job and soulmate, *existence* was the right word to describe it. Consumed by darkness in my mind, overwhelming everything, I did not *live*. I would not call my existence life, given that it was a word often employed to describe all the beauty and fun and purpose of the human experience. So bleak was this period, I had blotted most of it out. Even Tom knew little about my twenties and early thirties, and knew not to ask.

'Do you ever hear from your ex-husband?'

Enough was enough. I slapped the dashboard, hard.

Frustration, at myself, washed aside all fear of the man beside me and what he could do. 'No. No. None of that will help us find Tom. It was way before he was in my life and has nothing to do with right now. Don't ask again.'

We rode in silence for a while.

MARY

The first thing I think about when I wake is Lucy and just how much I hate that bitch. It's supposed to be summer, but it's freezing at ten to six in the morning. I'm in my car in the car park of the Serengeti pub, neck aching because my jacket is a shitty pillow. So, cold and in pain, I curse that bitch, who's probably still snuggled up in bed, and spreading out because Tom's half has only his cold imprint.

It's not just that though. Late last night I told myself to focus on possibilities, not likelihoods. So, I needed to convince myself that Tom might still be alive. This was because I started to worry what his body would look like by now, after decomposing for a few days under the hot sun, or beneath the cold water, or in the insect-infested soil. I had to fight against my belief he was dead, because it was better to imagine him living a new life somewhere, like Lucy claimed.

But it didn't work, and even trying to be positive about what had happened to my brother made coming back to reality feel like a head-on crash into a truck. This morning the feeling is even worse. Tom is dead and I am going to suffer the pain of losing him for years, and it is all that bitch's fault.

This thought clears the sleep from my head and I forget the cold and the neck pain. It makes me determined that it will be today. Today I'll expose that woman. Today I'll watch her be carted off to prison. Today I'll smile for the first time in ages.

From the back seat I can see partway down the main road and Baker's – a newsagent, confusingly – is starting to open. The owner, an obese fifty-something who – believe it or not – was a local junior bodybuilding champion, opens his door and slaps an ice-cream sign on the pavement. Then he flicks his door sign over, from CLOSED to OPEN.

I put my creased jacket on and take a stroll. It's too early for the cops and Lucy to arrive, but I rush across the road – how bizarre would it look if they came up the street and there I was, filling their windscreen? Even this wild thought gives another boost to my boiling Lucy-hate, as I fret about what poison she'll feed the detective during their cosy drive.

In the shop I buy a pre-packed sandwich for later and the last carton of apple juice. Since I was at this shop – what, a couple of years ago? – Mr Baker has invested in a tea machine. I buy one coffee for the caffeine and one tea for the taste. Then I wait at the till. The owner seems to have not heard the bell above the door because he doesn't waddle out until I rap a coin on the counter.

'Hello there. Visiting?' Baker says as he oozes from a doorway barely big enough for him. He looks a little puzzled because it's too early for tourists, so he asks if I've got family in the area. When I point out that my brother and his wife rent The Cascade, it perks him up.

'I saw police. And I heard they were down there because of a problem.'

So word has spread. Given his lustful eyes – and I know it's not me with my sleep-bedraggled hair and no make-up – he wants gossip, eager to be the focus of attention as people come at him to find out what he knows. I'm happy to give him some.

'It's my brother and his wife. His wife, Lucy, you remember her?'

He doesn't, until I mention Tom's full name and that he's an estate agent. Baker once got Tom to value his shop, so remembers him. And Lucy. 'So what's going on with the police and them two? Don't tell me The Cascade got burgled? That little bad 'un Badhen just got out of prison. He'd be the sort.'

Don't know any bad boy called Badhen, but good for him and his cartoon nickname. No one's going to care about his naughty escapades by day's end, if things go my way. 'Tom's gone missing and the police reckon Lucy's killed him.'

His jaw drops. 'You mean killed him at The Cascade? You're joking.'

'Wish I was. He vanished on Sunday and she's acting very suspicious. She says he ran away and left her, but there's evidence she hurt him. The police are coming today as well.'

'Wow. So there's no body? I'd search the ravine. They didn't find that old lady Grady, the one who went wandering, for two weeks. Head's messed up, can't remember anyone's names or anything.'

Don't know any Old Lady Grady, either. Is he having a laugh with these names? 'There should be crime-scene investigators and divers and search dogs and helicopters. It'll be busy here today. So get ready to sell all your doughnuts.'

He's almost bouncing with excitement. 'So Cullerton might be famous? No, isn't it infamous? Did she kill anyone else?'

Oh, a serial killer slinking around this tiny hamlet would go down a treat. Maybe Baker's imagining running the sorts of guided tours people take around Jack the Ripper's old Whitechapel stomping grounds. 'We're not sure yet. So keep an eye out for police cars and forensics vans.'

He wants to know more, but I tell him I've got to go make some enquiries about a machine that can search deep underground for bones. Outside, I check through the window and see he's already on his landline to spread the word.

Hopefully he's telling Lost Hope Pope and Floozie Suzie and the tale will spread like wildfire.

Gossiping about Lucy isn't something I'm proud of, but she deserves it. And it cheered me up. I don't want her to get away with murdering my brother, but it might take a while for the cops to arrest her. So until then, I'll make sure her life isn't a walk in the park.

I've already begun poisoning Sheffield against her and, starting with my little action in the newsagent, I'll see to it that she gets no peace in Cullerton, either. Or anywhere else. Even if she flees back to Germany, her evil act will be in hot pursuit. I'll see to it there's not a friendly place on the whole planet, no matter if it costs me an arm and a leg in plane tickets. And if she runs to hide on the moon, I'll email the guys and gals on the international space station so they can harass her. Hers will be one name Old Lady Grady remembers forever.

Warming thoughts indeed for a chilly morning as I sit alone in my car and eat my breakfast.

12

LUCY

My phone rang. I looked at the screen with dismay. 'This is something I hadn't thought about. Now that Tom has gone.'

'Who is it?' Reavley asked. We'd covered a few motorway miles in silence and he'd slipped into a kind of autopilot. Now he sat up straight, intrigued.

'Broadband cold caller again.'

After a brief flash of disappointment, the look on his face changed to one of confusion: why would a broadband caller cause me such upset? Before he could ask, I answered the call, but said nothing at first. But the caller probably heard a voice anyway: Reavley chose that moment to wave a fist at his window and insult a 'lunatic biker' who blew past us.

The voice on the other end spoke, asking if I was Tom Packham.

What? Did I sound like a man? I restrained an urge to be sarcastic. 'No, actually it's Lucy Packham.'

The caller asked if I had broadband and if I was happy with it.

'We've never had any problems. Tom and I have always been happy with what we had. Our connection has always been perfect.'

The brash caller insisted he could beat our existing supplier. I found myself getting annoyed. Sure, the man had a job to do and had no idea of the meteor that had struck my life. But shouldn't these people consider that some of those they call might being going through tragedy? He hadn't even asked if I was okay.

'Better? Ha, ha. Okay, let's hear what you've got,' I said a little abruptly.

He had various awesome packages and magnificent payment plans.

'Oh wow,' I said, heavy on the sarcasm. New broadband was the last thing on my mind, but I wanted to hit out at someone. I chose to reel this guy in. 'Okay, tell me your magnificent plans. In fact, just cut to the chase and tell me: what will this cost me in the long run?'

Before we got to that – how long had I had my existing broadband?

'Oh, a long, long time. And a long time to come.' Any problems with it? 'No, at the minute I'm happy. So why would I change things?'

Ah, but he had a deal to offer me. Despite his wasting my precious time, I was getting bored with burning his. I said, 'I don't really care about any sort of deal.'

But apparently he had a superb TEN YEAR special.

'Locked... *in* for ten years? You're dreaming. Ten years isn't happening. No amount of time will be happening, because I've got what I want already. And nothing you can offer will change that.'

But he was insistent that I'd be glad I switched.

'Look, get it into your thick skull. I'm not interested. If I was, or Tom was, we would have shown interest in you from the start. But we never did. Don't contact us ever again, please.'

I hung up. Reavley was waiting for an explanation. I said, 'Life has taken a fork. It's all different from now on.'

Reavley nodded, understanding.

In case he didn't, I explained. The life Tom and I had had together was over, but feeding that information to our world was going to take time. Like that broadband dealer, like our mortgage supplier and the post office, etc., and even some distant friends who didn't yet know – these people would all have to be told that Tom and Lucy Packham were no longer together.

The once-loving couple had taken different forks in the road, both setting upon brand-new, uncharted paths. And with each telling, I would again feel the stab of what had happened, like a re-tearing of a healing wound. The prospect, as Mr Broadband had discovered, was going to grate on me.

To my explanation, Reavley gave another nod. But this one was without conviction: acknowledgement of my words, but not acceptance of them. And no sympathy.

I could tell he still wasn't sure that I hadn't killed my husband.

MARY

The last time I visited this church in Cullerton, it was at Tom and Lucy's wedding. It's weird because when I try to picture Tom with a happy face, that's what I think back to. My handsome big bro in a tuxedo, newly hitched and grinning like a cat that got the cream. But I don't see that day as the happy-fest it was meant to be. Now I'll always remember it as the day he took his first steps down a fork in the road that would end in murder.

On the very same bench on the church's front lawn where I now sit, I could have saved Tom's life. As I'd told Reavley, Lucy had been grim personified that day. Keeping up a happy face had taken its toll on her and she'd crept to this bench for a break. I approached, meaning to have it out with her. I was going to tell her I knew she was only marrying Tom because she felt lost, but instead I stopped a few feet behind the bench, said nothing, and watched the miserable bride, her face in her hands. She had bunched her dress's mermaid tail behind her on the bench, but it had slipped through the gap between the seat and backrest and curled on the grass. So many had commented on her beauty that day, but I saw only mutton dressed as lamb.

Her slim, pale neck: I'd wanted to crush it in my hands. Oh, how easily I could have done so, and how that would have changed things. I would still be in the slammer today, but Lucy would be gone and my brother would be alive.

But I didn't strangle her, did I? In a moment I'll now admit was petty, I put a foot on the fishtail and ground it into the dirt. It was enough to satisfy me and I walked away, but Lucy never even knew I was there, and today Tom's dead.

From this bench, I can see all the way down the main road, with a slightly elevated view of the Kwaint Cottage Gift & Tea Room. Back when the joint was a pub, the couple who'd run it had knocked up The Cascade as a private getaway and the only way there was by the dirt track cut through the trees. So there was no chance I'd miss Lucy's ugly mug. I'd heard that the pub owners got mauled to death by wild game on safari. Lucy needs to go on safari.

It's early and there are a few people around, but the only other person in the graveyard is a woman about my age who's seemingly praying at a headstone a few metres to my side. Annoying, that, because I want to be alone. Where's all the tigers when you need them?

The tiger killings were probably good gossip for a month or so, until the next annual wheelbarrow race or whatever other strangeness these bumpkins use to pass the time. I wonder what village folk will think when they hear about the evil bitch who killed her hubby at the cottage. Maybe they'll decide the cottage is cursed and do an exorcism. The next marrow-growing contest won't be water-cooler chat if that happens.

'A lot of death involved with that place,' I say aloud. The woman at the nearby grave gives me a quick glance.

Death. Reminds me of the last proper sit-down talk I had with Tom alone, early on Saturday morning before he left to come to Cullerton. He'd popped in to Dad's house to collect something and, out of the blue, Dad had said he wanted his ashes scattered in Scotland, where he was born. It was the first time he'd ever mentioned such a thing and Tom and I had realised it was something we needed to prepare for.

We spent a few minutes discussing options, and then Tom's bloody wife interrupted with a phone call. She was out in the car, waiting. Even when Tom told her what we'd gotten talking about, she told him off for making her wait. Tail between his legs, he left the house and off they drove so she could have a sweet old weekend by the river.

Thinking back to that morning makes me sad. And angry as hell. It was the last time I'd seen Tom alive and the memory wasn't a good one. The last face I saw my brother pull was one of disappointment. His last ever words to me were *Can't keep Her Majesty bitchface waiting*. What kind of memory is that?

'She should be the dead one,' I say aloud. I hear a tut and see that the woman nearby is looking at me.

And speaking of bitchfaces: a car I recognise slips into view from beyond the Serengeti pub. Reavley's, with Her Majesty inside, nice and comfortable and warm. It's followed by another plain car, probably carrying members of his murder team. But that's it: no cop car follows. No forensics vehicle, no van with a canine logo on the side. That can't be right: Reavley's here without a search team? I don't like that. It's a bad sign.

Reavley's car stops outside the lone newsagent's. Only Lucy gets out, and heads inside. I wish I'd brought binoculars. Or not, in case I saw her smiling like she's having a nice day out. She's back in three minutes, and even from eighty metres away I can see she doesn't look happy. Good. My work in the newsagent's paid off, it seems. In fact, she seems angry, given how she slams her door so hard I hear it. Excellent.

'You think it's bad now, bitch? Life won't be worth living soon.'

The woman nearby looks at me, points, and says something about getting rid of my rubbish. Her finger's jabbing at an empty bottle of apple juice, just like mine, on the grass under the bench. I yell that it's not mine as she's scuttling away.

I decide to give it another half hour or so before I go say hello. Ten minutes in, a pair of Lancashire cop cars arrive and take the same turn into the Kwaint Cottage Gift & Tea Room car park and vanish. I give it another five, but no one else arrives. No dogs to search for human remains. No scientists to swab and bag and analyse as they tear apart The Cascade. I don't like this.

I decide it's time to go get in Lucy's face.

13

LUCY

Just a couple of miles from Cullerton, Reavley spoke for the first time in at least ten minutes. I saw a worry in his eyes.

'I'd like you to do a press interview today.'

I almost breathed a sigh of relief. The police gave press conferences when they wanted public help. It meant Reavley didn't suspect me of murder. But best of all, with Tom's face in the news, the chances of a reported sighting increased. I wanted him back. I was also buoyed by the prospect of proving to Mary that I hadn't killed my husband, her brother. It might sound petty, but I couldn't wait to see her face when he turned up alive. I'd go visit her arm in arm with him.

I had to check myself here though. It was a nice dream, but unlikely. Tom had left me, so a loving reunion wasn't on the cards.

'You okay?' Reavley asked. I must have zoned out for a few seconds.

'Yes, of course. I'm just nervous.'

'It's not like you normally see on TV. There won't be fifty

reporters asking questions. Just one chap I know. He's coming down here later. He'll feature the story locally.'

'No, I don't mean I'm nervous about that. Tom left me and caused all this. I'm nervous at the thought of meeting him again. My own husband of five years.'

'I understand. It can feel awkward sometimes even after a little argument, even if you've only gone into separate rooms. Lucy, are you okay with an interview?'

I nodded. But I had a worry. 'You said the story would be local. But Tom might be halfway across the country. He might not see it. The right people might not see it.'

'What we have to always keep in mind is that he's an adult with free will to go and do as he pleases. It would be a massive invasion of privacy if he's getting on with starting a new life and he's featured in the national news as a missing person. So we'll be using this story as a prompt for people who were in this area on Sunday, when he disappeared. Almost like a reconstruction. I'd like you to walk your route through the woods with the reporter. It may jog the memories of people who saw you together, and people who might have seen where Tom went.'

'Whatever gets my husband back.'

It appalled me to taste this lie upon my lips. Deep down I knew I wasn't doing this to get Tom back, because I had accepted our marriage was all over bar the signatures. *Whatever stops people thinking I killed my husband* would have been a more truthful statement.

As we passed the Serengeti pub, the marker for the start of Cullerton, I told him to pull into the road by the newsagent's, because I wanted a drink. He gave me a look as if he feared I was going to make a run for it, but the car slid to the kerb a short way later.

'You'll be back, won't you?' he almost pleaded. Then he did something surprising: he raised his eyes skyward, hand up, and said, 'Do you solemnly swear?' I gave him a long look, whose suspicion he read. 'I'm sorry. I know it's something Tom used to do. His sister told me.'

Annoyed, but unsure why, since it was his business to question all relevant players, I put up my hand. A heavily sarcastic tone accompanied my words: 'I solemnly do swear not to flee and make a new life in Australia.' I turned away before he could respond.

Although the bell rang in the shop, Mr Baker, the owner, was known to remain in the back room and allow his customers time to find what they wanted, so he wouldn't be waiting by the till. Sometimes the locals would ring the bell a second time then hide, to make him think he'd had a shoplifter who'd just bolted. For a laugh, I had done this on Monday when I came to meet the police, and I did it again now.

A few seconds later, I heard his footsteps. Then a pause as he surveyed his empty store. 'Anyone there?'

I gave it a few more seconds, heard him curse, and then I stepped out from behind the end of an aisle and waved. Last time, he'd seemed surprised, because he hadn't seen me since Tom and I made a trip back in Feb. This time his demeanour... I could only call it disgust.

'Sorry for the trick. Just a joke.' I headed towards the ambient drinks and saw there were no apple juice cartons. I asked if he had any in the stockroom.

'Not for you.'

I gave him a look, unsure of the meaning behind his tone. I might have assumed his words were accidentally barbed and that he simply meant there was no apple juice in stock. Except he still wore that disgusted expression. I knew then its cause was not my little joke. 'How's business today?'

'About to get a lot busier. Anyway, hurry up.'

On Monday he'd been full of smiles and chatter, but today

he was stand-offish, like an enemy. I realised he knew about Tom's disappearance. And what I had supposedly done to my husband. But it made no sense. Sure, the police had visited The Cascade with me two days ago, but we'd been in and out in no time, not a word spoke to a single local. He hadn't known the story on Monday, that was for sure. How could he have heard about it since then?

And then it hit me.

'Say hello to Mary for me if she comes by again.' I left the shop in a hurry, and back in the car updated Reavley. His analysis was:

'Word has a way of travelling, so you can't be sure Mary's gossiped.'

'Well we can find out later, can't we? Because she's here somewhere. And I have no doubt her plan involves a whole lot of trouble.'

MARY

Lurking on a tree stump just beyond the hole in the fence at the back of the car park is a uniformed copper, probably to stop people using the track. Ah, so new best friends Reavley and Lucy want no unwelcome visitors while they're cosying up. I see the copper early enough to make a turn in the car park. I'm seen, but he doesn't suspect anything. Tourists take wrong turns now and then, don't they?

I lay up my car off to one side, where he can't see, and head towards the back of the pub, where there's a gap between the fence and the enclosed beer garden. It's barely thin enough even for skinny old me and I get dirt marks on my clothing, as well as hurting my breasts. Ironing-board-chest Lucy could make it easily.

The track is shallower because it's longer and curves, but this direct downhill slope is steep. The undergrowth near the top is littered with old drinks cans and crisp bags and even unbroken pint glasses, from years of drunken idiots lobbing them over the back fence. If not for the high, thick trees, a big shoulder could land a glass on The Cascade's roof.

I emerge from the trees twenty or so metres later, near The Cascade's gravel-bordered open back garden. There's a detective puffing away on a cigarette at one of the chairs surrounding the firepit, but he's got his back to me. He just about jumps out of his skin as I crunch gravel underfoot.

'Hey, miss, you can't be here. Where did you come from?'

'Aaron?' I yell, then again, louder. By the time the detective has crossed to me, blocking my way, Reavley appears at the back door. Moments later, I see Lucy's face at the kitchen window. At least she's clothed.

At first Reavley is shocked to see me, then pleased. But despite his smile, he takes my arm and starts to lead me away. As well as the officer round the back, there are cops out front, too, so Reavley finds a bare spot by the side of the cottage.

'You shouldn't be here, Mary. Lucy said you were planning to come and cause trouble for her.'

'It's not a crime scene, nothing's been cordoned off, so I can go where I want. And she only doesn't want me here so she can sweet talk you.'

'That's not going to happen. She hasn't even tried.'

'And you didn't deny it's not a crime scene. Why is that? Why isn't it cordoned off, and where is the search team? You should be searching for evidence that Tom was killed here. There should be those people in white suits, dusting for things. And dogs.'

'We *are* searching the cottage. Mary, you don't see what we see. There's still a chance Tom walked off on his own two legs and until there's real proof of a crime, we can't just go in guns blazing. We certainly can't arrest Lucy just yet.'

He takes a deep breath. I wait: there's more to come.

'Some local people, including police, have decided to use their own time to search the woods and downriver for evidence of Tom. And although we're not tearing up the floorboards or anything, we'll still find evidence if it's there to find. But at the minute my team is just gathering an intelligence package.'

A very cop-like term, but it's just a shrug-off. I don't see what the cops see? I know loads of people go missing each year in this country, and the number that meet foul play is quite low. Most pop up unharmed. Some have chosen to uproot and go, and it's their business. Others are found but order the cops not to tell their loved ones where they are.

With so many innocent reasons why adults vanish, it makes sense that the cops can't just throw bodies into a hunt for a grown man if there's no obvious evidence he's had his head cut off. Tom was hardly a kid who vanished on the way home from school. So I *do* see what they see.

But the cops don't see what I see: a volatile marriage heading full-speed towards a brick wall, the steering wheel in the hands of a dangerous woman.

'You say you need intelligence, as you put it. Well, the best people to give you that are friends and family. That's my brother and I know him.'

'You're absolutely right. And there is something you can answer for me. Does Tom have a will?'

That question throws me off. 'Yes, he has a will. I helped him set it up when he was eighteen. And a pension. Before Lucy came along and spun her web, I used to take care of Tom's finances. I'm on his will as well as her, although I'm surprised she hasn't convinced him to remove me.'

'Look, Aaron, by asking that, you admit you need to know

what I know. So believe this, which I've said before and no doubt I'll have to say again and again. Tom wouldn't just run away without contacting people, especially me. Something bad has happened to him and you need to start believing that. You need to arrest Lucy, right now.'

Before he can object with more crap about evidence, or a spiel about statistics, I bombard him with the evidence against Lucy. And it's a lot. The missed monster truck show. The lies about where Tom was. The blood in the sink. The blouse burned in the firepit. The binned insulin. And the latest gem: Lucy's claim of a text message from a brand-new phone that is conveniently always turned off. If I was a cop, I'd snap the cuffs on her in a heartbeat. Tom's clearly dead.

'Clearly,' I repeat.

'It's not that simple,' he replies. Despite being out of sight of anyone, he's still holding my arm, although his grip is soft now, barely there. Not so much as for security as for reassurance. 'We have to prove it beyond doubt.'

'You told me how that's done. Proof of life, you called it. Has Tom used any of his bank accounts?'

'No, but murder without a body is hard to prove because–'

'I know, I've read up on this. The "no body, no murder" law supposedly comes from a case in Gloucestershire in 1660. A man called William Harrison went missing and his bloody clothing was later found, although his body wasn't. His manservant, John Perry, claimed his own mother and brother killed Harrison, although they denied it. All three were hanged, despite there being no body. Harrison turned up two years later, alive and well and with a story about being kidnapped and put into slavery in another country.'

'It's great that you know that, Mary, but–'

'But that was hundreds of years ago, and they didn't have today's technology. Has Tom been on Facebook since he vanished? Has he been to his doctor for insulin? Has he phoned his beloved sister? Has he put his name on any electronic forms or used his bank?'

He gives me a look that tells me to calm down. I know I'm getting worked up, and even in a whisper my voice is booming. I draw an imaginary zip across my mouth, to allow him to continue. 'Tom has been missing only a few days, which is not nearly long enough to satisfy a jury that he's dead. All we have is weak evidence so far.'

'What about the blood? Lucy's lies? The fact that Tom wouldn't just leave like that.'

His voice doesn't raise, so it's only the grip tightening on my arm a little that shows he's getting frustrated with me. 'Mary, you have to think about a trial jury. These are people who know nothing about Lucy or Tom or their history, so all they have is the evidence, and it has to remove all doubt. The blood, for instance. Lucy said it was an injury to Tom's finger. There wasn't a whole lot of blood. Can you tell me it's *impossible* that that blood came from a finger wound?'

Impossible? No. I have to admit that.

'Prior behaviour is no proof, either, Mary. Just because it's out of character for Tom to run away, to miss a monster truck, or to go somewhere and not tell his sister or friends, it doesn't mean they can't happen. Even all at once. Are those three things *impossible*?'

I don't answer that. 'And Lucy's lies?'

'None of it is enough to prove beyond all doubt that she killed her husband. You have to consider that you might be biased and unwilling to see exculpatory evidence.'

I look at him in shock. 'You think I've been dead against her, convinced she's killed him, and that I'm blind to her innocence?'

'It seems a little personal. You've been very quick to leap on all manner of things to prove her guilt. You didn't even entertain the notion that Tom could have left her. Is this why you didn't ask any of Tom's friends if they'd seen him?'

'What?'

'When you contacted them, all you did was berate and blame Lucy. You didn't ask a single person if they had heard from Tom.'

'And why would I? Lucy disposed of Tom's blood-soaked corpse. You need to get on the right page, detective. How about Lucy? Did she ask if anyone had heard from Tom?' His eyes tell me the answer before his mouth can. 'Exactly. And why didn't she? Because she knew their answer would be no. Blood-soaked corpse, remember.'

His eyes take on a look that captivates me. I think something momentous is coming next. 'She told me she thinks Tom was having an affair.'

I deflate. Not momentous at all, just more bullshit from Lucy. 'No way. Tom loves her. He's always talking about her. Buying her things. That's another Lucy-lie.'

'Can you be sure though? Affairs are pretty secretive.'

I shrug off his arm. His blindness is annoying me now. 'Tom's not the type. You think I'd berate him for such a thing, what with me and Lucy with pistols drawn? Tom knew he could tell me about an affair and I'd probably iron his shirt for their next date. So he would have told me, and he didn't. Because there isn't one. Lucy's just lying yet again. So who does she claim this mysterious woman is?'

'Lucy doesn't know. She has no proof. No texts seen on Tom's phone or emails or anything. Just a gut instinct.'

'Convenient. She knows no one would believe he just left, so she's invented a reason.'

'Well, the theory is out there, so we have to investigate it.'

'Don't waste your time. I knew Tom and I know her. Far more than you do. It's all clear in my mind.'

'I know. You're convinced beyond doubt.'

'And pretty soon you'll stop giving Lucy that final ounce of benefit of the doubt and get on my wavelength. You're not seriously considering this phantom woman tale, are you?'

He takes a step back, has a quick look to make sure nobody's listening, and says, 'I don't know what to think. That's how I have to do it. I have to suspect everything that defends her, but I also have to throw doubt on everything that points to her as a killer.'

I wait: again I sense more is to come.

'I spoke to her at her home yesterday and some things rang alarms. She had a limp handshake and didn't meet my eyes, which I always think is a bit of a giveaway. She didn't like it when I asked to have a look around her home. When I told her I wanted to search the cottage, she didn't like that. She gave a long pause before she agreed. She was unhappy about telling me about her arrest for assault. And she didn't let me take Tom's computer.'

'Why would you want Tom's computer?'

'Just to analyse it. There might be some deleted emails, or a search history that sheds a clue. It's standard to look at someone's computer. The whole time I was there, she acted funny and it gives me concern, I admit. But my opinion doesn't matter. The evidence is all that matters. At the minute, there's not a whole lot pointing at his being dead. Or even why they'd reach such a point.'

Does he mean there's no evidence that Tom and Lucy had a falling out? Is he for real? 'What about the argument the night before he went missing? Lucy threatened him with a knife–'

Here he cuts me off with: 'Lucy said the argument with the knife wasn't that bad. She had a knife and fork and they were at dinner.'

I add the bit I couldn't before he cut me off: 'The text

message Tom sent me said she was a crazy woman and she pulled a knife on him. You should get the CCTV from that pub and you'll see. Look, Aaron, you'll soon find out theirs was a very volatile relationship. Tom was a big man and often he was able to restrain Lucy, so she couldn't hit him. But she tried to a lot. And this time she got him. Did you know she's planning to sell his car?'

'How did you know that?'

'He told me she'd mentioned wanting him to. You need to find that car. But how did *you* know?'

'There was an email on her account. But she said Tom wanted the BMW valued.'

I almost laugh. 'Tom was looking at ordering a biometric security device. A fingerprint scanner locking mechanism. Check his emails and you'll see that. There's no way he was going to sell that car because he'd already promised it to me when he got another one.' It takes another moment or two for the truth to hit me. 'She's planning to sell it now he's dead. She's hidden it somewhere till this all blows over. This wasn't just a random act. My God. And the police are blind. What will it take to convince you of what I already know? A confession? You haven't even asked her if she killed him.'

'The moment I ask her that, I alienate her. She'll get a solicitor. I have to act as if I accept most of her story.' He paused. 'But it's good timing that you ask me that. We have a reporter coming to chat to her. We're going to put the story out there in the hope that someone's seen Tom. But partly I've arranged it because I want the reporter to ask that million-dollar question. I've got a behaviour analyst who'll review the tape.'

Why didn't he give me this beautiful news earlier? Lucy will be asked, under camera, if she killed my brother, and thousands of eyes will see right through her act, and know she's an ice-cold murdering bitch. I love it.

14

LUCY

In order to follow the route Tom and I took through the woods, the reporter and his cameraman, DI Reavley, and a pair of uniformed officers had to cross Low Man Brook using the walkway across the top of the waterfall. I went first, with more confidence than when I had been with Tom because the lack of summer rain since the weekend had allowed the water to become tranquil. No one would get dragged over the waterfall if they were dunked, so we made quick time.

The reporter was a skinny man, easily in his seventies, which I hadn't expected. I got the impression he was a long-time stalwart of the news programme *Calendar*, probably having cultivated important friendships way back when ITV Yorkshire was called Yorkshire Television. I had seen the programme and it and its reporters seemed family friendly, so I didn't expect a Jeremy Paxman-like grilling. I had worried that Reavley wanted me to face taxing questions so he could watch and study.

However, once inside the woods, the reporter started barking orders like a drill sergeant, and here I felt the first itch of concern that I might have made a mistake in agreeing to a TV interview.

He told his cameraman exactly how far in front of us to stand and to make sure he didn't 'bloody trip', then he instructed Reavley and his officers to remain 'no less than eight feet behind and four feet beside us'. And finally, when I stood by his side, he grabbed my arm and pulled me a little closer to him. There were shafts and curtains of sunlight pouring through the treetops, but it was still quite dim and the cameraman had to turn on a spotlight atop his camera.

Once he'd confirmed that we looked good and the police weren't in shot, the reporter was all smiles. We would walk slowly, he said, and stop a couple of times so we could face each other and the camera could be moved to perform over-the-shoulder shots. I was nervous and wanted to throw up.

It began the way I was promised. The old reporter asked me to tell the story of the last time I'd seen my husband. He led me in with, 'So, you were walking side by side, as we are now, just a happy couple out for a summer's walk. And then what happened?'

As we strolled slowly, with the cameraman walking backwards ahead of us and the police dawdling behind, I reran that Sunday morning for the viewers. But I was told not to bring up the argument, so there wasn't much I could describe. I avoided the fact that Tom and I hadn't walked side by side, but far apart, with me trailing behind like a dutiful Victorian wife. I didn't mention the tree root that tripped me and that I'd had to raise myself without help. I left out his insult that I couldn't even walk properly.

The viewers of *Calendar* were destined never to know that my husband told me to keep up if I could and went ahead, smoking his electronic cigarette, and that I hobbled home when it became clear he wasn't going to return full of guilt.

Instead, they were given a bogus tale that made him look good. I hurt my ankle and tried to convince Tom to go ahead without me. He said no, because we should stay together. I said yes, because I didn't want to ruin his day. He insisted: he would help me get home and bathe my foot. I insisted: go and finish the trek he'd been looking forward to.

The next and final part was true though: 'And then he disappeared round that corner there, and I never saw him again.'

The cameraman whirled around to capture where I was pointing, as if they might just catch Tom still there.

The reporter stopped and said it was time for our first over-the-shoulder shot. I faced the smaller man and tried not to look at the cameraman literally put the camera over his shoulder to capture my face, and my reaction.

And this was where it all went wrong.

'You both came in separate cars, is that right? So when you left the cottage that next morning, Tom's car was still there? And you left his clothing and belongings in case he came back?' He gave his necktie a jerk, as if it was too tight.

I was a little puzzled because he'd run through what he would ask me, and this question hadn't been listed. Plus, this was a fact I'd only told to the police. With that camera on me, I didn't dare look at Reavley, the tale-teller. A little perturbed, I crossed my arms over my chest, hugging myself as if it was cold. But it was for mental warmth. I nodded in answer to his question.

The camera was behind the old man, so his face wouldn't show to the world. I alone caught the slight leer he gave at my response.

'The local Cullerton pub, the Serengeti,' he said. 'It has CCTV that covers the single main road out of the village. Your car was captured leaving the village at 08.18 in the morning. But what's puzzling is that Tom's car was also spotted. Leaving the village at 7.46. Before yours. So Tom's BMW couldn't have been still at the cottage when you left.'

I was shocked and couldn't keep it off my face. I glared at Reavley. 'You didn't tell me the police had found CCTV. So Tom came back to the cottage just after I left?'

I was desperate for an answer because this was important. If Tom had returned to the cottage that early, it must have been because he wanted to catch me before I left. Had my leaving upset him? Was that what this was all about? Tom had rushed back to make amends and, finding me gone, assumed he didn't mean that much to me, which had prompted him to abandon his life? It was an extreme reaction, because a typical response would be to go home, but that didn't mean it wasn't possible.

Reavley didn't get a chance to reply: the reporter stepped between us and demanded an answer to his own question. I wanted to slap him. 'When I left I stopped near the shops, and I sat there a while. I left the cottage about seven.'

'You say you went in a shop? Seven is too early to shop. None are open at that time.'

'No, no, I didn't go in the shops. I just sat in my car, thinking. Tom must have just missed me when he got back to the cottage, and then headed out of the village before me. He must have not seen my car parked by the shops.'

'Well, the police checked all the cameras. There aren't many in such a small village as Cullerton. But the exterior of a few of the shops are covered, and there's no video of your car stopping.'

I thought he was trying to catch me out with a careful selection of words. Asserting that there was no video of my car stopping by the shops wasn't the same as claiming I'd been recorded driving straight out of the village. But only the guilty would fall for this tacky trick. 'I did stop. I parked about halfway between the gift shop and the Serengeti pub, outside the dry cleaner's. I stopped to think because I was torn between heading on and going back. Tom must have driven right past me. I now wish I'd not chosen the wrong alternative.'

The reporter said, 'You had Tom's blood on your shirt, didn't you? Which you burned so the police couldn't analyse it.'

I was horrified. 'It wasn't so they couldn't analyse it. It was ruined, so I got rid of it.' My gaze went left to right to left repeatedly, like someone watching a tennis match. The players were the reporter and Reavley, who'd extended to far more than giving this obnoxious man information. He had set up this interview as an ambush.

I tried to turn and go, but the reporter put a hand on my arm. 'Mrs Packham, you need to address these questions. Why was the text message your husband apparently sent from an untraceable pay-as-you-go phone first activated in Sheffield on Monday morning?'

I was shocked. Reavley had traced the phone, yet neglected to tell me.

'And why was that text sent from the vicinity of your home?'

This was more shocking. Sent from close to my house? But that would mean... 'Tom had been home? My God. He must have... been scared. Too scared to come in... and...'

'Are you saying he drove to your house, waited outside because he didn't want to see you, and sent the text from there? Does that sound plausible?'

I couldn't find adequate words to explain, but decided I didn't want to. I shrugged off his arm and started walking, fast. I realised too late I was going the wrong way, deeper into the woods, but I didn't stop. Taking a long route around and back to my car was preferable to going past my accusers. Besides, I didn't have a car here, I'd just remembered, so heading back to the cottage would mean I'd have to ride home with Reavley. The last thing I wanted.

'Why was his half-full insulin bottle in the dustbin?' the reporter said, now following me. He and the cameraman were both in pursuit, although the police officers had stopped to watch.

'There's no evidence of another woman,' came next, louder because I'd put a little distance between us. I made the mistake of taking my eyes off the path to look round. My foot caught an exposed tree root, perhaps even the same one that had snared me when I was with Tom. This time I only stumbled, but it caused me to veer off the track. And I kept going into the undergrowth; at least the fool wouldn't follow me in his expensive shiny shoes.

And he didn't. But, standing there, being filmed, and backdropped by three intrigued police officers, he held out his microphone like a singer urging the audience to roar, and yelled a final question. This one pierced me as if he'd thrown a spear at my back, actually causing me to stagger forward and drop to my knees, a palm slamming hard into a sharp stone jutting from the earth.

I ignore the fiery agony and rush on at speed, with tears streaming down my face. I hear Reavley call my name, obviously upset that his vile trick has turned so sour, but I blunder on through the undergrowth, down the slope, towards the ravine, determined to sail out over that chasm and bring the ultimate end to this wretchedness.

MARY

Keep away. That order is a little vague, or at least that's my read on it. When Reavley told me to keep away from Lucy while she was doing her interview, I chose a distance. Thirty or so metres.

That was what he meant by 'keep away': come no closer than thirty metres. In my eyes.

I decide to cross the water at a spot away from all eyeballs, but it means going into the woods. Some fifteen metres after it leaves the clearing, the brook starts to go downhill and a short way after flicks right to run into the ravine. Here it drops steeply in places, straight down in some spots like steps.

Crossing at the bend is a bad idea because the riverbanks are steep and slippery, and dark because of the thick canopy. But I go across here because the end section of a chain-link fence is nailed to a tree on the far side. I plan to follow the fence, but that's not the only reason for choosing this spot. The end of the fence was originally connected to a concrete post, but that came loose and toppled into the brook. It's angled into the water in such a way that it bridges half the eight-feet gap.

Tom once told me that Lucy's too scared to cross this way, so they use the walkway over the waterfall. That just makes me determined to make the leap, so I'm not a scaredy-cat like her. And I do, no problem. A few seconds later I'm up the bank on flat ground again and following the fence.

It runs all the way along the edge of the ravine to protect idiots walking at night. Tom once told me that people liked to steal the concrete posts and I can see he's right. As I follow a faint track alongside the fence, I see places where chain-link panels lay flat in the undergrowth or hang out over the chasm like metal tongues because posts are gone.

At one point I have to walk a little higher up the slope because there's a section some twenty metres long with no barrier at all. Scary. I continue through the undergrowth until I find a flat tree stump, and I plonk my butt to wait. For Lucy.

I've seen those TV programmes like *Faking it: Tears of a Crime*, which show people pretending to be distraught as they cry and moan for the return of missing loved ones they actually killed. Usually they just want to fool everyone, but some of these evil bastards actually like the limelight. They enjoy the idea of playing a role and having control. I wonder which type Lucy will be. Scared and defensive, or shoulders back and lapping it up? Either way, she won't have the skills to pull it off. I can't wait to see.

As the minutes drag by, I play scenarios in my head and wonder which I'd like the most. I see Lucy as a broken woman, dropping to her knees under a barrage of questions from the reporter and tearfully confessing all. Nice. I see her getting so upset that she flees and is chased through the woods like a hunted coed in a schlock slasher movie. Better. I even imagine a Colonel Jessup-like moment from the movie *A Few Good Men*:

Did you order the Code Red on Tom?
You're goddamn right I did!

Perfect. I want that one. I want her to get so flustered and out of control that she sinks herself before she even realises it.

It's a long time, maybe an hour, before I hear people coming my way. I hear feet making the walkway across the river rumble, even though it's a hundred metres away. And then I see them enter the woods via the main path higher up the slope. Reavley and two cops in uniform. The reporter and a man with a big camera, like something from the 1990s. And the bitch.

They stop almost level with me, just thirty metres away. The reporter seems to jab and blab some orders, and then they all walk. The cops keep back while the reporter and Lucy walk next to each other, and the cameraman leads the way, backwards, aiming his machine.

I can't make out what they're saying at this distance. I stay low down so undergrowth hides me and creep like a sneak thief. I match their pace, all the time watching Lucy. Her mouth's moving, which means she's giving the reporter her practised lies. God, I want to scream at them. I imagine it would look quite funny on TV that night if the viewers heard some unseen person shout *bullshit*, especially if it echoed and Lucy and the others had no idea where it came from.

Then they stop walking. The reporter and Lucy face each other and the cameraman moves behind him, so his camera gets Lucy's reaction in close-up. I can see the lens over her shoulder, as if the machine is actually secretly aimed at me. It's happening. Reavley told me he'd use the reporter to put awkward questions to her – veiled accusations, actually – and I can tell from the old man's body language that he's started the attack.

I wish I'd chosen to be uphill from them, because then I wouldn't have Lucy's back to me, and I could have seen her ugly mug. But I'll see it tonight on TV.

I thought Lucy would love playing the pleading, sad wife, but I'm happy to see that's not the case. Her body language says she's not having the time of her life out here. But still she has that brashness. No broken woman, then. The reporter asks a question and then shifts his necktie, and Lucy's response is to cross her arms defiantly.

She doesn't want to do this, but she's not scared of him. No woman who killed a man as big as Tom would be worried about this little rake. Hopefully that rage of hers will burst out for the world to see.

Lucy takes a step back and turns to leave, so no, she's not Colonel Jessup. The reporter reaches for her arm. I wonder what he's just accused her of. I reckon it's to do with the bloodstains on her blouse. No, the dodgy mobile phone message off Tom. I itch to get closer. I want to feel the discomfort pulsing off her. It might even crackle like a power line.

She flicks off his grip and off she goes – deeper into the woods, fast. So, she's the schlock slasher coed. The reporter begins following her with his cameraman. He yells something, but I only catch one word. *Insulin*. Oh, I'd forgotten about that one. Then he asks something else and this time I get the word *woman*. Maybe he just challenged her bullshit about Tom having an affair.

I see her trip and stumble, and then she cuts off the track. I get a frightful moment when it seems she's aiming right for me, and how the hell would that look on TV if I was suddenly standing there? But then she veers, heading downhill on my left. I see the pain on her face and actually, genuinely wonder if she's about to leap off the edge and smash to a pulp hundreds of feet below. Am I so blessed?

The reporter and his cameraman don't look prepared to kick their way through the tangled undergrowth, unfortunately. From up on the path, he thrusts out his microphone and shouts, and this time I can hear everything.

'You recently increased the life insurance on your husband, Mrs Packham. From five hundred thousand to one million pounds. Is that why he's dead, Mrs Packham? Did you kill your husband out here for the life insurance payout?'

I love it. But Lucy doesn't. The cops planned this mammoth accusation in order to see her reaction, but they can't because she has her back to them. She's only ten metres from me, though, and I get it in ultra HD.

With a sneer of anger on her face, Lucy tries to kick at something on the ground, perhaps a squirrel, but she misses and sprawls to her hands and knees. When she struggles up and continues, I see blood on her palm. When she reaches the faint track I'm on, just three metres from me, she turns away and runs alongside the broken fence. Somehow, she didn't see me. I glance up at the cops and the reporter, but nobody's prepared to follow her. How sweet of them, letting her have some time alone to compose herself.

I'm not so sweet.

I follow, keeping low so nobody sees me. This means I can't move fast and the gap between Lucy and me widens. I catch up a little when she reaches a point where a missing post means the fence leans right across the track, forcing her to duck to pass underneath. A little way on, she looks round to make sure she's alone. She's not, of course, but she's focused on the main track, not the teeny path we're on, and she doesn't see me. Blessed I am. She moves on, but slower this time because she thinks she's lost her pursuers, the silly mare.

And then, when she reaches another spot where two concrete posts are standing tall and immobile but the panel between them is mysteriously missing, she just stops. She approaches the eight-feet gap, stands just inches from the sharp edge, and stares out over the ravine. I know she feels the danger's over for now, and with it her pain, and she won't jump.

She's wrong about the danger part.

I step uphill into the undergrowth so that her peripheral vision doesn't catch me. She doesn't hear me approach, too focused on the view. I stop five feet behind her, still surprised that her cat senses haven't jangled at someone so close. The world is silent.

I wonder if she stopped here for a reason other than the calming view. Is her mind casting back to the events that altered our lives? Had Tom been in that same spot, looking out across the land, and had she been standing where I was, staring at him with the same hatred I burn into the back of her head?

'Is this where it happened?' I say. She whirls, shocked. 'Is this where you pushed him to his death? If I look down there, will I see his body?'

15

LUCY

Somewhere out there, in one of the towns and villages scattered across the portion of the world laid out before me, a woman like me was getting a promotion, or winning a bike race, or making love to a man. The world was a beautiful place.

No. Somewhere out there, a woman like me was getting fired, or breaking bones in a bike crash, or getting assaulted and raped. The world was an ugly place.

Sometimes a stunning view like this could darken my mood. I would imagine all the people out there, living and laughing and loving, and it would make me think about the bad in my life. I would become jealous of those people. During bleaker moments, though, a kind of opposite applied. A focus on the grim aspects of the world, of people consumed by debt and pain and despair, could help me realise that my problems, in comparison, were small fry.

It didn't work today, and how could it? I had never sunk so low in my life, even back in Germany when I was target practice for a drunken monster. To many, the fracture of a marriage hurt like a stab wound. Being abandoned without warning was like having that knife turned inside you. Being left for another woman? Salt in the wound. Now add to that a suspicion of murdering your husband, and anyone would understand why this pit of despair was one I couldn't ever fathom escaping from. It was a boiling, constant ache in my gut.

But suddenly I felt an even worse pain in my head as it was yanked backwards.

'Is this where it happened, you bitch?'

It was Mary. Somehow, she was here, right behind me, and I was unable to turn or even move because she had a fist in my short ponytail. My scrabbling feet, as I tried to move backward, sent loose dirt and stones cascading over the steep edge. But I couldn't back up because her little body felt like a rock-solid post up against mine.

'Is there where you pushed him to his death? If I look down there, will I see his body?'

'Let me go,' I yelled, struggling. But she forced me forward a few inches, and I froze. The message was clear: struggle and you go over. If I ever doubted she thought I'd murdered her brother, that was impossible now.

'If I throw you down there, will you land next to my brother's body?'

MARY

'Well, why don't we find out?' Lucy yells at me, with an evil grin.

We're five feet apart, but it takes her half a second to jump across the gap between us and grab my shirt collar. She hauls me past her so fast I almost trip over my own feet. I wish I had. The next thing I know, she's behind me, a fist in my collar still and one in the hair at the top of my head, and I'm inches from the sheer edge of the cliff.

I try to back away, but she's bigger and stronger and pressed up against me and there's no going anywhere. Except over that edge.

She bends my upper body forward and I can't stop it. My head is out over the ravine and I'm staring down at the tiny brook and jagged rocks far below. Now she doesn't even have to push: just letting go would send me sailing away.

'There, can you see him?' she hisses. 'Is he down there, broken and dead?'

'Let me go, you maniac,' I yell. I flail with my arms, seeking to grab one of the concrete fence posts, and manage to clamp a hand on to one. But only for a second. Lucy lets go of my shirt collar and stabs her fingernails into my hand, which breaks my grip. Before I can try again, she jerks me to the right, dead centre of the gap in the fence, and my fingers hit nothing after that.

'It's what you hope for, Mary, isn't it? To see him down there and have all your dreams come true. Well, look close and you'll see him.'

Even though I'm full of panic, I realise that she's as good as admitted murdering my brother, but instead of relief there's only a massive wave of fear. She's admitted murder only because she knows I won't be telling anyone.

Because she's going to throw me to my death.

'Don't do this, Please...'

16

LUCY

'...Please, don't do this.'

But Mary's reply to my terrified plea was the wild cackle of a soulless lunatic. Knowing words would not save me, nor hoping she had a change of heart, I threw back my arm in a desperate attempt to break her grip on my ponytail. I jammed my fingernails into her flesh on the back of her hand.

Mary gave a shriek of pain and let loose my hair. 'You damn bitch,' she roared at me. I pushed back against her small frame, turning at the same time, and managed to slip past her. As fast as I could, I thundered through the undergrowth, up the hill. I knew that my longer legs would outrun her on flat ground. I needed to get to the track before she caught me.

'Get back here, you murdering bastard,' she hisses at me, far too close: she's right behind me, although my own ragged breathing prevents me from hearing her feet in pursuit.

As soon as I hit the track, I heard my name shouted from somewhere back towards the cottage. Back where I had left five men in shock. The safest course of action would have been to head that way, but even though I was terrified, I still felt anger at Reavley because he had dragged me into this hellish day. So, in that split second, my judgement clouded by swirling emotions, I turned the other way and ran deeper into the woods.

My plan, once I was clear-headed enough to prepare one, was to get to the Fox and Hound, call a taxi, and ride the hell out of this nightmare.

MARY

Lucy laughs, a low, sadistic noise, and trips me to my knees. I think this is the end, but then her foul hands release me. I scramble to one of the fence posts and throw my arms around it, knowing it's my only chance.

But she's leaving. I watch her stomp through the undergrowth, up the hill to the main track. I hear Reavley yell her name, having spotted her, but the thick undergrowth and my downhill position mean I can't see him or the others.

'You got lucky this time,' she calls to me once she reaches the track. Then she gives me a wave and jogs away. But not towards Reavley. Instead, she flees the other way, deeper into the woods. And just like that, the monster's gone. But I'll see her again, for sure. When I tell Reavley the snarling bitch tried to kill me, he'll fast-track her arrest and I'll goddamn be there when it happens. Bars will be between us the next time we meet.

It's my chance to go. I rush up the hill, to the track, and there, some hundred metres away to my right, are the cops and the journalists. I could be there in fifteen seconds. Driving home within half an hour. Outside Tom's house, watching Lucy get cuffed, before lunchtime. But I pause.

Now I've calmed, my idea of getting her arrested for attempted murder doesn't shine so bright. If I tell Reavley what happened here, he might think I'm full of crap. He told me to stay away. He told me Lucy thought I'd come up here to cause grief. Everybody just watched Lucy run away from them like a soppy girl and now little old me is standing here instead – and the cops are supposed to believe she took time out from skedaddling in tears to try lobbing me off a cliff?

New plan. I take a casual walk towards the group of men. When I'm spotted and pointed at, I even wave. All part of the act. Seeing me, Reavley says something to the group and they stay back as he meets me halfway. I do a good job of smothering the turmoil in my gut, but he doesn't.

'What the hell are you doing here, Mary? Did you see Lucy?'

I'm still in shock at my near-death experience, but I smile. 'I came to look for clues. I was hoping Tom might have dropped something, if he walked through here with Lucy. Yes, I did see her. I was down by the ravine edge and I saw her up here, running past. Why was she running?'

'What happened to your hand?'

I look down. The back of my hand is bleeding where Lucy stuck a claw in. I nearly tell him the truth, because the injury is proof she turned rabid. But I don't, because it's no proof at all, is it? So I moan about a thorny bush and he accepts this.

'Speaking of hands,' I say, 'have you noticed that Lucy's wedding ring is missing?'

'I did, yes. She said she left it at the cottage. That's not important though.'

'Did you find it during your search? You didn't, did you? You know she disposed of it, don't you?'

'No. But if Lucy believes Tom is having an affair, she might just–'

'Oh balls,' I cut in. 'No one stays married to a corpse, that's why she disposed of it. It's gone forever.' No reply to this, but I know he's not buying it – or won't give me the benefit of admitting the missing ring is dodgy. I move on.

'So, detective, did the reporter accuse Lucy of killing Tom, like you said he would? What was her reaction?'

I know he did, because I heard parts of it. Thankfully, Reavley doesn't lie to me. 'He did. But she was already walking away, a little angry with him. I tried to call her back. I hope she doesn't suspect I set the whole thing up.'

I also heard the reporter ask her a question about life insurance. I've been thinking about this. It was just another angle to feed my Lucy-hate, but maybe I'm onto something. If I croak it, my life insurance policy goes to Dad. Tom's doesn't. Lucy will get a windfall instead. But if Reavley won't bring it up, I'll do it.

'I was close to Lucy when she was with that reporter. I heard him shout a question at her about life insurance.'

'Mary, did you sneak up on us? I thought I told you–'

'Listen to me,' I cut in. 'That reporter said the policy on Tom had been increased. What did he mean? Is this about money? Please tell me it's not?'

He pauses for a few seconds, perhaps considering whether to answer my question.

'Tell me, Aaron. Earlier you asked me if Tom had a will, and now you're looking into his life insurance. Lucy is the sole beneficiary. And she's registered as Tom's financial attorney, so she's got control over all his money. She increased the policy, didn't she? Without his knowledge.'

'Yes. A few weeks ago. But before we start assuming Lucy planned to kill her husband for money, let's take a step back. First – and I need you to hear me on this – there's no concrete proof he's dead yet. Also, the law doesn't let you collect life insurance if you kill someone. It's the Forfeiture Rule. Basically, it means you can't benefit from killing someone.'

'But that's not proof she didn't do it. I've heard many news stories about people killing to get life insurance. She might not know that rule.'

'Well, she'd know the terms of the insurance policy. Insurers don't pay the killers of policyholders.'

'Maybe she didn't read the small print. You don't know if she knows that or not. None of this is proof that she didn't...'

Here I stop myself as something clicks into place. He's just pissed on the idea of Lucy killing Tom for a payday – yet he asked the reporter to quiz her about it. But why? Maybe blasting this motive apart isn't about defending Lucy. Maybe it's about defending me. From the truth.

'You don't doubt it at all, do you?' I say.

He tries to act like he doesn't know what I'm talking about, but it's too late.

'Tell me, Aaron. You know something. What is it?'

Finally, he relents, perhaps one second before I might have slapped an answer out of him. 'Tom is missing. If we don't find proof of life, then at some point Tom will be declared dead. With no body, no crime scene or evidence of violence or a murder weapon, there's a chance she could avoid a murder conviction. Then there wouldn't be much in the way of stopping Lucy from collecting a big insurance payout.'

There's more, I just know it. Instead of asking, I grab his arm in both of my hands, like a silent plea. He gets it.

'I saw Lucy's emails. Various ones from the insurance company. I saw the email confirming the policy increase, probably a copy of an arrangement made by letter or on the phone. I don't think Tom ever saw that email because it wasn't in the insurance folder. It was in the recycle bin. It had been deleted.'

17

LUCY

When I arrived home, the phone was ringing, but I missed it by seconds. I'd turned my mobile off and, suspecting who'd tried to reach me, checked for missed calls. There were three, all from DI Reavley. Good, because I wanted to talk to him. I so badly shook with emotion that my finger missed the redial button with its first jab.

'Lucy. Are you okay? I tried ringing. Where did you go?'

I'd hoped that time to think during my taxi ride home would mellow me towards Reavley, because he was only doing his job. But the opposite had taken place. I'd had a chance to analyse events back in Cullerton that morning and I was angrier than ever. That he suspected me of murder wasn't my focus any longer; rather, the mechanics of how he'd gotten that message across. After this phone call, I planned never to speak to him again, unless I was arrested, but right now I wanted to tear into him.

'Tom's damn sister was there, in the woods. Did you know about that? I bet you brought her along, just like you brought that reporter so he could accuse me of killing my husband. You set the whole thing up, you bastard.'

I was torn between hanging up and awaiting his reply. I don't know why, but I chose the latter. But he said nothing. When I spoke next, some of my manic energy had dispersed.

'I really don't know what's going on here, Reavley. No, I do. You think I killed Tom. Killed him and got rid of his body. That's what you think.'

Again he said nothing, and again the silence had a calming effect. The detective had let me combust some rage. I also realised I hadn't asked a single question.

'Why don't you just arrest me or tell me you believe that Tom ran away, just so I'd know where I stand and wouldn't have these confusing thoughts.'

'My job is to find the truth, Lucy. I walked into this investigation in the way I always do: knowing nothing. If I genuinely thought you were a killer, you'd be in a cell right now.'

'But you haven't said you believe me. And you've doubted things I said. You think I made up that text message Tom sent me, don't you? That I sent it to myself, just like Mary says?'

'I'm just collecting information. Lucy, it's my job to believe nothing I'm told and listen only to evidence. I'm not on your side and I'm not on Mary's. If you tell me a flipped coin is heads and she says it's tails, I go look for myself. You want the truth? I don't know if you killed your husband. I'm just being honest.'

Honest? Deceptive, more like. I'd just put to him a question of my guilt, and he'd sidestepped it. But, again, being suspected of murder wasn't my focus here. I started to pace the living room.

'Am I supposed to be impressed by your honesty? I'm not, detective. I'm too busy being angry at how you've gone about this whole thing. You think I lied about Tom's car being at the cottage when I left on Monday morning, because you've got

CCTV showing his BMW driving out of the village before mine. Totally understandable, but I would have preferred to be hit with that in a jail cell, detective. That and the text message accusation. But instead, you set me up to be ambushed in front of a TV camera.'

'I'm sorry about the way he put questions to you, Lucy. I didn't put him up to that.'

'What I'm most angry about is that you and everyone else, including that reporter, seem to have blinders on. You're so determined that I'm guilty that you missed the point. Don't you get it still? Before my car, after my car, doesn't matter. Two cars. The CCTV showed Tom driving away. Don't you see that that means Tom left the village alive?'

'Well, that CCTV is all we have. We don't know who was driving it or where–'

I couldn't believe what I'd just heard. 'What do you mean, you don't know who was driving? Who else would it be? You've just proved my point that you're determined to think the worst of me. All that crap about evidence and finding the truth and your little example about the coin? I think if I said heads and you saw it was heads, you still wouldn't believe it.'

There was a pause, and when he came back, the detective spoke in a breathy voice that I read as restrained anger. 'Tom's registration number has been put into the ANPR, that's the Automatic Number Plate Recognition system. It's used in conjunction with our police databases and we can track vehicles all across the UK, even retroactively. In the days since Sunday, when that pub CCTV captured Tom's BMW leaving Cullerton, there have been no flags. Thousands of cameras use the ANPR network and none have seen that BMW. It's highly unlikely Tom's car has travelled far beyond Cullerton, and certainly not using any main roads.'

It was another veiled accusation and I'd had enough.

'Detective, you've searched my house and the cottage, and I don't want you coming back. You have enough to be going on with without me. Your good friend Mary can fill you in on anything about me or Tom that's still puzzling you. The next time I see you, either have proof that Tom is alive and well or have handcuffs in my size. Goodbye.'

I hung up and shivered, as if feverish. I had to sit down immediately and did so on the floor. I felt Reavley had deserved to be reprimanded for his actions today, but I regretted my final threat. If he was as emotional as I was, he might just decide the handcuffs option was favourable. I couldn't shake the notion he was coming for me this very moment.

But it wouldn't help to let such a fear get me down. Worrying about an arrest all day, and tomorrow and every day after that would turn me into a wreck before too long. I had to try to get on with my life.

After a few minutes I felt able to operate as normal. I ate a banana for the energy and opened the back door to let Zuzu in. There was no sign of him. He'd been out all night and hadn't touched the treats I'd put down. I hoped he hadn't gone to look for Tom.

The thought reminded me of an old story about a loyal Akita dog called Hachikō, famed for waiting at a train station every day for his master to return from work. One day his owner had died at work, but the Akita had continued to turn up at the station at the same time every day, for nearly a decade.

God, what a silly thought. I needed a bath to clear this tension. I wanted to leave the back door ajar for Zuzu but couldn't because of another silly thought. I didn't want a team of police sneaking inside and arresting me in the bath. Get a grip, Lucy.

While soaking, I noticed blood under one of my fingernails. Mary's, from where I'd dug my fingers into the back of her hand to get her to release my hair. I scrubbed it away just in case I got arrested in the next few minutes: if DI Reavley saw that blood, he'd assume it was Tom's. I imagined him accusing me of moving Tom's body after I'd run away from the reporter.

That damn stupid thought led to another. I was trying to convince people that he'd left me, and they seemed intent on proving I'd killed him, and all this while nobody was really considering the third alternative. That my husband had hurt himself out in that area of maze-like woods and rocky chasms and was either dying or dead. Suddenly, I couldn't shake the image of him laying out there, gravely injured and trying to crawl out of a ditch, and begging for help.

I wanted to leap out of the bath and rush back to Cullerton, and run through the woods and deep into that ravine, calling out Tom's name in hope of hearing a weak moan. Instead, I sank low in the water and topped it up with a gush of tears.

Later, while drying my hair and staring absently at the wall, I received a text from Reavley in which he told me that, because of the urgency to locate Tom, my interview would be aired on the *Calendar* programme at 6pm that very evening.

That message was like a magical cure for depression because I immediately got my act together, just like that. I'd spent so much of today worrying about what everyone thought of me that I'd ignored the opinion of the only person who mattered. Me. I knew the truth of what had happened to Tom. He was not dead in a ditch and he hadn't been murdered by his wife. He had walked away from his life and was shacked up somewhere with a new woman.

I wasn't going to let suspicious idiots influence or upset me. If Tom saw that news programme, he'd realise the trouble his silliness had caused and would contact someone. To me, Mary, Reavley, it didn't matter. As long as the world knew he wasn't dead, so I could get on with my life. I would have the last laugh.

Around half five in the evening, I grabbed a glass of wine and settled in front of the television. The nerves came back. I counted down the minutes until the news programme started. By the time it did, I was on glass number three and a shivering wreck.

MARY

At home I find Dad in the living room, asleep in front of Sky News. To pass time, to get my mind off things, I decide to clear out the shed. As I open the door, a rake that must have been awkwardly balanced falls forward. I catch it and stare at a pair of gardening gloves dangling from the hook hole by the index fingers jammed into it.

Tom's gloves. The house is loaded with things he bought for Dad, but for some reason these gloves set me off. Maybe it's because it was last summer when he last wore them and the garden has turned wild since: a reminder of time gone by. Of change. I take the gloves into the living room and sit and bawl my eyes out.

Dad wakes up and sees me crying, but he looks like he's got no clue what to do. I point at the TV, where the news is sad and depressing, and he makes a connection. He's asleep again within thirty seconds. I cry for a long time after the programme has finished.

The reason I'm crying is a new worry: the Unlawful Killing (Recovery of Remains) Act. Not yet passed as of 2019, this is a law designed to stick it to killers who don't spill the beans about where they left dead victims. Since non-disclosure causes immense pain to families, for instance me – without Tom's body, I can't have a proper funeral – these secretive assholes can be denied parole. Forever. Right now this law is working its way through parliament, and if passed would make sure Lucy spent the rest of her worthless existence slopping out.

Currently, parole boards paint such killers as in denial of their crimes, which is no tasty recipe for a stroll out the main gate. It's no guarantee, though. I need that law to pass, or there's a good chance Lucy could make that walk one day. She'll waltz home, and Tom's skeleton will stay buried.

The cops will carry on looking for Tom long after a cell door bangs shut behind Lucy, but not forever. They'll go hard at a whole bunch of valleys and woods and abandoned buildings up in Chorley, but every day they find nothing, hope will dwindle and they'll get a bit lazier. As they need to widen the net, the search will slow down. Days will pass as they figure out the next spot to send the backhoe. Then weeks.

Then one day some bastard who runs a desk will moan about manpower and budgets and they'll stop looking. Maybe once a year they'll get a clue and go dig. But if they never find him, there will be no closure for the people who loved Tom.

The word is a joke. Closure? No such thing for me. I'll get used to Tom's death, to not having him a call or drive away, but how can that door ever shut? I can't forget my brother or miss him beside me. In time, his buddies will move on. With all the planning and activity that comes with a trial and a funeral, Tom's murder will be a constant itch, but once one dead body is in the ground and one living body is locked in a cage, their minds will shift to other things. They'll think of him less and less, and then not at all, or only on his birthday or whenever he's mentioned by me.

But there will be closure for Lucy. Oh yes. She'll get used to prison life, she'll make pals and get new hobbies and ten years from now she'll be a proper part of that world and content with it. Maybe even happy with it. Years will roll by and one day a bunch of suits will decide she's paid her dues, learned her lesson, have a nice day. That's something I don't even want to think about. Lucy back on the streets, her old crime forgotten in her eyes, and Tom's sister still hunting for his body. Twenty years for her, a life sentence for me.

And this, as nasty as it sounds, is a best-case scenario. I know DI Reavley still has doubts a killing took place. Lucy wouldn't be the first killer to die in her own bed, old and happy, with Tom's fate a cold, forgotten mystery.

At six, when the *Calendar* news programme starts, I head upstairs to use the TV in Father's bedroom. I grab a glass of wine, because I'm going to enjoy watching that bitch squirm.

The show's host talks about an appeal to find a missing man, then introduces a report from their reporter. The piece starts with a shot of Cullerton from somewhere near the Serengeti pub and a voiceover explains that we are in an idyllic little village in Lancashire, where Tom Packham was with his wife at the weekend when he went missing.

They show a picture of Tom and Lucy on their wedding day, each with a hand on a knife to cut the cake, both smiling. Next, the reporter is outside the cottage, taking a slow stroll towards the camera, giving us more background. Then it cuts to him and Lucy in the woods. I lean forward and stare at her face. She's sweating with fear.

Then I get a shock. When the camera cuts to a shot over the reporter's shoulder to show Lucy's face close-up, I see a little dark blob behind her, deep into the trees. The trees aren't in focus, but I know that blob is me, hiding in the undergrowth. It actually makes me laugh, which was the second-to-last thing I expected from this news report.

The last thing I expected comes next. The camera cuts back to the reporter, standing outside the cottage alone. He appeals for help – if you were in this area last Sunday morning, did you see anything? Then the screen shows a police hotline number to contact. And then it's over.

What? Where the hell is the portion showing Lucy wilt under accusations? Did the cops order the TV station not to air the juicy parts of the interview because it was wrong to accuse a wife of murder during an appeal for help in finding her hubby? Did they slice the best bit out because they needed to free up time for another story? Was that bitch having an affair with someone at ITV Yorkshire?

I'm so angry that I flick my wine right across the TV, although most sprays the curtains behind it. This news report was the best chance to force Lucy's hand. The uncut performance would have drawn out those who knew her with holier-than-though-my-ass revelations. Social media would be afire with people ranting that she was a killer. The cops would be forced to start considering Tom murdered instead of missing. And Lucy would crack under the weight of accusation from all sides, finally admitting she killed my brother.

But instead she just got portrayed as a saddened wife, due only a soaking by a rain of sympathy.

I calm myself. It's a setback, that's all. The war is not lost. The public can still be shown her black heart. The truth can still be forced out of her. If not by the cops or a TV show, well, I'll have to do it all by myself.

18

LUCY

I ended up finishing the bottle of wine, but not to drown my sorrows. The opposite in fact: a celebration. The reporter who'd sliced me to pieces in Cullerton had obviously had a change of heart when it came time to cut his report. That or he'd been forced to make changes by the police or his superiors.

The final edit had no mention of the – I admit – suspicious evidence against me in Tom's disappearance. No angle that I was guilty of harming him. No nasty questions and accusations. No video of my storming away through the woods. And, best of all, it had finished with a plea for anyone with information on Tom's whereabouts to come forward. At least some people believed Tom had left me.

I went to my bedroom window and peeked through a chink in the curtains, to see what kind of effect the news report had had on my neighbours. For half an hour I had knelt there, back aching, and watched for activity.

A nice couple had come across with a wrapped gift, which was a particularly good sign, but I didn't answer the door. Same for an old lady with a tray of flapjacks. Same for two other door-knockers, one of whom yelled through the letterbox, asking me to call round if I needed a chat. It seemed that the TV show had gotten me some fans.

But some people had seen the news report in a different light. When later I took the wine bottle out to my recycling wheelie bin, a man up the street putting oil in his car stopped to watch the entire event. I waved but he didn't wave back. He just stared. Other faces at windows suddenly vanished when I looked their way. Nothing on that news report had made me look bad, but a missing spouse will probably always look suspicious to those who devour true crime TV channels.

But silly crime shows weren't the reason, were they? I had to stop kidding myself. Mary had been yelling outside my door a few days ago and the police had turned up, and six months ago I'd been arrested for assaulting Tom. Those events would guarantee that I would never totally wash myself clean of suspicion, especially on this estate. I would probably have to move house soon. A fresh start. Or, to quote a term of my mother's that I use, a new square one.

I didn't feel too dejected by that thought because this house, this area, would always remind me of Tom, and every day decant depression into my system.

'Unless you crawl out from under your damn rock, Tom, you bastard.' I had to keep reminding myself that this nightmare would end the second my husband reappeared. And he would. He couldn't hide forever.

As sunset arrived around nine in the evening, I got another knock on the door, and a peek through the window this time showed a man in a suit under a jacket on my step. I recognised him as one of the detectives who'd accompanied Reavley and I to the cottage that morning.

He imparted some news. And showed me some pictures.

He got down to the news immediately, even before I'd taken a seat in the living room: 'We've found what we think is Tom's backpack.'

I sat and put my arms around myself. It took a few seconds for me to realise that he wanted me to ask, so I did. 'Where?'

It had been found jammed between two rocks in Low Man Brook, a few hundred metres downstream and deep in the ravine. He stepped forward and held out an electronic tablet to show me a photograph. It showed the area of river, taken from the bank. I could see something small between two rocks poking out of the frothing waters, but at this distance it was impossible to determine what it was.

He swiped the screen to show another photo. Same angle, but zoomed in. Now it was clear that it was the strap of a backpack between the two rocks, with the whole bag visible under the surface. The next photo showed that backpack after rescue, laid on a plastic sheet on the grassy bank.

I couldn't read the detective's expression. Not sadness at bringing me bad news, that was for certain. 'I need you to look at these items and confirm: is this your husband's backpack?'

He started scrolling through photographs. The first showed the backpack wide open, exposing its contents. All of them Tom's, I instantly knew. I saw folded tracksuit trousers. I saw a water bottle in the outside pocket. I saw his electronic cigarette in a little net pocket inside. I saw his balled-up spare socks.

Next came those items, still wet, laid out on the sheet, with a hi-definition close-up photograph for each one. The tracksuit trousers had a pinkish bleach stain near the hip, which I remembered. The socks were his fluffy red ones, which Mary bought for him. The electronic cigarette was black, with a picture of a monster machine and the word Animal.

'Yes, it's Tom's,' I said. 'Tom goes everywhere with that vape and I remember him puffing on it as he waited for me to climb onto the walkway. I don't know why he'd get rid of his bag.'

The detective gave a sympathetic nod, but the next instant saw him return to a cyborg-like dedication. 'Do you know how the bag got in the river? It appears to have washed downstream and jammed in the rocks. But you said you'd crossed the river and were walking through the woods.'

'It must have rolled down the hill.'

'I don't understand.'

'The main track through the woods has little offshoots here and there, like rungs in a ladder. Some of them go downhill towards the ravine.'

'But there's a fence.'

'It's got missing segments. The bag could have rolled off the edge. Or, because he's big and strong, he threw it all the way off.'

The detective flicked at his screen. The following picture was a close-up of one of the backpack's straps. It showed a red mark on the fabric. My jaw fell open.

I knew it was blood.

The detective's eyes were still on me. They'd never left. 'Blood. It was kept dry because the strap was above the water. We'll get it analysed. But do you know how this would have got here, if it's Tom's?'

His sympathy, as I suspected, was faked. His questions struck me as ten per cent curiosity and ninety per cent allegation. 'Did Reavley put you up to this?'

'I'm sorry?'

'Coming here, pretending to be on my side, and then trying to catch me off guard with accusations. Just like Reavley did with that reporter. Trying to ambush me. You think that blood proves Tom is dead, don't you? You're all ignoring the fact that Tom drove away in his car. That he sent me a text message from right outside this house the day after he left me.'

'Mrs Packham, I'm just here to gather information on–'

'That's what Reavley said.' I stood up. He took a step back. 'I've told the police already that Tom cut his finger on the tap in the cottage. He must have transferred blood to the bag when he put it on. Look, I don't know if you believe me or not, but now I get to ask questions. Are any of you people not on the Nail Lucy Taskforce? Is there anyone actually trying to find my husband?'

His answer, surprisingly, was the sincerest he'd sounded. 'We're still searching for him. But if he was wearing this backpack when it went into the river, and we don't know for sure, then he could have been washed further downstream and even now held under by a current somewhere. That's all I can tell you.'

I laughed in frustration. I couldn't help it. But it immediately put a frown on the detective's face.

'This isn't a laughing matter, Mrs–'

'Oh yes it is, detective. All of you are funny, the way you're completely ignoring every single thing I tell you. You think this backpack being in the river is further proof I killed my husband, but I think Tom tossed it away because he didn't need it. Not if he had clothing and stuff and another vape at his other woman's house. I said this to your boss and I'll say it to you. I didn't kill my husband and if you think I did, arrest me. Until then, or until you find him living in another house with another family, leave me alone. Get out.'

I didn't wait for him to comply. I pushed past him and fled upstairs, where I sat on my bed and listened. Half a minute later, I heard the click of my front door closing. At the window, I watched him drive away. I could see some of my neighbours watch, too. I wanted to open the window and scream at them:

I'll prove you all right by murdering Tom after all, when he finally shows his damn face again.

MARY

I nod: yes. 'Are you going to bring Lucy down here, too?'

'No. We did it by photographs. I sent one of my team.'

I had just arrived at Reavley's police station in Woodseats, where he met me in the car park. When he gave me a bell earlier to come down and view what they thought was Tom's backpack, found downstream from the cottage, I drove as fast as I could. I wanted to confront Lucy and see her fake shock when someone shoved the backpack under her nose. It's gutting that she's not here.

'How did she act?'

We start walking towards the building. The sky was losing light fast. It made me realise how tired I was. This has been the longest day I can ever remember.

'My man who spoke to her reckons there was... contradiction,' Bennet says. 'There was something off about her demeanour, but he didn't feel she knew the backpack was in the river.'

I would have read her better. I know the woman like these strangers can't. They're treading so lightly around her they've got blinkers on.

It wasn't a question and Reavley knew this. He started on some excuse or other, but I didn't let him get more than a couple of words out. 'Any flags on Tom's BMW yet?'

During the same call bringing me here, Reavley had told me all about the ANPR system and what it meant that my brother's car hadn't been flagged: it definitely wasn't on the move and hadn't been for a while. So, Tom had left his phone behind and now abandoned his prized BMW.

Both massively out of character, yet the cops were doing nothing. What would it take to get these people off their arses and nail Lucy – her walking into a police station with his severed head in a box?

Annoyed, I say nothing to Reavley as he leads me inside and to a room where Tom's stuff is in plastic bags laid out on a table. And it *is* Tom's stuff, I see that as soon as I get through the door. His backpack, his trousers, his water bottle, his vape with a picture of Animal on it. I confirm it for Reavley with a loaded sentence:

'Yes, these items you found dumped in a river are indeed Tom's prized possessions that he'd never throw away.'

'Are you okay?' he asks. He puts a hand on my shoulder, but I step away so it falls off. I approach the table and look at the backpack, which has a bloodstain on one strap. It makes me shiver. No, I'm not okay, but it's not for the reason he thinks. Maybe hundreds of other people have been in this room and broken down in tears at seeing a missing loved one's belongings laid out like some jumble sale. Not me. There's no hard-hitting revelation here. I've known Tom was dead from the start.

I ask, 'Did Lucy have some bullshit story to explain why Tom's stuff was found in the river?'

He's not comfortable answering this and I know why. Sure enough, after telling me Lucy claimed Tom tossed the bag when he left her, Reavley tags on: 'It proves nothing though. It's not enough for us to arrest her. Or even to upgrade the missing person's to a murder investigation. But it's a piece of the jigsaw.'

Jigsaw? Eventually, I'd like the full picture of what happened between Tom and Lucy on Sunday morning, but right now I don't care about the why and the how. I just want the cops to cotton on that my brother's dead and that his wife made it so. Then a fire will be lit under their asses. Even if they can't do Lucy for murder, at least they'd give finding Tom's body a better shot.

But the worrying, the hoping, the ups and downs, it's all

wearing me out. Right now, the grief of the last few days is weighing me down and I need to get away, clear my head. I want to sleep. Such a long, awful day.

'I need to go back home,' I say. 'I'm tired.'

'I don't think you should drive. Not after this news.'

No argument there. Reavley arranges to have my car driven home. I ignore the young detective constable behind the wheel and he seems happy with this. Until we arrive. As we pull up next to a cop car waiting to take him back, he tries to lift my spirits a little:

'It all takes time, but we get there in the end. If Tom's wife killed him, she'll go down for it. Believe me.'

How can I believe a guy who just used the word *if*?

LUCY

I found evidence of the wide divide in opinions about me on my doorstep. Two notes, left by people who'd awaited dark in order to slip down my garden path unseen. One was scrawled on a cut-out portion of a cereal box and the other bore neat script on scented paper. You could probably guess which was which.

Poor dear. I'm sure your husband will be back. I bet he's gone off binge drinking with friends. Hope you are well.

I hear those arguments you and your man have. I know you buried him out there. Hello prison for twenty years. Justice is coming, killer.

I peeked out my bedroom window, hoping to see who'd left these messages, but the street was empty because it was past ten at night. I watched for a few minutes, but the handful of people I saw come and go about their business paid my house no attention, and didn't appear to be actively trying to act ignorant. I considered looking in people's wheelie bins for a chopped-up box of Shreddies, but wrote it off as pointless. I wouldn't be confronting anyone even if I found evidence of the culprit. It would also look pretty strange if I was rooting through rubbish late at night.

I also learned that social media had picked up the *Calendar* story. I did have a Facebook account and around a hundred friends, but I used it only to snoop. To me it was like reading through people's diaries. I didn't look often, perhaps an average of once a week, and hadn't created or commented on there in months, not even in response to some of Tom's silly posts. But that morning I decided to take a look.

I skimmed through messages from people from my history, seeking insults and accusations, and those were there, but the overall gist was pleasant. But I was about to learn that people were more comfortable tearing me apart on Tom's profile.

Amongst the friends asking where he was, wishing him well, and urging him to get in contact with them, I found myriad negative comments, too.

The landlord of the Serengeti pub in Cullerton mentioned a 'spat' between Tom and I on Saturday night. Two of Tom's co-owners of his monster truck had mentioned their visit to the cottage to pick him up last Sunday evening, remarking how weird it was that he had vanished without word – *weird* was also their opinion of my behaviour when questioned about Tom's absence. Friends of theirs, not known to me, had commented things like: I was a bitch to Tom; he could do better than a freak like me; I was a wrong 'un.

It seemed he'd mentioned me often to his friends, and not flatteringly. I wasn't sure how to feel about that. Then I was sure: sod them, they weren't my friends.

I wasn't surprised to find that Mary had been replying to many of these comments and posts, and, of course, she wasn't kind. But she did avoid calling me a murderer, although that was probably in order to avoid getting her Facebook account barred. The comment that stung the most was:

This woman has messed up every relationship she's ever had. Her parents sent her away, she has no friends, and now Tom's gone. Even her cat ran away.

The bitch. The awful bitch, saying such a thing and tagging a joke on to the end.

It was true that I didn't have contact with my family – I'd lied to Reavley when I said I saw my parents once a year. Back in Germany, when depression and the abuse that fed it became too much to bear and I fled my life, I didn't tell my parents.

They had been strict with me and determined to make sure I did something worthwhile with my life. It was my mother who'd arranged my role in Germany and they'd put a lot of effort into it. But I was suddenly back in England, with no job, no partner. A failure. Maybe I would have been the prodigal daughter, but I was weak, and I secreted myself away. There I was, right back in England, and they didn't even know. At that point, I hadn't spoken to my mother or father for four or five years, so hiding in plain sight was easy.

Eventually, after I was married to Tom and working, I did make that important phone call.

But in the nine years since there had been no contact. They seemed to have accepted and understood why I'd left Germany, but I hadn't told them the whole truth. My tale had erased any mention of abuse by my husband, instead promoting the notion that our marriage had simply fizzled out. This lie had been spoken years ago, but still it stung, still it made me feel like I'd betrayed them, that I was an embarrassment to the family.

And it was for this reason that Mary's scathing two-line assessment of my whole life, based upon the fragments of truth I'd allowed Tom to know, pierced deeper than she could ever have intended.

I soon found something that gave me a rare smile during this dark period. It seemed that the *Calendar* news item had caught the attention of the eagle-eyed and a trend had started. Bigfoot had apparently come to north-west England.

When I searched for a hashtag someone had created – #LancashireBigfoot – I found posts from all over the country, the vast majority in no way connected to me or Tom or anyone we knew. I cycled through dozens of screenshots taken from the news report, some with creative borders, many with captions and with Bigfoot himself circled in pen. And my face in all but the cropped ones in zoom. There I was, out in the woods, talking to a reporter, and there deep in the trees behind me, lurked a dark humanoid figure.

I knew Mary had been loitering in the woods, in order to have accosted me so soon after I ran from the TV crew. But this was a shock. She must have been watching and following us from the outset, darting behind trees like a cat on the hunt. At any other time, this would have really upset me. But how could it now? Mary was Bigfoot. She would know about the trend her grainy, skulking figure had started, and I hoped she was burning up with embarrassment.

But my joy didn't last. Amongst all the messages of condolence, the accusations, the offers of help, and a thousand Bigfoot jokes, there was nothing from Tom. My reason for agreeing to the TV interview had been to prompt my husband into making contact, and so far it had failed. Why hadn't he? It was a question I'd asked myself a hundred times.

Tom might not have seen the news report, or be around anyone else who had, so there was always a chance over the coming days. But I didn't believe this. The police had been in contact with all his known friends, friends and colleagues had been in contact with all his remote family, and his family would have made their own enquiries: there was just no way that in this digitally-connected world Tom wouldn't know that his sudden absence was big news. Yet he hadn't been in contact with anyone. Why?

The police and some local people had searched the woods around the cottage and asked questions at various pubs, shops and other establishments in the area, all to no avail. Nobody had seen Tom and I together. Nobody had seen Tom on his own in the woods, or anywhere beyond them. Why?

I'd considered that Tom was punishing me by remaining hidden even though he knew people suspected me of murder, and would return when he was bored. I'd wondered if he was simply playing a major practical joke and enjoyed watching everyone scratch their heads. I had thought about the possibility that he was locked away in a remote cabin somewhere with his new woman and somehow didn't know he was in the news – perhaps his new lover was someone in the public eye and had a lot to lose if an affair became knowledge.

In the end, it didn't matter which. All three scenarios surely had to end with Tom one day making an appearance, alive and well. I needed that, and not just to avoid getting arrested for murder. I needed it for my own sanity. Even I, the only one who knew the whole story, had started to find it harder and harder to ignore the notion that... that Tom could be dead.

Had something happened to him after he sent me a text message on Monday? Accident in the middle of nowhere? Murder by someone else? Like his new lover or her jealous boyfriend? A monster truck rival? Back in Tom's estate agency offices, Reavley had asked about disgruntled clients, so could Tom have made a lethal enemy through his business dealings?

While these random, unsubstantiated, and headache-inducing thoughts were pinballing in my mind, I absently scrolled through messages on my Facebook, not really paying attention. Until one name zapped me out of my trance.

The name was Fischer and the message simply listed a phone number and an order to call her. Her profile showed a handsome middle-aged woman, backdropped by a sun-blasted beach. It brought a tear to my eye.

For a few minutes, I sat with my phone and my old friend's number on the screen, finger poised over the call button. But I just couldn't bring myself to make the call. In the end, I sent a return Facebook message with my number. I felt it was easier that way.

The woman called me almost immediately. I answered with a shaking hand.

'Is this a life insurance scam?' she said. 'First thing the police will look into, so I doubt it will work. I imagine there's many a wife or husband who's innocent of murder and actually goes to prison just because there's a big life insurance payout. So did this husband of yours deserve it, and will the cash go to me when you're in prison?'

She gave a laugh, which told me she was joking. Her next words explained the dig: 'Just thought I'd get that awkward shit out up front, so we're not skirting around it. I guess we've got a lot of catching up to do. So, tell me what happened.'

Before I could do that, I burst into tears. In Germany all those years ago, the last thing I had done in front of Leona, as I was about to board a plane, was get emotional. Now here my old friend was, and hearing me cry once again.

MARY

Bigfoot. I'm so annoyed.

After being dropped by the cop, I had headed back out and visited a late-night newsagent to get some colour photocopies.

My plan was to get changed back home and then hit the streets – starting with Lucy's road.

But now, as I return to the house, Dad calls out from upstairs. I find him in the bathroom, laying on the floor and in pain and soaked.

Straight off I can tell he's pissed himself. Turns out he rushed to the upstairs toilet, twisted his ankle and hit the deck, and had to relieve himself on the floor because he couldn't get up. It's not the first time I've found him in a bad spot. And it's not the first time Dad's decided he's magically a lot more able-bodied than he was the day before. He doesn't like to piss in the bottle he keeps by his armchair.

I'm also guilty of not paying attention to what happened last time. I couldn't lift him back then, but still try now. He's got skinny legs and arms, but a big belly, and he's heavy. I can't even sit him up. I can't imagine how long it took him to drag himself upstairs.

'Tom will help,' he says through the pain. I can see his ankle's bent funny: broken for sure.

'Tom's too far away, Dad. He can't come. I'll get an ambulance.'

He's right though. Tom has helped Dad after a fall many times, and gotten him changed and into his chair. But he's never going to do that again, so now I have to sit with Dad, smelling his stinking mess, while the ambulance ambles its way to us. It's another upward gear change for my Lucy-hate and it staves off the tiredness of a long day.

They let me ride with him in the ambulance. I call Reavley on the way but get no answer. Dad's wheeled into the accident and emergency department. The room's pretty full despite the late hour, but we do get a pair of end chairs and a space beside me. I brought my handbag and it's got some of my photocopies in it, so I dump one on the empty seat beside me. Nearby, a thug of a young man with a fist wrapped in a blood-encrusted necktie gives it a long look, but he doesn't say anything. Maybe he can't read anything except comics.

DI Reavley sends me a text, but might as well not have bothered. It says he's sorry for not answering, can't talk right now, but if I'm calling for an update, they have nothing new yet. Enquiries are progressing. He'll let me know. In other words, no arrest team is about to boot in Lucy's front door.

'Dad, I have to pop somewhere. You'll be all right here.'

'Don't leave me on my own, Mary. Where you going?'

'It's important. You won't get seen for well over a couple of hours, and I'll be back by then. Can I go?'

I'm already getting up. Dad says it's okay and I kiss his cheek and scuttle off. A couple of people who probably overheard give me a funny look, but I send it back with interest. They don't know my problems and should keep their noses out.

I jog across the road to the dark car park and actually get beyond the barrier before I remember I didn't come in my car. That's Lucy's doing, confusing me with all this stress. I grab a taxi from the rank outside.

'Where we off to?' the driver asks.

'Tom's house,' I say, before realising my silly mistake. Lucy's really messing me up now.

19

LUCY

I spent an hour on the phone to Leona and we filled the time with biographies. I told her all about my life since I'd returned to England. Leona was the only person who knew everything about my time in Germany and I had always been buoyed by being able to pour my heart out to her.

As if sensing I needed the same boost now, she didn't allow me to talk about the happy moments with Tom. It was the low points she insisted on hearing, and I happily obliged. I might even have overplayed the gravity of some situations, especially my almost non-existent relationship with my parents, just to force that much-needed sympathy from her. Then it was Leona's turn.

After leaving Stuttgart, Leona had started a pottery business with her mother and made quite a career of it. Her old boyfriend had attempted to get back in touch, but Leona had not only shunned him, she'd gravitated away from men altogether. On holiday in Hawaii, she had met a rich girl who later became her fiancée, and now Leona had been living in Honolulu for six years. They had married last Sunday.

I was immensely happy for her but that joy was tinged with a modicum of sadness: as one marriage had birthed, another had died.

That brought me around to how she'd heard about Tom having left me. A news programme broadcasting to the middle of England wouldn't reach Hawaii. Leona told me she'd made some good friends amongst the surfing community in Hawaii, one of whom was from Norfolk, which did get *Calendar*. But how did...

'I'd showed them your Facebook in the past. My friend recognised your photo.'

'My Facebook?'

'I looked you up here and there, Luce.'

That brought a tear to my eye, in part because I hadn't checked for my friend on social media. It made me feel heartless. 'But why didn't you contact me?'

'You seemed to be happy. I was back from a bad time in your life.'

The tears came faster as I understood what she meant. I had fled Germany to escape everything and Leona must have assumed that contacting me would stir up old memories, ancient fears, and reawaken the black mood that had virtually defined me in the final months before I got on a boat. But there was a painful irony.

My time overseas, more than half my life at that point, had eroded all former friendships, leaving me virtually alone and unknown once back in England, and I had many times wanted to keep in contact with Leona. I had never made that phone call or written that letter because Leona, too, had begun life afresh and I'd assumed she wouldn't want to be burdened by the moans of some depressed girl she once knew. I should have known better.

I should have realised that soulmates don't just cast each other aside. I wish I had called her every day. I wished she lived right next door to me. And I told her this.

'I feel bad for not contacting you sooner, Luce,' she said. 'But we'll make up for that when I see you. Which I will, soon.'

'I'd like that. A visit would be nice.'

Probably to relax me, Leona turned the conversation to world events and celebrity news. And it worked. Despite midnight looming, I felt vibrant and eager to move about. I put the phone on speaker and cleaned the kitchen as we gossiped. I almost danced around that room, in fact, and couldn't remember when I'd last felt so... comfortable. I realised I'd gone too long without a good old chat with a female friend.

'I've got cash, Luce,' Leona said when we found a spare moment between giggles. Luce was a nickname only she ever used. 'So you're coming here to visit, my treat. To Hawaii. When you've gotten through these problems.'

'I don't know. It's far, and...'

'Now just stop bullshitting me. Who do you think you're talking to?'

I started to cry as I realised I was misjudging the bond of eternal comrades. Deep down, I knew exactly why I hadn't made close friends since returning to England. Fear of having to talk about my past, fear of being judged for it, fear that I didn't deserve love, all of which were symptoms of a self-esteem cracked by mental abuse. And Leona knew this. She knew I was scared that something might have changed between us and visiting her in a strange country might turn out to be a bad idea.

'Okay. I'll visit at some point.'

'Don't sound so rubbery. Be concrete. Be certain. I want you down here within a week or so.'

'Okay. For certain.' I paused. 'I'm sorry about this, Leona. I'm sorry that you didn't find me to be the happy person I promised I'd be.'

Leona's response made total sense: without this tragedy, we might never have reconnected. 'Besides, happiness is on and off. I bet if I'd called you on any of a thousand earlier days before today, your promise would have been fulfilled. Why don't you promise again? Go on.'

On the day we'd parted, I'd told Leona that the next time we spoke, I'd be a happy person. I made a promise. Now she wanted me to do it again.

'I can't. Because I want to talk to you every day, and it will take longer than overnight to fix my problems. But how about this? I promise you that when you next *see me*, I will be a different woman. Strong and happy. No longer the depressed wimp you knew.'

'That's a transmutation I'd love to see. Deal. We'll bet a bag of jelly babies.'

I laughed, remembering some of our long chats in Leona's bedroom, where we'd lie together on her bed and toss jelly babies into each other's mouths. My best-ever friend, yet one I'd barely told Tom about. Her use of a fancy T-word for *change* reminded me of Tom, who loved to show off his vocabulary. I uselessly wondered how this pair might have gotten on.

Leona decided to end our catch-up there for the time being, given the late hour. I knew she'd opted for that precise moment in order to leave me on a happy high, and it made me love her all the more. I suddenly loved the idea of getting away from everything and jetting off to Hawaii for a week or so.

But soon after I'd been left all alone, my demeanour became dark and depressing to match the rest of the house. Sending my mind back in time, or across the waters to Hawaii, hadn't erased my problems. Now, they came back hard. While talking to

Leona, I had ignored four other calls, plus two on the landline, and someone rapping on my front door. There would be more to come. I was still wired and figured sleep would be impossible.

I tried to read a book on my phone – *Perfect Lie* by Claire Sheldon – but something was bothering me, making concentration impossible.

Despite Leona's idea to get 'that awkward shit out up front' we hadn't talked about events post-Sunday. Leona knew all about Tom and our life together, the good and the bad, but she'd relied upon social media gossip to learn about my husband's disappearance and the role the police considered I'd played in it. I felt incomplete having neglected to tell her my version of this part of the story, and I called her back. She picked up before the second ring, as if expecting me.

But before I could start the story, there was a new knock at the door. This time, though, the caller didn't simply wait for a response. A male voice called through the letterbox, introducing himself as a reporter from a local paper. He wanted to talk to me and I should feel obliged to, because the public had a right to know.

Right to know? That claim, which journalists had been hiding behind forever, annoyed me so much that I rushed to the door and yanked it open. I didn't care if the neighbours across the street were watching me through pulled curtains.

Before me stood a handsome young man in a shirt and tie, which immediately gave me the idea someone had sent a pretty face in the hope that would get me to talk. 'The people don't have the right to know my private business and you don't have the right to hassle me at home. Now piss off.'

He seemed to like my anger. I was sure my previous two words would be quoted in bold and italics, front page. 'If you didn't kill your husband, then you'd talk to me.'

'I am. I'm telling you to get lost.'

He held up a sheet of paper. A leaflet. My jaw dropped and I snatched it off him. 'And what the hell is this you've done?'

'Not me. They're everywhere.'

And they were. I glanced beyond him, out onto the dark street, and I could see a woman across the road standing on her doorstep, watching. In her hands was a square of paper, surely the same leaflet. Further down, I could see a similar shape stuck to a lamp post. Good Lord.

The one in my hands had a picture of me at the top, underneath which was the word MURDERER. Below that was my name and: YOU MAY HAVE HEARD ABOUT THE DISAPPEARANCE OF TOM PACKHAM, FROM SHEFFIELD. HE DID NOT RUN AWAY. THIS IS HIS WIFE AND SHE KILLED HIM.

If I hadn't been holding the evidence, I wouldn't have believed it. But it was real. And I had no doubt it was Mary's brainchild. Her vendetta against me had just hit a new level.

'So what do you have to say about that? For our readers?'

'Piss off. Go talk to my husband's sister. She's having a love affair with a convicted...'

I trailed off, aware that I'd nearly made a big mistake. Mary would jump at the chance to slaughter me in the newspapers.

But I had his attention. 'Convicted criminal? Have you got the sister's address?'

'Look, just go away.'

Then I heard a noise from my phone, still clutched in my fist. Leona was speaking. I'd forgotten she was there. I held the phone close to my ear and heard her say, 'Put him on, Luce. Put that bastard on the phone.'

I held out the phone and the reporter took it. He listened, but said nothing. And after he handed it back sheepishly, he turned and left. I gave another glance up and down the street. The late hour didn't seem to matter to some, who'd been drawn to their windows and doors. For their entertainment, I tore up the leaflet and tossed the fragments into the air, but as a bold statement it backfired when the wind cast them against my face and chest.

I slammed the door and rushed back into the living room. In the silence, I heard Leona's tinny voice begging me to speak. 'I'm sorry, Leona. Sorry. I'll call you later. Just give me time and I'll tell you the truth.' I hung up before she could respond. I knew she'd wait for me.

My thoughts turned to Mary. I bet she was very proud of her little smear campaign. I bet right then she was fast asleep with a smile on her lips, dreaming of exciting additional ways to tear into me come the new day. There was no way I could sleep, so I grabbed my shoes, planning a drive to try to work away some of the tension.

Later, still unable to sleep and trying to concentrate on the TV, I heard my phone give a text message beep. A new unknown number. But not a troll or a well-wisher this time.

It was Tom.

MARY

When I arrive back at the hospital, close to midnight, Dad's gone. I figured he'd still be waiting in the A&E waiting room, but the woman at the desk tells me he was seen and booted out quickly because his ankle was only sprained. They got him an ambulance. She asks me why I didn't stay with him, like it's any of her damn business.

At home, I find Dad in his armchair and in a rare foul mood. The first thing he tells me is that his taxi ride cost triple because the driver had to half-carry him to the front door, and the sod stole his watch.

'You got an ambulance, Dad. They told me.'

'So where's my watch?'

'You haven't got that watch anymore, Dad.' I've heard the taxi story many times. It happened on a drunken Hallowe'en night, way up in Fife. In the 1960s, before he'd even met my mother.

'Tom will tell you. Where is he? In the Den?'

He's talking about a treehouse Mum and Dad had down at the bottom of the garden of their big home. As a kid, Tom would hide there if he broke something of mine while I was at work. Which happened a lot because he liked to snoop in my bedroom. The treehouse was always the first place I looked for him, yet he always hid there. But those days are long gone. Dad's getting badly confused, probably because he hasn't napped for a while.

'No, I checked the Den.'

'Where is he? Where did you go?'

If he'd pushed it, I might have told him, then and there, that Tom was dead and I went to his killer's housing estate to spread the word. But instead he turns to his TV and seems to forget about me.

Soon he's asleep, bless him. I wish I could, but I'm still buzzing with the urge to do something. I toss a blanket over him and head back out. I'm eager to see the effects of my work.

Even so late, a crowd has gathered outside Lucy's house. I park and force my way through people, careful to avoid the rakes, spades, baseball bats and knives they're waving about. This far back, everyone's fairly quiet, just watching, but closer to the house the mob is angrier, screaming their hatred of Lucy. Stones are thrown, busting all the windows. Someone yells *charge* and a mass of bodies pours into her home like water busting a dam. I love it.

As Lucy's dragged out by her feet, I grab a petrol bomb off the woman next to me and launch the bottle at the bedroom window. It sails through a hole in the glass and the crowd whoops as flames fill the room and lick at the night sky.

Lucy is screaming, which is music to my ears. I force through the crowd as it moves down the street, to the nearest lamp post, and fight my way to Lucy. There is rope in my hands, whose noose I loop around her neck. The crowd cheers and I toss the free end over the crossbar of the lamp post and haul the murdering bitch off the ground by her dainty throat and...

Who the hell am I kidding? I turn onto her street and get exactly what I feared. Nothing. Not a rake or petrol bomb in sight. The street is dead-of-night silent. Just a run-of-the-mill late-evening splinter of suburbia. My leafleting campaign has achieved sod all, except maybe snidey remarks behind locked doors.

I cruise past Tom's house and see all the curtains are shut. The leaflet I stuck to Lucy's garden gate is still there, same for one I taped to a lamp post. A couple of others flutter in the street, which is a bit puzzling because the remainder got slipped through letterboxes. Maybe people tried to join my campaign by pinning them up outside, but didn't do a good job. But, again, who am I kidding? I've tried to convert these folk and their response: tossing my leaflets right in the street. Earlier, I saw an aeroplane flying a banner advertising a birthday: if only I'd had that idea instead.

Further up the road, a middle-aged man with a comb-over and a dog eager to drag him away is looking at a leaflet on another lamp post. I pull up next to him and wind my window down.

'Have you read it?'

Trying to see my face in the dark, he squints at me for ages, while his dog tries to get to my car. 'I know you. You're his sister, aren't you? You put these up? News said he was missing.'

'Oh no, that was wrong. They didn't report the whole story. My brother was already dead.'

He yanked the leaflet off the lamp post. 'And who says she over there killed him? She's hardly been arrested.'

'I know she did it. The police are gathering evidence.'

'Sound like horse manure to me. She'd be arrested if she did it.'

He tears down the leaflet, balls it, sticks it in his pocket, moves on, slipping out of the puddle of light from the lamp post and into darkness. I don't complain: some people will root for Lucy. I do wait until he's not looking and put another leaflet on the lamp post.

I turn the car and head back. I honk my horn as I zip past Tom's house, just to make Lucy get up and investigate.

At home, I head up to my room. It's been such an intense day I'm surprised I'm not a walking zombie. A few hours ago I was ready to doze standing up, but now my brain's buzzing with the intensity of recent events. No doubt that bitch is sleeping like a princess. I've got no chance. The best way for me to relax is to work on another letter to Richard, my death-row pen pal.

When I first started writing to him, I avoided complaining about insignificant little things in my life because his problems were so much worse. I stuck to sweet and sunny things because dudes stuck in dingy cells will want uplifting stories, right? Not Richard. He loves to hear about apple juice leaking in my fridge or losing an earring down beside my car seat, because those things, the dross of normal, everyday life, are like tales from another planet.

He loves me pissed off, but not unhappy, so tonight I write about a plate jamming in the dishwasher, and I avoid anything to do with Lucy or Tom. It's hard.

I'm still writing the letter at past two in the morning, when my phone rings.

It's Lucy.

I answer in my usual way: open the call, say nothing.

'Tom sent me another text.' She sounds emotional. She's a fine actor. 'He's alive, just like I told everyone. Mary, can you hear me? I will send it.'

She hangs up before I can blast her. I watch my phone, waiting. The text comes a few seconds later.

Saw you on the news stop looking for me im not coming back but i think its kind of funny everyone thinks you killed me this is new number again so i cant be traced im travelling in order to send the text so tell cops not to look for me wherever they trace this.

There's an eyeball icon for the word 'I', everything's spelled right but without punctuation, and like me Tom often calls the police 'cops'. It damn well looks like a Tom text, but if I know that, you can bet Lucy does. This, like the last message, is bullshit. But this time it doesn't make me see red. I must be exhausted because I've got no fight in me. When she calls a few seconds later, even I'm surprised by my response.

This time I break tradition and speak first. 'I need him, Lucy. I need to bury him. Where is he?'

At first she seems confused, because she says, 'He didn't say. Did you read the text?' Then she seems to realise that I used the word BURY. 'Don't you believe it was him? Mary, it was Tom. I've just told the police, and they're coming here. Tom is alive, Mary.'

The phone feels heavy in my hand. My head's heavy on my neck. It's an effort to speak. Everything's suddenly catching up with me and I'm worn out. My words are flat, robotic, no anger, no emotion of any kind. 'He's not alive, Lucy. You know he's dead. The police are looking for his car and it's not flagged up on any cameras, so it's not being driven. I want you to just admit it.'

She pauses, dismayed that her convoluted trick hasn't worked.

'Lucy, please. I am trying to get on with my life. I can accept that Tom is dead. But not that his body is missing. For the funeral, we need him. His father misses him. We need his body. Where did you hide him?'

Now she finds her voice, but needn't have bothered. She wastes it on more lies. 'No, he's alive. I don't know how else to convince everyone. He sent me a text. They can trace where it came from. I didn't do anything to him. He ran away from me. From all of us.'

All the threats over the past few days, all the evidence thrown in her face, have achieved sweet sod all. She burned me out and I'm weak and I've got only one weapon left. The sickening last resort. But I've got no other choice.

I slip off the chair, falling hard onto my knees. One thuds into my pen, dropped on the carpet, but I don't even feel the sting. Impossible given the agony in my mind. I clutch the phone in both hands. I cry. And then I beg. I urge her to find her soul, and end this pain, and give me my brother's body.

But the tears, like her lies, are a waste of time.

'He's alive, Mary,' she yells down the phone. In a fit of rage, I lob the mobile hard against the wall. I hear a deadly crack and a piece of it breaks free, and the device lands with a thud on the carpet. But, unlike Tom, the phone's not dead. From across the room, I hear her tinny voice, screaming from the phone, repeating the same words, like a stuck record:

'I didn't kill him, he's alive. I didn't kill him, he's alive. I didn't...'

20

LUCY

Just before I'd called Mary, I'd left a text for DI Reavley. He didn't return my message or call, and I figured this was because of the time, but a mere nine minutes later I heard a car pull up outside. From the bedroom window, I saw a plain car and a police car. Reavley.

I had just hung up after my failed call to Mary and my face was a mess of tears. I wiped them away as I rushed downstairs and opened the door, with my phone in my hand, ready to show Reavley the message from Tom. I didn't care that I was barefoot and in pyjamas.

But Reavley wasn't there. I had failed to note that the car wasn't his, or realise that a dead-of-night visit by police can't be good news. It was one I didn't recognise and the plain-clothes black female who got out was unfamiliar, too. I froze on my doorstep as my heart leaped. Nine minutes since my call – too quick for Reavley to have received my message, allocated someone to visit me, and for that person to have made her way here. And why were a pair of uniformed officers needed?

They weren't here because of my text to Reavley, I realised. They had already been en route.

'Where's Aaron?' I asked, using Reavley's first name to project a sense of intimacy.

The female led the way into my garden. She was a lot younger than me and I wondered if she was police staff rather than a detective. But I got my answer when she flipped open her warrant card and introduced herself. A detective sergeant. Was Reavley busy? Was this woman part of the night shift?

'Are you Lucy Packham?'

'Yes. Where's Aaron? Did he get my text?'

'Can we go inside, please?'

I didn't even turn; I backed up, right into the living room, and all three officers followed me inside. I didn't say a word. I had a horrible feeling.

The female detective said, 'Lucy Packham, I am arresting you for the murder of Thomas Packham on or about Sunday the sixteenth of June...'

I dropped into an armchair, numb, and barely heard as the detective cautioned me. I gave only a nod to the question of whether or not I understood why I was being arrested, and only a weak headshake when the woman held up a pair of handcuffs and asked if she was going to need them.

I lifted my mobile, to call Leona – why, I wasn't sure. What did I expect from her, to do what she did with the reporter and send these police away with a few stern words? But the female detective ordered me to hand it over, which I did.

Told to get dressed, I was accompanied upstairs by the female detective to find clothing. The officer seemed so distant and robotic that I didn't even speak to her, let alone ask again for DI Reavley. I got into canvas trousers and a jumper and running shoes: clothing I knew I'd be warm and comfortable in for a long period. Clothing I knew I could sleep on a hard cell bed in. Was this really happening?

Outside, I locked the front door, but the detective took the key. I didn't look up from the ground as I was led to the police car and put in the back. But once inside that protective bubble, I allowed my eyes to roam. Faces at windows, all along the street. Every day for the last few, I'd given my neighbours something to gossip about. In that moment, I never wanted to show my face on this street again.

I heard another vehicle coming down the street. For all of two seconds, the fast approach of those headlights elevated my hopes. But when the vehicle drew to a stop on the other side of the road, I deflated. Not Reavley, rushing here to tell his colleagues they'd made a terrible mistake.

Mary.

I could avert my eyes, but not my ears. 'You had this coming, you murdering bitch.'

Still I refused to acknowledge her presence, even when there was a mammoth thud against the window, as if she had charged the car like a raging bull.

'I hope you rot in prison forever for killing my brother. Your life is over.'

I was glad I'd been arrested. My call to Mary had flipped her over the edge, even though she'd seemed pathetic while begging on the phone. I worried what might have happened if she'd arrived and the police weren't here. Would she have kicked in my front door and attempted to throttle answers she craved out of me?

I kept my head in my lap, eyes screwed shut, even as I heard a scuffling beyond the door and Mary yelling to be let go, and the police desperately trying to calm her. She had been restrained. When finally I did open my eyes, it was all over. The police car was moving, following the detective's vehicle. But when I looked out the back window, I saw those same bright headlights right behind. Mary was following us.

My mind replayed her final words, again and again, because she was absolutely right. My life was over.

MARY

I follow the cop car a short way, then pull into the side of the road. This silly car chase suddenly seems futile. Why am I doing this, at this early hour? Lucy's in custody, which is what I wanted. There's no point in trying to hound her at the police station, and I wouldn't be let in anyway. The wheels of justice will punish Lucy and I can take a stride back now.

That thought leads to another: the future. What's next for me? It's something I haven't thought about since all this started, but now I can't shake the idea out of my head. A big life overhaul, that's what I need.

I don't want to put my dad in a home, but I reckon it's about due. For a long time now, I've wanted to move to America, but having to look after my dad and keep an eye on Tom always made this impossible. It isn't now. There's nothing for me here except Dad and I don't think he'll live too many more years, and even if he does, he's becoming too much work for me to handle alone. He needs to be in a care home.

I head home to find more proof that he's losing it. In another of his otherworldly feats of stamina and perseverance, he's managed to get out of the house while I was gone. I run upstairs to check the bathroom first, then his room – mine's always locked – and while in there I spot something out the window. The motion-activated light on the shed is on.

And there he is, soaked in its light, down at the bottom of the backyard, where the weeds have overgrown in an area of decorative stones. Fixing that is another job Tom was meant to do and now never will, because of his bloody wife.

As I go into the garden, Dad takes a seat on a kitchen chair he must have used like a Zimmer frame to get all the way down there. I don't know how he managed it on his ankle. When he sees me jogging to him, he calls out.

'Where are the trees? Who cut them down?'

That tugs at my heart. I know what he's referring to. He must have gotten confused and thought he was back at his old digs, and had come searching for Tom in the treehouse. When I get to him, I'm such a mix of emotions – anger, despair the top two – that I blurt something I had no plan to tell him for a while yet.

The shed light goes off, turning the world black for a second until it flicks on again as I enter its range.

'Tom is dead, Dad. He got killed by his wife. You remember Lucy? *Fawlty Towers*? She's going to prison. You won't see either of them ever again. I'm sorry.'

'Tom? What do you mean? When, how?'

He's backlit by the light, but I can still see that his eyes look misty. I don't think of Dad as someone who's lost his mind and has bouts of clear-headedness, or the exact opposite. He's more like a pendulum that swings between both, so neither is the norm, and neither should really be called a 'period of'. Bad news doesn't lose him and it doesn't clear up the murk; it just depends which way he's swinging when it comes. My outburst was stupid, impatient, but he's in a murky zone.

'You won't see either of them for a while,' I repeat. 'Tom's had to go on a business trip.'

There's a little confusion as his brain works on what I just said while still remembering my earlier words. But he gives a nod. 'Hard work. I had to leave your mother for long periods, too.'

I'm not sure this is true, but I give a nod as well. I feel even worse now for almost telling the truth and then doing an about-face, and I'm about to compound it.

'Let me help you inside, Dad, it's late. And I have to talk to you about something.'

Dad's condition has sometimes been a sore point between me and Tom. According to Tom, Dad has dementia and needs professional help, but I've always been opposed. I know Lucy thinks I don't care about him, but it isn't that. I was always scared to get a diagnosis. I needed to think my Dad did not have a debilitating condition, just... the murky moments. I needed someone in my life since Tom got married, and I couldn't feel that I truly had someone who cared about me and would be a real friend if I knew Father had dementia.

But now, I accept it. I have to. Because things have changed in my life.

I take his arm to help him. 'What about the chair?' he says. 'It's good to have you around, Mary. I can't dance around like I used to.'

The timing of his words only adds to my sense of guilt, because I'm about to tell him about my plans to leave the country and put him into care.

21

LUCY

'Where's DI Reavley?'

'Busy,' was the response.

Reavley hadn't made an appearance yet, but I had put that down to the late hour. It was almost 3am when I had been booked into the police station. The police had taken my photograph, fingerprints, and a head hair root for DNA. They'd asked for a blood and urine sample, but these I had the right to refuse, so did. They had searched me and taken my phone. They'd demanded to know if I had used drugs that day and if I was likely to harm myself.

I was told I could nominate someone to be notified of my arrest. I thought this meant a phone call, but I wasn't allowed one. Instead, an automated message would be sent. Leona was the sole person I considered alerting, but she wouldn't be able to help and this would only frustrate her. I hadn't spoken to my parents in years and when I finally got the will to break the reformed ice, it absolutely wasn't going to be with such a depressing and embarrassing addition to my biography. Nobody else would care.

'Tell DI Reavley,' I said. It was a genuine request, but the look I got seemed to say, *Oh, you think you're being clever?*

'DI Reavley knows you're here. He authorised the arrest.'

That was a shock.

Afterwards, they locked a cell door behind me. It was bland white except for some signs on the walls and one on the ceiling above the bed. The walls told me I'd be prosecuted if I damaged the room, offered me drugs counselling, and that BAZ WOZ HERE 5/2/19. I lay on the bed attached to the wall – more like a shelf – and closed my eyes, but didn't even try to sleep. My mind was frantic and in a nearby cell someone was kicking a door and yelling threats to the police.

Weirdly, I did sleep – the weariness of a long day, perhaps – and there was no Infinity Dream. I put this down to the stone cell I was caged in: no chance of floating away into deep space. I needed one of these at home.

Around seven in the morning, I woke with a new resolve. The shock of a late-night surprise arrest had worn off. Now, it was a new day, I was refreshed despite only a few hours' sleep, and I knew I'd get to tell my story and end these allegations. I was no longer scared of going to prison, but annoyed that the police had made such a blunder in arresting an innocent woman. The first face that came to see me got an earful. My attitude surprised me as much as it did the officer.

'Where's Reavley? I want to see that liar.' No longer 'Aaron'. The detective had deceived me from the very start, his mission to see me convicted for murder.

'Busy.'

'Fitting up someone else, I imagine. When is my interview?'

'Patience.'

'Wore thin long ago. I want my breakfast, and then I want my interview.'

I was fed a vile microwaved all-day breakfast in a white pot and offered legal advice. There was a duty solicitor at the station. He was supposed to be independent of the police, but I had my doubts.

'If this solicitor is someone who works here a lot, there's probably a few cosy friendships developed. Maybe a Christmas party he photocopied his bum at and made everyone slap his back. Get me someone else.'

'Well, we'd have to contact the Defence Solicitor Call Centre. This'll take time to get someone down here. It'll delay your interview.'

I'd seen enough police shows on TV to know I couldn't be questioned without a solicitor present, except in serious cases, like murder, and then only with the permission of a senior officer. Obviously that hadn't been authorised. However, I had been asked if I wanted legal representation, which meant I could refuse.

'Then we can do the interview without. I agree to answer questions without a solicitor present.'

He seemed to like that. I also know the police don't like interference when interrogating and would rather I didn't have a legal rep by my side. I had nothing to hide, so no reason to have a referee for our chat. He said he'd go 'have a word' with the custody sergeant.

When he was gone, I lay back on the bed, folded my arms under my head, and waited. I stared up at the sign on the ceiling, which simply said BE POSITIVE. It reminded me of how Tom liked to plant such feel-good signs above our bed, to start the day with a good attitude. I *was* positive. I was quite certain that later today the truth would emerge and I'd be free of this whole mess of being suspected of murder.

I closed my eyes and smiled.

MARY

At five o'clock Thursday morning, I wake with new energy, and half an hour later I have my mind on a plan and my wheels on the motorway. In The Cascade there are ornaments and knick-knacks in drawers and all sorts of other bits and bobs that belong to my brother, even though other people rent the place here and there. Since I only ever visited when Tom and bitchface stayed there, it always felt like my brother's second home, so I feel I need to strip it of all that is him.

Maybe it's a way of distancing our family from Lucy, or maybe it's just for something to keep me occupied while I wait for news from detective Reavley. The drive puts me in a good mood and makes me think I'm doing something worthwhile.

But as I unlock and push open the front door of the cottage, I immediately feel a sense of emptiness like you wouldn't believe. I'd never been here when the place was unoccupied, but it's not just that. Something feels wrong. It reminds me of a visit to York Castle and standing where people were executed. A coldness that shouldn't exist in a building in the summer.

In that moment right there, I realise I can't leave my home city. It had been my plan for when this was all over, when Tom's funeral – with his body – was done and when his bitch killer was getting gang-raped in a prison shower. Tom had once used the term 'a new square one' and that was what I had my mind on: a life away from the land I'd grown up in. Nothing around me that would fire bad memories. Nothing to remind me of this hellish period of my life.

But now I know I can't leave. I need the comfort of order, of the known, the regular. I have a life here, for what it's worth, and

I can't kick it to the kerb. I can't run from the pain. That bitch's vicious, selfish, insane actions aren't going to force me to bury my head in the sand of some faraway city. And if I need some kind of exposure therapy to kill my anxiety, then this cottage, ground zero of my suffering, is a place I need to *avoid* avoiding.

It's hell imagining what might have happened here last weekend. I don't reckon Tom was killed in the cottage, but the blood in the sink and on Lucy's blouse... it's hard to shake the idea that *something* went on here. Despite the icy feeling I get with this joint's walls wrapped around me, I go deeper inside. Upstairs to the bathroom.

The room's clean now. No, sterile. A fine job by Lucy to shift evidence, oh yes. But I don't think the bathroom is the murder scene. Tom didn't cut his finger on the tap, but there wasn't enough blood to suggest he was cut down here. So what happened?

Did she slice him and the fight paused until they were outside? Was the blood from a head wound that left him concussed enough to be easily led outside, to a ready-made grave in the woods, or the river?

The cottage is so neat and clean, the area so picturesque, that every theory I've got seems far-fetched. This postcard setting doesn't gel with the idea of murder. But something happened inside these walls that chopped a path to an evil act. I need to know how, and why.

In the bedroom, I stare at the double bed and wonder how things went so pear-shaped. No, I don't like Lucy, but for a long time Tom was happy with her. They had laid on that bed together, made love together, and no one back then could have foreseen how messed up it would all go.

I hear the crunch of wheels on the dirt track outside and rush to the window. A cop car pulls up outside. Then an unmarked car. I look far to the left, where I can just see the exit of the track that curves down from the Kwaint car park. A white van is next, then another cop car. As the van draws up, I see CRIME SCENE INVESTIGATION printed on the side.

As the vehicles rustle up outside the cottage, I lay on the double bed, on the left side, which was Tom's. I pull my phone to call DI Reavley. He answers immediately.

'Thank you, Aaron. Thank you. Has she confessed?'

He doesn't ask what I thanked him for. 'Mary I can't really talk now. We haven't interviewed her yet, but we're going to search her house and the cottage this morning. I'll update you later today.'

'Aaron, you're taking this seriously. Thank you again. I won't get in the way.'

'In the way? Mary, whatever you're planning, don't. You need to stay away. Don't come to her house, don't go to the cottage. Look, I have to go. Chat later.'

He hangs up and I burst into laughter. Outside, I hear car doors slam and voices nattering. Since I can't just slip away without being seen, I go nowhere. I look up at the ceiling, where my brother has pinned a sign saying MORNING SUPERSTAR. It was his way of starting the day with a positive outlook. I wonder if he stared at that sign last Sunday morning, expecting a fine day, no clue he'd be dead within hours.

It didn't work for Tom, but seeing that sign now fills me with positivity, especially against a soundtrack of chatting coppers and crime-scene investigators.

There's all manner of heartache ahead of me – arranging Tom's funeral, giving evidence at Lucifer's trial – but I still get a feeling that this long road is coming to an end. Vile Lucy's in custody. Investigators are opening up her worthless life. Today the truth will come out and a killer will be charged with murder. From this point on, things will start to improve.

I close my eyes and smile.

22

LUCY

My interview wasn't until the middle of the afternoon. Reavley still hadn't visited me and he wasn't part of the interview team. I was due to be grilled by a pair of detectives I'd never seen before. I was suddenly nervous, even though I had nothing to hide.

One was a grizzled middle-aged man who looked as if the joy of the job had long left him. He'd probably heard every lie imaginable from that chair and was adept through experience at discerning them. The other was a woman whose eyes somehow struck me as clever. Here, I believed, was someone university-educated who'd rely on some *-ology* or other to work out if I was being deceptive. She was younger than me, which I didn't like.

After stating names and the time for the file, the female explained why I'd been arrested and asked if I had a reply to it. She was very robotic. A career woman for sure. No kids. No Netflix subscription. I was playing detective myself.

'I didn't kill my husband,' was my reply. 'He left me.'

She pointed out that proof of life enquiries didn't back that up. Tom the loving son, nephew, cousin, brother, business partner and good friend hadn't contacted any of his family or colleagues or friends since Sunday. Tom the frequent social media user hadn't made a single online post or reply to post since Saturday evening. Tom the owner of two bank accounts hadn't made any transactions. Tom the member of society hadn't left a footstep anywhere in the world since I'd claimed he walked out on me.

'But he sent me text messages.'

My reply solicited a slight grin from the robotic lady, and I knew then I had stepped into a trap. She had a sheet of paper with text messages on it, many of them circled in pen. Tom's messages to me. She pointed a number of these out, including that horrible one from Saturday evening, when we ate at Cullerton's local pub: God why did i marry this crazy woman she pulled a knife on me.

'I've explained this to DI Reavley,' I said. I had to take a sip of water because my mouth was like a desert. 'Where is he?'

'DI Reavley is helping to co-ordinate the search of your house and the cottage in Lancashire. We know of the explanation you gave him. How about this one?'

She pointed out another message. We went through a series of texts sent by Tom over the last six months, three of which were to me and showed clear signs of a marriage in trouble. But the remaining three were the most worrying. One to his business partner at the estate agency:

I will work for you tomorrow i need to get away from this lunatic hold the sunshine road house i might be the new tenant soon ha.

One to a friend:

Im not bringing Lucy she is having one of her turns.

And one to Mary:

Arguing again if i dont call tomorrow come dig me up from the backyard.

I was shocked. All I could say was that our marriage, like many, was a little unstable but no shambles, and that although I could get upset, I certainly wasn't the volatile weirdo Tom seemed to have made out.

The detective didn't reply to that, other than to make another sheet appear. Emails this time. Now I had to explain why I'd cancelled a holiday to Paris we had planned for October and had accepted a lost deposit.

'Tom said he had work to do on that date. He wanted me to cancel it and said we'd book another shortly. But it's Paris, the City of Love. Couples with bad marriages don't go there, do they?'

No answer to that. Next: why had I emailed the local leisure centre to cancel Tom's swimming direct debit? Both of which had been done on the Saturday before he disappeared.

'Tom asked me to do that as well. He said he was bored of swimming.'

Why had I sought a valuation on Tom's car and enquired about advertising it for sale on the Auto Trader website, even though the valuation query had been on one day, the advertisement query two days later – and on the day in between Tom had renewed his car tax for a whole year?

'But Tom asked me to do that, too. I was puzzled that he wanted to sell the car. I didn't know he'd re-taxed it.'

Why had I emailed Tom's pension company to try to cash out early? I explained that Tom had wanted me to end the pension scheme early because he believed he'd be a property development millionaire by the time he was fifty and wouldn't need that money. Continuing to pay into one was akin to admitting he wouldn't realise his dream.

I hadn't agreed, but Tom had put his foot down. Despite giving me power of attorney over his finances, he still made some rules. Ultimately, though, the pension provider had stuck by a clause that forbade Tom from taking his funds until he was fifty-five.

'So these things, the cancelled holiday, the attempt to cash out his pension, and trying to sell the car, they weren't because money is short?' the detective said. 'We spoke to one Peter Smith, co-owner at Packham/Smith Estate Agency. The agency is doing well, but a few years ago Tom got his partner to sign an agreement dictating that neither man can dispose of his equity unless both do so through a third party. According to Mr Smith, Tom set this up to prevent you getting hold of that money.'

'What? That's not true. Why would I want him to sell his business?'

'For Shangri-La. Does that name ring a bell? Mr Smith said you wanted Tom to build you a large office at the bottom of the garden. You were quite insistent.'

'Well, that's true. But I didn't ask him to sell his business. Certainly not enough times to make him set up some kind of silly agreement with his business partner. You're wrong. Peter's wrong.'

More sheets of paper materialised. She showed me a copy of Tom's life insurance policy. After that came a letter I'd written on the computer seeking to increase the policy, plus the return letter confirming the change from the insurers and an email copy of it.

She said, 'It was a level term policy at fifty-eight pounds a month for a five-hundred-thousand-pound payout. Increased by twenty-seven pounds a month for a whopping one-million-pound payout upon Tom's death. One million pounds. That's a lot of money. No contingent beneficiary, just one primary. You.'

Even I felt that my answers sounded suspicious, but what else could I say bar the truth? 'I have attorney control of all our finances, so, yes, I made the arrangements. But Tom wanted the increase. He asked me to do it.'

'There seems to be a lot of things Tom asked you to do in a short time before he disappeared.' There was that horrible word again: disappeared. 'Did he also ask you to delete that email? It was in your trash folder.'

'I don't recall that. If it was me, I must have hit delete by accident.'

'Tom has a will. We found a copy in his safe at work. Do you know who he's left his estate to?'

I didn't like the way she asked that question. It was leading. Not simple curiosity. I had a bad feeling I wasn't going to like what she said next. 'Yes, I'm on it. With Mary and Tom's parents. A three-way split.'

And another sheet of paper. Of course, it was Tom's will, which as far as I knew he'd last updated two years ago to remove his mother's name following her death. But it had been redrafted again since, I saw. The new version was just four weeks old and didn't include the names of his father or sister.

I was the sole heir.

I shook my head. 'I didn't know that. I didn't know he'd changed it. I...'

The detective was trying to make me wilt under her glare, and it worked. 'We have a statement from Peter Smith. He opened the safe for us. He told us that Tom had mentioned changing his will a month ago. According to Mr Smith, Tom told him you were unhappy with the will and told Tom to change it.'

'No, no way. I knew nothing about that.'

'You told Tom to remove his sister and his father from the

will, leaving just you as the sole beneficiary to his estate. And Tom swore Mr Smith to secrecy. He was to tell no one about the change ordered by you.'

I couldn't sink any lower. My mind was fried. Was she right but I had no recall? Had I given Tom those instructions? I rubbed my face with my hands.

'I see your wedding ring still hasn't returned. We didn't find it at the cottage. Why did you take it off in the first place?'

'To clean. The blood that was in the sink and on the floor. I didn't want to stain the silver.'

'You didn't wear cleaning gloves?'

'I didn't think. I just went to do it. I put the ring on the windowsill. I thought I did, anyway.'

She showed me a printout, which I barely looked at. 'Well, it wasn't there. Let's get back to the text messages. Mainly the one Tom sent. It says here he sent that message at one fifty-seven this morning.'

'No, I'm not listening to this,' I said, sternly. 'It's starting to make sense what you people think. You think I killed my husband and I did it for money.'

'We're open-minded, but why don't you tell us why you think we think that?'

The old answer-a-question-with-a-question tactic. I didn't have the will to argue individual points any longer. I wanted this interview to end and the quickest way to achieve that was to let them do most of the talking. I said nothing.

The older detective put a large plastic evidence bag on the table. In it were the four pay-as-you-go phones I bought in order to try to contact Tom. Purchased last night, they had been left in my car when I was arrested. The female asked why I needed untraceable phones. It was a sly question.

'I didn't buy them because they're untraceable. Tom knows my number and I didn't think he'd answer my calls. I thought if I called from an unknown number, he might answer. The extra phones were in case he blocked me and... I could try again with another number he wouldn't know.'

'But why did you go all the way to Bradford to buy them?'

I knew my answer would invite scorn, but it was the truth and I wouldn't refuse to state it. 'I needed a drive. I needed to unwind. I only had the idea to buy the phones while I was out.' Then something hit me. 'How did you know I was in Bradford?'

She had a receipt. 'Because we had a surveillance team on you. You were followed. You were watched going into the twenty-four-hour store where you bought these four phones, for cash. Well, I say four...'

She showed me the receipt, which had COPY printed across it – they must have gotten it from the store. She showed me where it said I had bought five mobile phones.

'I used one to try to call Tom. Like I said, I wanted to use new phones so he wouldn't know it was me. I tried to call him after he texted me last night.'

'So where is untraceable phone five?'

That word again. 'I'd used it. Tom would know the number. So I had to throw it away.'

'You threw it away? But what if Tom tries to call it?'

'But I texted him, too. He knows to reply to my main number.'

Now, with a clear, predatory glint in her eyes, she laid the call/text log printout and the receipt on the table, side by side. 'Look where the message from Tom's new phone, sent at one-fifty-eight this morning, was traced to.'

It was Bradford.

She then pointed at the transaction time on the receipt. 'You bought those phones at one forty-nine in the morning.'

'Yes. I couldn't sleep.'

'You need to explain this, Lucy. You went to Bradford and

bought new untraceable phones, and by shock coincidence Tom sent you a text message from Bradford just eight minutes later. That's twice we've had a bizarre coincidence.'

It took me a moment to fathom what she meant. The first text Tom had sent had been traced to the vicinity of my house; now this second one had been pinpointed as coming from another area where I just happened to be. That couldn't be coincidence. My heart thumped. 'My God. He's... he's watching me. Tom is watching me. Is that it?'

The detective shook her head. 'No, we have a different idea. We think that after we pointed out the first supposed text from Tom was sent from close to your home, you learned your lesson. So you decided that the next text from Tom would come from somewhere far away. You chose Bradford. You didn't know you had a surveillance team though. Where is untraceable phone five?'

I hung my head. 'That's preposterous. You think Tom didn't send me any texts? Preposterous.' It was all I could think of to say.

'We have a few unwritten rules here. One of them is that when someone insists on using the toilet as soon as they come into the station, we think it might help to check that toilet. In case we find something hidden.'

The male detective didn't have much to do, but his latest action was performed like the main event. He laid another plastic bag on the table. Another mobile phone.

The female lifted it and waved it in front of me. 'Found in the cistern in the toilets. Untraceable phone five. Brand new, bought from Bradford last night. All this phone has ever done is send one text. To your main device.'

She let the accusation sit between us, awaiting my response. Unable to bear the silence, and the stares, I gave in.

'Yes, I did send those texts to myself. Because everyone

thinks I killed Tom. It was silly, I know. I wanted to stop people accusing me. I know Tom is alive. He left me. He's out there with his new woman, and he's laughing at me. You'll find him soon, and then you'll know I was telling the truth all along. I did not kill my husband. I don't want to answer any more questions.'

'How about one more?'

Now they brought a tape recorder into the show. I was told I was to be played a recording found on my seized computer. I had no idea where they were heading with this and when I heard my own voice say, 'Halloa! Unten dort!' it didn't make anything clearer. I immediately recognised it as the recording I'd made a few days ago. Instead of reciting the German translation of Charles Dickens' ghost tale *The Signal-Man*, I'd instead begged for Tom to come home: *Bitte nach Hause kommen, Tom.* I remembered it well.

Or so I thought.

'Zur Hölle mit dir, Tom, du bastard...'

I stared at the tape recorder in shock as more words I didn't recall uttering spilled from it. It was my voice, but I had no recall of them.

The female detective had done her research well because she translated from memory: 'To hell with you, Tom, you bastard. You deserved everything you got. Rot down there in hell. Rot in eternity for what you did to me.'

I had to put both hands on the table for balance. The room seemed to wobble.

'Mrs Packham, people who've run off to start a new life don't rot in hell. Only the dead do. I think you know it's time for the lies to stop. Tell me the truth. All of it. I want your version of what happened. Everything you did. Everything you thought. Everything.'

The room stopped wobbling. My head cleared. I had no path

before me except the one I had been loath to travel since this nightmare began. 'Where do I begin?'

'Where does anything begin, Mrs Packham? The beginning.'

'The beginning,' I said, tasting the word.

I cast my mind back, seeking the point where I had first felt my entire life might be about to unravel. *Your version*, the detective had said. A certain somebody was going to cast major doubt on my tale.

'You'll get two versions of this story. But Mary is a liar. Don't believe her. Not one word. What I'm about to tell you is the truth. And it all started with a terrible accusation...'

MARY

Finally, the cops are getting off their arses, doing what they should have done on day one, and it's a beautiful sight. Crime-scene investigators booted me out of the cottage and they're inside right now, forensically examining the whole place. Detectives are going door to door, hunting witnesses and CCTV. The woods and miles of streams and brooks and rivers are going to be searched.

The media has heard about the police circus here in Nowhereville and invaded with their cameras and pretty reporters and vans with satellite dishes. The population of Cullerton has just about doubled today as the search for Tom's body and proof of his murder blows up. It touches my heart. I hear there's even a plan to use drones with thermal cameras, and apparently those bad boys cost £50,000 each. Tom's getting the care he deserves.

A bit earlier, the owner of the Serengeti pub, a pal of Tom's, rustled up a search team of locals. Fifteen or so bumpkins arrived at the Kwaint car park to offer their help, although the cops said hell no. So they planned to circle around the area and enter the woods from the far side.

I was in the cark park when they arrived, overheard their plan, and asked to join their group. Here I am. One lady's brought a dog to do some sniffing, but she can't seem to get it to give a toss. A man has his own drone, but it won't fly straight and he's trying to sort the calibration. Others seem to be here just for the gossip, or to get out of the house for an hour. It's all a bit amateur as a search party goes, but it's fifteen extra pairs of eyes looking for my brother.

Three cars carrying five each park in the Fox and Hound car park and our group heads into the woods. I can't hear any people traipsing up ahead, so the official search team hasn't travelled far. The plan is to meet them somewhere in the middle, whether they like it or not. I was in a car with a wiry old man in battered jeans and a thick shirt. He kept looking at me throughout the journey and now, as the mob breaks apart inside the woods, he's still at it. In case he wants to chat me up, I stay by a lady's side so he can't.

But after a few minutes his stare gets really annoying and uncomfortable and I break away from the lady to give him the chance to approach. It's not like he's here alone with me, and even if that was the case, I doubt the old fart is going to try to grab a tit.

Seeing his chance, he slinks my way. No direct approach, but a sly one, as if we'll bump into each other, oh, by accident. I find that even more uncomfortable, so I just stop and stare at him. When he realises I'm ready to chat, he dumps the farce and comes straight over. But he stops a few feet away.

'John Regan. I do the gardening.'

I realise I know a bit about this guy. Tom's mentioned him. The village folk rallied round his wife when she was dying, way back in the eighties, and since then he's repaid that debt by doing odd jobs and gardening for free. In secret: people have woken to find their weeds pulled or shed roofs re-felted during the night. At first, there was a funny supernatural buzz about these dodgy goings-on, until Regan was caught red-handed. He's kind of known as the village odd bird, but he's not sacrificing chickens or anything, and he's very sweet and well-liked, so they let him get on with it.

'You've been staring. What do you want with me?' I ask.

'I saw the news. Your brother. Your brother's wife. I need to tell you. I saw the police here, but I keep to my own business. I had no idea until I saw the news.'

Like most. But something about the nervous twitch in his feet, the way he keeps looking to make sure no one is noseying, makes me realise he's got something secret to tell me. About Tom. I lunge at him and grab his arm. 'What is it? Do you know something about Lucifer?'

'Who? No, I...'

'Lucy, my brother's bitch wife. Do you know something?'

'Mrs Packham... your brother's... yes... his car... I don't want to get in trouble, I had no idea. The car. She paid me...'

Here he pauses, looking worried, as if not sure he wants to say more. But he's just mentioned Tom's missing car, so he's going to continue. I literally shake him – what, what?

'She paid me to...'

I listen in absolute horror as he spills his tale. When it's done, he starts to apologise, but I push him away and pull out my phone. I'm so nervous and angry I can hardly dial. He's watching me, but from a safe distance. I'd wring his neck if he was in range.

Reavley answers with, 'Mary, are you still–'

'The gardener just told me he dumped my brother's car. She said they were going away, but there were vandals... going on holiday, but the vandals, so he drove... he...'

'What? Slow down.'

He's right. I'm so worked up I can barely breath, never mind get my story straight. 'Lucy told the gardener they were going on holiday and didn't want to leave the car outside their house, or at the cottage. Tom didn't take his car when he vanished. The gardener did. Lucy paid him to hide it and tell no one.'

23

LUCY

Without a thumbs up from an officer authorised to extend my detention, I could only be held for twenty-four hours before I had to be charged or released. That custody clock started at around two thirty this morning, so I had only eight hours left when I was told I was going to be released on police bail.

After telling my story, I had requested the duty solicitor and one had called me an hour ago. He'd informed me that new laws tried to force the police to conduct investigations within twenty-eight days, after which I couldn't be kept on bail. He expected the police to sidestep this by releasing me 'under investigation', which meant no time limit.

The good news was that this set no specific date to return to the police station; the bad was that it would be like living in limbo. With the former, I would have been charged or released on that set date or even before, but the latter meant I had no clue when or if the police would want me back. A knock at the door or summons to the station could happen weeks or even months from now, and in the interim I'd worry just how far the investigation had progressed.

There was something terrifying about going about your daily business while knowing a gang worked behind the scenes to take you down. Plus, the standard bail-imposed restrictions, including who I couldn't have contact with (Mary was one, which was a silver lining in this dark cloud) had no end in sight.

But the bail was a good sign. After my arrest the police had searched my house and come daybreak another team had been down at the cottage in Cullerton, yet they must have unearthed no incriminating evidence because I hadn't been charged. My main mobile phone and laptop, both seized and scrutinised, had also divulged nothing.

In the end, I didn't care about anything other than getting out of the station. When I was escorted to the desk to be processed for release, I walked with a spring in my step. I soon lost it.

The custody sergeant got a phone call, right there in front of me. After it, I was told there was a delay and promptly escorted back to my cell. My feet dragged. The door had been shut behind me only a couple of minutes when a face I'd been asking for all day appeared.

'I'm not sure I want to see you after all,' I told DI Reavley.

'I didn't come because you asked,' he replied from the doorway. His stance and tone told me he wasn't here to explain, or apologise. I knew he was about to make my day worse. 'I decided to inform you of this myself. We found Tom's BMW.'

I turned away to face the blank wall, fully aware that he'd paused because he wanted to see my reaction. I wouldn't play his game.

'It was half a mile away, under a tarpaulin in a corner of the car park of the Naga Indian restaurant in Abbey Village. A couple of remote back roads will get you from Cullerton to that spot, so that's why ANPR didn't flag it. Guess how we found it.'

There was no need to guess. I was done with lying. 'John Regan, the local handyman.'

'And do you know what we found inside?'

Of course. I turned to face him. 'Tom's suitcase full of his clothing in the boot. My jeans with his blood on them.'

'Lucy Packham, I am further arresting you...'

Car theft. Not sexy and not a touch on murder, but detention for a new offence would restart my custody clock. I didn't care. Game over. I broke down into tears, but I wasn't upset that I'd been caught. The weight of guilt, of deceiving the world and dishonouring Tom's name by lying about him, had become too much. I cried because I was relieved it was all over.

'I killed him,' I said when Reavley had finished cautioning me. 'I killed my Tom.'

PART II

24

MARY

'She admitted it. She admitted killing Tom.'

I nearly drop the mobile. Dad's looking at me, so I rush into the kitchen to speak to DI Reavley.

'Really? She said she killed Tom?'

'Told us the whole story just a few minutes ago,' Reavley replies.

I sit down, right there on the floor, and it's hard not to cry down the phone. A great weight has been lifted. The last I knew, sod all incriminating was found at the cottage or in Lucy's house, and I'd started to fret that there wouldn't be enough evidence to doom her. I'd started to imagine what life would be like with my brother's murderer living free just minutes away, laughing at all those she'd run rings around.

Well, it's something I never again have to worry about. The bitch has confessed, which means she'll plead guilty. No trial, so a quicker route to a jail cell. Perfect.

'Are you okay?' Reavley asks.

'So I was right to always use the past tense.' It's a strange thing to say, but my mind's out of whack.

'Yes. I'm sorry it's that way.'

I tell him I'll call him back shortly and hang up. I go upstairs and sit on the toilet with the door shut, and here I blubber like a little girl. Lucy's confession might guarantee she'll get what's coming, but it's also the final nail in the coffin. Tom's coffin. Even though I'd never doubted it, there had always been that slight chance I was wrong, that Tom was alive somehow, somewhere. Not now. I wish I'd been wrong.

I take a few minutes to try to let this sink in, or at least penetrate the surface, and when I'm ready I call Reavley back. 'I'm okay, so don't ask, please. Thank you for this. Without you...'

'No, without *you* we wouldn't have gotten this far. You had it all worked out before anyone else. If you hadn't been onto Lucy from the start, who knows how long it would have been before, well, before Tom was even reported missing.'

I don't know if it's the right question or not. Maybe it's wrong to ask, and maybe it's the first thing grieving relatives want to know. But I have to say it: 'How did she do it?'

'She said she hit him on the head with a rock and he fell into the brook. She thinks he drowned.'

How the bitch slaughtered my little bro is something I've tried, and failed, not to dwell on. I had to tolerate all manner of scenes behind my eyes because there was zero as to what happened that day. Her slamming a rock into Tom's head is a horrible image and I'll never wipe it out, but the thought of him drowning is much worse. I want to pound that monster into dust, and I want to scream, but I settle for, 'Dad will be very upset. Everyone will. Why did she hit him?'

'She told the whole story, including how she planned to fool everyone into thinking Tom was still alive. There were some accusations against you of harassment, but she's not planning to make anything official.'

'Did she plan the killing?'

'No. Spur of the moment. An accident. He provoked her, she said. She admitted there was no affair.'

I don't like this. Spur of the moment? Accident? 'Provoked how? That's a lie. She's trying to get a lighter sentence by saying she killed him by accident. If that was true, she would have said it from the start, not try to pretend he was still alive. It's bullshit. You don't believe that, do you?'

'Mary, I should tell you that her confession has prompted the Crown Prosecution Service to agree to an involuntary manslaughter charge. She got a solicitor before she made her full confession and wouldn't give it unless that charge was accepted. They'd like to know your thoughts on that. A guilty plea, no trial, straight to sentencing and prison. I'm required to inform you of this. How does a manslaughter charge make you feel?'

Perhaps if I kick and yell enough, I can get a manslaughter changed to murder, but I doubt it or Reavley would have mentioned that option. Murder was exactly what Lucy did, but I don't care what her file says, I just want her locked up. If manslaughter can do it, so be it.

'I don't care, as long as... Wait. Her confession. You never said how Tom provoked her. I asked, and you avoided it. Aaron, what did she say he did? I need to know.'

'I know you do, Mary. That's why I came ready. I shouldn't really do this, but... I've got a copy of her recorded confession. Perhaps it's better to hear it from her mouth. I can bring—'

'No, don't bring it. Play it. Play it for me right now, down the phone.'

He doesn't object. He doesn't try to change my mind. He knows it's a fight he can't win. So he plays the recording. I grip the phone tightly as I hear Lucy's voice as she prepares to tell me how she killed my brother.

LUCY

'...This, babe, is where things transmogrify.'

With those words from Tom, he took a puff on his electronic cigarette and bent down before me. On all fours, fingers gripping the sides of the metal walkway bridging Low Man Brook, I looked up at him – and he blew a cloud of smoke into my eyes. Suddenly blind, my grip tightened on the handrail for fear of tumbling off. But despite being locked in place, my hands were suddenly wrenched free and I felt myself tumble backwards.

With a gong-like clang, I landed on my back hard enough to vibrate the walkway. I realised that Tom had pushed me while I couldn't see. I felt a throbbing on my shoulder and knew he'd used a foot.

He bent over me, and grabbed at my jeans.

'Let's do it here.'

'No.'

But he wouldn't take no. I fought his hands, but they were faster and stronger, attached to those big shoulders of his that I had no hope of outgunning. I had loved those shoulders for eight years, but not right then.

He undid the buttons on my jeans and tried to pull them down, but they wouldn't go far because he'd moved my legs apart to kneel between them. He lunged forward, slamming one hand between my legs and clamping the other around my throat. He spat in my face and licked it away. I said nothing. I couldn't move.

In the next moment, he grabbed my jacket and twisted me. I

felt my shoulders and head scrape over the perforations in the metal and the next moment, nothing – my upper body had sailed out over the edge. I had to stab my left arm backward into the water as a prop, where I found purchase on a rock. The fast water splashed over my shoulder, coating my face and hair and going into my mouth.

In that moment, believing he planned to drown me, I had no choice but to snap my legs around his waist and grab the walkway with my free hand, forcing my fingers painfully into the perforations. I was locked tight, but utterly defenceless.

And he knew this. Sitting back on his knees, he ran his finger through his hair and said, 'Let's see if we can get those jeans off now.'

The stinging cold pain in my submerged hand turned my focus to it, and I realised I had one option only. With my legs around him and left hand welded to the walkway, I dragged my right arm fast out of the water, arcing it towards Tom's face. By this point his eyes and hands were on my jeans again as he tried to rip them down the open join: he didn't even see it coming.

The rock in my hand slammed into his left temple, knocking him backwards with a high-pitched yelp. My legs were still clamped hard around his waist, but his toppling weight easily tore him free. I saw him overbalance and plummet out of sight over the waterfall.

Without his body to anchor me or my right arm as a prop, I fell backwards into the water, catching my shoulder hard on a rock. The powerful flow threatened to suck me under the walkway and also over the waterfall, but I was still attached to the walkway by my left hand. I got my feet down and hauled my upper body onto the walkway.

'Tom!' I screamed. My eyes searched the river and I momentarily glimpsed his backpack and the back of his head through the frothing water as he was carried away from me, fast.

He was face down. Seconds later, he'd passed beyond where the trees either side crowded the edge and was lost from sight.

I lay there, calling for him, for I don't know how long. A long time, until my voice was hoarse. But eventually I willed up the strength to get moving. My fingers had swelled where the walkway perforations dug in and it took a long time to free my hand. By the time I had crawled off the walkway, slid down the hill and staggered to the cottage, my jeans were virtually dry.

I sat on the doorstep, and that was when I realised I still clutched the tennis-ball-sized rock in my right hand. With no strength to throw it, I placed it into a plant pot by the step.

Inside the house, I stripped off my torn jeans and noticed blood on one inner thigh, which must have come from Tom when I struck him. I got fresh trousers. My blouse was quite dry under my jacket and I didn't change it; nor did I notice blood on the sleeve. My mind was consumed with guilt, but not so much what I'd done to Tom as the story I would tell the police.

The truth was the only correct option, but that would only hurt both of us. Tom was already dead, nothing would change that, and I saw no point in adding to that suffering. Blunt and callous as it sounds, my thinking was: a funeral was guaranteed, so why add a trial into the mix? I did not believe I deserved prison for reacting as I had to attempted rape. Tom had pushed me. I had responded without thinking. But he was dead, and by my hand, and I knew I would go to prison. My life would be over.

I would not throw my life away because of one stupid error, a one-second mistake.

So, when the police found Tom's body in the river, I would lie. I would say Tom and I had gone for a walk and we'd argued, and he'd abandoned me in the woods. It would be assumed that, walking alone, he'd fallen in the brook, hit his head on a rock, and drowned.

The blood on my jeans would look bad, so I put them in a bag to dispose of. That, I knew, was the point of no return.

Hours later, still no knock had come at the door. I checked local news on the internet, including social media, but there was no word. I knew Tom's body hadn't been found. I knew there was a chance it could be held under the surface by a current or had washed up somewhere remote. He might not be found for days.

Or ever.

Late in the afternoon, I sat by the firepit out back and assessed everything. Tom had been due to head out to watch his monster truck perform at an event that night and there would be concern if he didn't show. He was back at work tomorrow, Monday, and another absence would raise an alarm. I was also worried that his body would wash up on a bank and be discovered, probably this evening. I needed a story and after half an hour by the firepit, I had it.

If Tom's body wasn't found today, then tomorrow morning I would leave a fake note for him saying I'd gone home. When his friends called because he'd missed the truck show, and his business partner because of absence from work – or anyone else, including his sister – I would tell them that Tom and I had argued and he'd chosen to stay at the cottage for a while.

We'd brought separate cars, so my story of travelling home alone would be accepted. Eventually, people would try to visit him up there, but find him gone. Seeing his clothing and car still at the cottage, they would search and eventually find his body. A terrible accident. I would have to act shocked and despairing. Such emotions hadn't hit me for real yet, only a blinding numbness.

It was this numbness that became my downfall.

Mary turned up that night because Tom hadn't answered his phone. From the very outset, she was suspicious of my story that

Tom had gone out, in part because of my mistake of leaving Tom's blood in the bathroom. Her threat to involve the police caused me to contradict my story in places, like when I said he'd texted me even though he'd left his phone behind. I wasn't thinking straight. And things got worse after she'd left. Instead of sticking to my plan, I created a stupid new one.

So, that evening I packed Tom's things into his suitcase. I sought his insulin, but it wasn't in the medicine cabinet so I figured he'd had it in his backpack, even though he'd had a dose before we set out. My brain seemed to be half a minute behind my actions, as if I were an onlooker, watching someone else perform.

I also knew I had to get rid of his phone. I had to pretend he'd taken it, but nobody could be allowed to call it because he'd never answer. I microwaved it, which killed it within a second. Tom had actually shown me that trick some months back, when he'd cooked my phone because I told him off for a mess in the living room. Just to be certain, I then put the SIM card in a frying pan and broke the phone into pieces. The battery, SIM and pieces sank to the bottom of the brook.

I burned my bloody blouse in the firepit.

I knew the local gardener was due round to do some work early in the morning. I would pay him to take the car and hide it. My story was that Tom and I were using my vehicle to drive abroad, and we wanted his car to be kept somewhere safe. I warned him not to look in the boot because we had a camera and would know. He was to keep hold of the key until I needed it.

It was done. Now, when friends came to the cottage for Tom, they'd find him and all his belongings gone. My stupid new plan? To pretend Tom was having an affair and had run off.

That night, I sat on the doorstep and cried, probably for the majority of the dark hours. At that point, I prayed my husband was still alive. Every noise out in the woods made me stand up, praying it was Tom stumbling through the undergrowth in his desperation to return to me.

My hope and panic got so great that I didn't take my eyes off the brook, just in case Tom tried to clamber out and come home. I convinced myself that he might have survived. I didn't care if he ran to the police and I got locked up for attempted murder. Even if I couldn't have him back and I got locked away, I just wanted him to be alive.

But the hours passed. Tom didn't stumble out of the woods, bloody-headed and confused. He didn't drag himself out of the river. Reality finally slipped by my denial: Tom was gone forever.

It was such a bad plan, and I knew that come the morning. The shock of Tom's death and the accusations by his sister had thrown me out of whack. I knew if his car and clothing were gone, yet he was found dead near the cottage, I would look very guilty. Better to go with the original idea of pretending Tom had stayed at the cottage.

Even now, I don't know why I didn't. But I didn't. I put Tom's suitcase and my bloody jeans in the boot of his car, paid the gardener to take the vehicle away, and then drove home.

Mary's outright suspicion, so without real basis, made me react without thinking when she again turned up on my doorstep, this time back home. For some reason, when she demanded to see Tom, I told her he was ill in bed. I should have stuck with the story of Tom remaining at the cottage. But I knew she would believe nothing I said, and it forced me into behaviour I have regretted ever since.

I pretended Tom was still alive, but I knew I needed proof. I no longer had his original phone, so my idea was to have everyone think he'd bought a new device. Which he texted me from. After the error of sending the first message to myself from inside my own house, I travelled to Bradford in order to perform Tom's second contact.

These actions might seem like those of someone who planned Tom's death, but I promise that is not the case. I have admitted causing Tom's death and trying to cover it up, but I am standing by my claim that all of the evidence that suggests premeditation is coincidental. Any time that I said Tom asked me to do something, like value his car, or cancel his pension, or any of the others, that is exactly what happened. It includes the increase to the life insurance on Tom. I absolutely did not kill him for money.

I wish he was still alive.

25

MARY

It's raining on Friday morning when I go to Sheffield Magistrates Court to hear Lucy plead guilty. In order to avoid the paper-shifting, seat-taking build-up in the courtroom, I decide to land there fifteen minutes after the start time of 9am. What DI Reavley told me last night hadn't sunk in properly and I was about to find that out in a bad way.

I park in a nearby Premier Inn car park and head over to Castle Street at a slow stroll. Close to the ramp to the court entrance is a large brick mural on the end of a building. It's made up of 30,000 bricks of different colours to create a picture of a man wearing a muffler and a hard hat. A few weeks back someone graffitied it with a curse about miners and the newspapers scalded the vandal, partly because he had no clue the man in the mural was actually a steelworker.

I think about Lucy and the judgement she's got coming. I hope no one gets it wrong.

When the cops carted her away, I figured she'd seen the last of freedom. Murder is a mandatory life sentence, but that's not on the cards. The Crown Prosecution Service agreed to a charge other than murder because the evidence against Lucy is feeble.

There's no body, so no jackpot evidence from a post-mortem. If she'd not confessed, or she'd denied hitting Tom, the CPS would've had the devil of a time proving she killed him. Even if they found Tom's body and he had a head wound, it was caused by a rock from the brook, and her slimeball defence team could say Tom got the injury when he *accidentally* fell into the water. Too much of a headache, so: involuntary manslaughter.

Basically, they took the killer at her word that what happened that day happened. Unless Tom's body turns up full of stab wounds, history isn't going to remember Lucy as a murderer. This thought gives me wobbly legs as I approach the ramp.

But, oh, the hits don't stop there. Manslaughter sentences are varied, and it's up to the judge what she serves, and it'll be based on all the 'key elements' of the case. And a lot of those elements favour that slimy bitch. Even though she tried to cover up the crime, she's admitted it and shown remorse. Her nasty bullshit that Tom tried to rape her adds provocation and self-defence into the mix. Then there's the fact that Lucy's cracking him with a rock didn't actually cause his death, because he drowned.

We've only got her word for that. But they took her word, didn't they?

And, finally, from Reavley I learned about 'victim impact statements'. He tried to lift my spirits when he told me this means I can stand in court and try to influence the judge's opinion. So, if I can turn on the waterworks as I stammer through the emotional and psychological nightmare Lucy's evil put Tom's family and pals through, the judge might give that bitch a little extra?

I seriously doubt it. Lucy's good at raining tears when she needs sympathy. She'll thrive in front of a jury, and use all her emotional manipulation tools like a wizard. They'll eat out of her hand after she sets that quivering lip going. She'll cover herself by painting Tom as the bad guy, and I wouldn't be surprised if they carried her out of there on a damn sedan chair while the court prepared a rape charge against a dead man. I won't risk writing a statement that'll be pathetically overshadowed.

That's just me being sour, of course, but can I be blamed for it? The starting point for a manslaughter charge, unbelievably, is two years, and Reavley doubts Lucy will get slapped with much more than that. He even warned me that there's a snippet of a chance she could land no prison time, given all the factors in her favour. A suspended sentence or community service? For killing my brother? Is that justice? *I* will kill *her* if that happens.

No matter the final result, at least the bitch will be facing a jail cell today. Reavley told me that all cases start in the magistrates' courts, but magistrates can't try murderers and have to boot these cases upwards, to the Crown Court, even if they know a defendant plans to plead guilty. At what's called a Plea and Trial Preparation Hearing, Crown Court judges will either sentence her or remand her to await sentencing – or send her for trial if she suddenly decides to fight the charges. Today is about little more than acknowledging the case needs to go to a higher court because magistrates can't bail killers, either. So even if Lucy is destined to waltz free, it's not happening until her case is heard by the Crown big dogs, and that could be weeks, even months. She'll wait out that time on remand, in a cell, and I'll take that because it's better than nothing.

And when all's said and done, Lucy will suffer whether she escapes prison or not. Once a guilty plea is entered, that's an immediate conviction for manslaughter. Lucy Packham will officially be a killer and that tag will follow her everywhere like a rabid pet dog. Ever and always. It's not much of a win, not even close to justice, but it'll have to do.

When I step back from the mural, something whacks into me, sending me staggering.

'Christ,' a woman yells.

I turn to see a tall, black lady in a skirt suit, but on her stockinged knees, surrounded by papers from a briefcase. She's probably usually very elegant, but right now she's panting, scrabbling to collect her papers. Even though I was minding my business and she barrelled into me, I feel sorry for her.

'Let me help,' I say, and that makes two women on their knees, collecting her work. She spits apologies in a constant stream, until she sees it's quite annoying me. I pass papers and she stuffs them into the briefcase. When the ground is clear, I have to help her to her feet because her skirt's so tight she can't open her legs without lifting the skirt. One of her shoes is gone. I see it by the mural. I pick it up, but can't see the missing heel anywhere.

'Oh, sweetie, don't bother looking, I lost that heel earlier. I'm on the clock. I'm so sorry for barging into you.'

I hand the shoe over, tell her, again, it's no problem, and ask if she's a solicitor.

'Sweetie, wish I could chat, but I can't help you right now, but call me, yes?'

'No, I just wondered, because the court is–'

I don't get to finish. The lady thrusts a business card into my hand and limps away on that broken heel, fast.

I'm about to fold and forget her card, but something makes me look long and hard at it. Louisa Beckham, a barrister. I don't have the foggiest about the difference between a barrister and a solicitor, but they all know the law, and that means she can help me.

It's just occurred to me: I've got no one to advise me or fight my corner in a court. And I might damn well need someone in the future if that bitch Lucifer appeals her conviction, or demands her own autopsy on my brother's body, if it's ever found. She's got someone to work courtroom magic, and I want the same. I jab the barrister's card into my purse as I head towards the court.

I stop halfway across the ramp. I can see Reavley waiting for me near the doors, but it's hard to rouse the urge to press on. Against the bland court building are a contrast of characters. For every suit that's probably a solicitor or judge, there's a drab tracksuit. Yobbos out front are smoking and being noisy as they wait for their cases to be heard. Those people, added to the grey sky and colourless rain, suck away even more of my resolve. I stop walking. Suddenly, I don't want to be here. There seems no point.

And then I see her.

Lucy pushes through the double doors ahead, with a man in a suit by her side and three casually dressed chaps behind. The man beside her is clearly her solicitor because he's trying to protect her from the others. They're reporters who must have been in court. I don't see cameras, but the three men are shoving their phones next to her face for a soundbite. Lucy and her slimeball defender walk fast to escape them.

I don't get it. It's only twenty past nine – surely the hearing can't be over already? Surely a convicted killer hasn't just been told to be on her way? In a grey skirt suit, she looks smart and ready to give a bullshit impression to the court, but she also seems unhappy, so whatever's just happened, it wasn't to her liking. I see her wiping her eye as they both scuttle towards me, ignoring questions from the reporters. I back up against the side railing, shocked. What's going on?

She's watching the ground, listening to the slimeball, and doesn't notice me. Not until I give her both barrels.

'Where are you going? Tell me they didn't let you walk out?'

Even then, it's only a quick, disappointed glance I get. Her solicitor moves on to her other side, between us. 'Mary Packham? You can't talk to my client.'

They're past me a moment later. I don't follow, but I'm not done yet. 'You can't just go home. You've got no friends, you can't talk to your neighbours, even your stupid German language job involves sitting alone in a room making recordings. Where can you go? Who can you turn to? Nowhere, to no one.'

'You need to stay away from my client by court order. Do you understand? Stay away from her and her home.'

Court order? 'Even this idiot isn't on your side, he's just being paid.'

Giving me her back makes me angrier and I think about starting a fist fight. It would be stupid because she's bigger than me, and she's obviously got power to overcome a man like Tom, so I'd come off worse. But it would get her bail snatched away.

I just watch them leave.

'Mary.'

I drag my gaze away and back towards the court building. Reavley has just exited and is coming my way.

'How can it be over already?' I ask while he's still some way out. 'What's happened?'

He waits until he's by my side before answering. Apparently, the courts are sticklers for timetables and her visit today was over by 9.08. She'd been in court for eight minutes.

My head starts to pound. 'But why did she just walk out free as Larry? She should have been locked up until the case goes to Crown Court. You told me magistrates courts can't bail killers.'

He looks a little embarrassed. 'They can't. But they did ask her if she planned a guilty plea, and she said yes. At that point the court has to pass the case on as fast as possible. The barrister Lucy's solicitor appointed made a lot of smart friends over the years, and one of them is now a murder-ticketed circuit judge who's a fan of video chat software. He was sent the papers early this morning, so he was ready to go. I've seen this run-of-the-mill process a hundred times, and today it just got fast-tracked like I've never known. Right then and there in the court, the magistrates accepted the circuit judge's video call, and he granted bail. Bang, done. The barrister must have had a hot date waiting, because she got out of there so fast she broke a heel. I'm sorry.'

Wait, broken heel woman? That was the bitch who got Lucy released? I wish I'd stepped backwards from the mural with my elbow raised, so I crushed that damn woman's nose. I hope it's a truck she runs into next time. It burns my tongue that I apologised to her, not knowing what she'd just done to my world.

But she's only a tiny part of the machine that let my brother's killer go. 'But why did they let a killer just waltz out of there? Bailing killers is uncommon, that's what you said.'

'I told you this could happen, remember? They figured there was no risk to the case with her being free. She won't flee the country or threaten witnesses. And there's still that fragment of doubt that Tom is dead. Her barrister made a good argument.'

Unbelievable. 'She's been in a mental home, Aaron. I know that it's hard for evil murderers to get bail, so how did such a danger to society manage it?'

'The court doesn't have that information as far as I know. Accessing years-old foreign medical records is a long and tricky process, and there's no need. She's pleading guilty.'

He's not fooling me. 'This is political, isn't it? She cried rape, and the almighty powers can't jail a non-convicted raped woman who accidentally killed her attacker.'

He seems a little embarrassed, probably because he's a cog in the machine of the almighty powers. 'I don't know. But they bailed her. And there's a restriction on the media being able to name her or publish her face. She's also not allowed to talk to them, go into Cullerton or even back to her house until the police searches are over. And she has to stay away from you and Tom's family.'

That explains why her solicitor told me to not go near her. But it's hardly party-throwing news. I can't believe this. Today Lucy should have experienced her last slice of freedom, but instead she might have seen her last prison cell. And she won't be cut to ribbons in the papers, either. She can just go back to her cosy little home and sleep in an empty bed, like nothing's happened. I need to sit down.

But instead I perk up. I'm getting used to working out Reavley's face and know when he wants to say something important. Something I probably won't like. 'What is it? Tell me.'

He leans his elbows on the railing, so I copy him, and we stare out like a couple enjoying a beautiful view. 'A few puzzling things, that's all. Some of my team are having doubts. Still no body.'

Yesterday he'd told me that Low Man Brook 'isn't exactly the Suez Canal', and there were shallow places where anything bigger and weightier than a paper boat would get caught up on rocks, just like Tom's backpack had. But the search teams had so far followed the brook all the way to the other end of the ravine, where it entered the River Darwen, and found zip. There were still deeper sections yet to receive the divers, but nobody was brimming with confidence.

'But don't forget the water is mostly gone. It was deeper and faster when Tom vanished because of the rain.' It actually pains me to say this because it feels like siding with Lucy. I'm still not sure she didn't bury him out in the woods. That blood found in the bathroom at the cottage has me convinced Tom's death didn't happen the way she reckons. I think the truth would mess up her plans to get an involuntary manslaughter charge and a short prison sentence.

He pauses before saying, 'Possible. We'll search the Darwen itself afterwards, of course.'

He's still got that look. Not the river searches, then. Something else. I ask him to spit it out.

'On Tom's business computer from his estate agency office, on his work email address, we found a purchase confirmation email from an online company called Banas, based in India. For something called a Timesulin. It's a pen cap, costs about fifteen pounds. The package was delivered to the estate agent office two days before he went missing. We searched that office yesterday afternoon, while Lucy was being interviewed, and found no trace of that product.'

'I don't understand. Why is a pen lid important?'

'It's not just any old pen lid. The Timesulin fits onto an insulin pen to help you keep track of when your last injection was. I didn't realise Tom used injection pens.'

Now I get it. I wish I hadn't. 'Are you saying he had insulin pens so didn't need his bottle? That he dumped it himself in the bin back at the cottage? Why would he waste insulin? He wouldn't. Lucy dumped it. Please tell me you don't think she's innocent in some way? There's so much other evidence against her.'

'Just a puzzle, that's all.'

He's making my head spin and I can't hide my frustration. I step away a few feet. 'No, it's not a puzzle, detective. You can't find Tom's body and now you think he's got a secret stash of insulin. You think he might be alive, don't you?'

'No, I'm not saying that. There are just some unanswered questions.'

'You found no proof of life. No digital footprint, as you call it. And she admitted it.' I say this so loud, almost a shout, that it turns heads. Reavley looks worried about my volume, and takes my elbow, starts to lead me away along the ramp.

'My God. So where is he? Hiding? So you believe Lucy's bullshit that Tom is playing some practical joke on the world? Hiding out in a bush somewhere, suffering, just so he can have a giggle? Or with this phantom woman he's having an affair with?'

He doesn't answer until we've stepped off the ramp and onto a little patch of grass. 'I didn't say Tom was alive, Mary. If I thought that, we wouldn't have just whisked his wife into court. But I didn't expect this reaction from you to the possibility that Tom could be alive.'

'That's because I'm not bloody stupid, Aaron. If there was a chance Tom was alive, I'd jump all over it. How dare you say I don't care? I know Tom is dead and you bastards better not stop believing that.' I slap his hand off my elbow. 'I still don't believe a word that bitch wife of his says. There was no rape attempt and she didn't kill my brother by accident. You'll realise that when you find his body. So if it's not in the river, stop thinking about conspiracies and dig up the woods. See if she chopped him up and burned him in that firepit. But you better find him. Because I'm not having his funeral without a body.'

I'm shaking with rage. This is all beginning to reek of some freaky nightmare. I've had enough and I want sod all to do with any of this anymore. I take off right then and leave him standing, amid the raining confetti of that foul barrister's business card.

LUCY

I was secured a room at a hotel near Meadowhall shopping centre and sneaked in by a colleague of my solicitor, like someone under witness protection. I was free, and not under any kind of house arrest, but I still felt like a prisoner.

Despite a gag order by the court that prevented my name and picture being published by the media, previous interest in my case meant many knew who I was and what I'd done. And many weren't happy with me. I wasn't allowed home until the police released my house from their investigation, but I wouldn't have gone back anyway. I wasn't going to go anywhere, full stop.

My plan was to hide in this hotel room until my plea hearing in ten days' time. I wasn't thinking of any point past that because it was just too painful.

The TV couldn't hold my interest, nor a book, so I passed the time in one of the usual ways I cope when feeling down and dejected. I cleaned. The room was fairly spotless anyway, so I set about doing things no cleaner would have. I scraped limescale from the inside of the kettle. I stripped the bed just so I could redo it. I dusted high corners of the walls. I scraped dirt out from around the buttons on the TV remote.

I would do it all again later. I had ten days of life to waste, before the day when my life got wasted forever.

The only high point of it all was when I found a lucky charm under the bedside cabinet. It was a real acorn, baked and painted, on a little chain. I clutched it and wondered about whoever had lost it. But I needed luck, so I would not hand it in to reception.

All this cleaning wasn't just to burn time though: I was trying to avoid an awkward phone call. Eventually I realised I was making things worse by waiting, so I put my face to the window, stared out across the world that vilified me, and dialled a number from memory.

When my friend, Leona, answered, she sounded suspicious: 'Who's this?'

I realised that she wouldn't have this number. The police had seized my registered mobile and my solicitor had provided a cheap pay-as-you-go device so he could contact me. When

Leona heard my voice, she lost the suspicious tone and replaced it with one of urgency.

'Luce? Oh, sweetie, how are you? I tried calling your other mobile.'

'The police took it to analyse it for evidence. I'm sorry.'

'I know. They answered my call. Wouldn't say why they had the phone, wouldn't tell me where you were, but they did start trying to ask questions about you. I told them to piss off. You got arrested, didn't you?'

I broke down into tears. Leona said nothing while I composed myself, simply waited for me. I knew it was time to tell her the truth. Somehow, it was easier down the phone.

So I told her everything. Everything. Afterwards, I said I needed a moment and I hung up. I composed myself and called her back ten minutes later. During my confession, she hadn't said a single word and when the tale was told, I'd hung up before she could respond; now, while her phone rang, I prayed that, somehow, she had missed my tearful tale.

I would keep it secret if that was so. It was not fair to burden her with my problems so soon after we'd rekindled our relationship. And I didn't want her to hate me. She was my only friend in the whole world.

But she'd heard it all, and she didn't sit in judgement. Leona answered with, 'Do the police have this phone number you're on?'

'No, my solicitor hasn't given it out. They have to contact me through him.'

'Good. They might record your calls or something. Just in case – hey, bozos, leave my girl alone.'

I gave a laugh, but it was mostly forced.

'Keep calm and keep in contact with your solicitor,' Leona continued, 'Look, I don't mean to panic you, but I want to make sure you get no nasty surprises. If the police are still searching your house, they're not happy with involuntary manslaughter.'

'I don't understand. They accepted my story.'

'Because they've got nothing without it. But there's still time between now and your next court case.'

'Time for them to do what?'

'To find something. Some piece of evidence to give them a murder charge.'

I felt cold. Would they do that? Even after we'd made a deal, they would seek to stab me in the back? 'How do you know that?'

'You've got them over a barrel. They don't want to be over a barrel. And I bet, like any company, they want results, numbers. I've been reading up on your laws over there and looking at how some cases played out.'

I was a fool for not realising that, of course Leona would have kept up to date on my case. After learning that some suspected me of murdering my husband, how could she not follow developments? She would have already known of my arrest, perhaps even my court appearance, yet with all this evidence against me, she hadn't accepted any of it. She hadn't once doubted my version of events. Suddenly, I felt awful that I had been unfaithful to our loyalty.

'I'm so sorry I lied, Leona. I should have told you. Right from the start, I should have admitted the truth. But I didn't want you to hate me.'

'No, no, no,' she said. I can picture her clutching the phone with both hands, her face also wet from tears. 'Luce, you'd have to kill my spouse, not yours, for that to happen. I'm sorry that Tom is dead, and I feel for his family and all who knew him, but my priority is you. I'm always on your side. And I'm not upset that you didn't tell me. You had to do it in your own time. Look, let's not talk about that right now. You don't need the worry. I'm going to come and see you. Soon. I'm coming down there and we're going to lock ourselves away and have fun.'

'That would be nice.' I meant that, but doubted it would happen, at least the way she outlined it. More than likely, our first meeting in years would be in a prison, with glass between us and guards listening. But the fantasy was calming. 'We could just sit around here, in my hotel room, watch TV and chat about nothing.'

'Well, some of that chat will be about your court statement. You will have to give a statement in your defence, right?'

'I'm not sure. At the sentencing, my barrister will give what they call mitigating circumstances. I think it means she'll talk about me in a way to try to get sympathy, so I get a lesser sentence.'

'Perfect. You should read it out yourself. The judge will lap it up.'

I seriously doubt it. No matter how sweet and innocent I sounded, no matter the provocation for the assault on Tom, it would all be undone when the court got to hear what was called a victim impact statement. Mary would stand before the judge and slaughter me. She would paint Tom as the vulnerable prey of Lucifer, and by the end of it everybody in that room would doubt society could function in safety while I was free. I wouldn't be surprised if even the court reporter helped the mass drag me to a makeshift gallows. I won't waste my time making a statement that will be embarrassingly eclipsed.

But I didn't say that to Leona. Instead, to make sure she didn't worry, I told her I would do my best.

She paused. I knew something uncomfortable was coming. 'I called your parents.'

I took a few deep breaths. 'How did you know? I mean how...'

'I just found out where they were and called them. We had a long chat. And they want to hear from you.'

I really didn't know how to feel. My parents had never respected me and I had no silly dreams that my new infamy could do anything but widen the chasm between us. I just had to ask how much they knew, but I didn't get the chance. Soulmates can virtually read each other's minds.

As Leona proved when she said, 'They know some of the story, Luce. It was in the news the other day and they know you got arrested. The police contacted them for a lowdown on you.'

Now I knew what to feel: anger. Damn the police for bringing my parents into this. And terrible fear: 'Are they… okay? I mean, with me?'

Leona didn't answer that. 'Look, I have to go. I'm going to call you back in two hours, at five o'clock. Okay? We'll talk then. Make sure you're by the phone. Exactly at five.'

She hung up before I could reply, and my heart sank. My parents hadn't tried to contact me during my recent descent into hell and now I knew why. If they had been forgiving towards their only daughter, Leona would have told me. If they had told her they wanted nothing to do with me because I'd spread shame across the family, she would have kept quiet. And she had just refused to answer my question. I didn't have the mental strength to call her back.

But I was due a mammoth shock two hours later. When the phone rang on the dot of five o'clock, it wasn't Leona's voice I heard. 'Hello, Lucy,' my mother said.

26

MARY

Dad's in his armchair, watching TV, when I get back from court, but he immediately waves the cordless phone at me. 'Some newsperson called. They've got Tom's bag off the police. Did he lose it? You have to call them back.'

Dad's pendulum is swinging into the murk again, which is good, though that sounds bad. If I understand him, a reporter found out about Tom's bag being found by the cops and he's been begging for an update from the family. The tosspot might even have said that Tom was dead, but Dad has misunderstood.

I take the phone and go into the kitchen to check the missed calls and messages. It rings in my hand. The screen says it's Mrs Johnson, a nosey neighbour up the road. I'd put her in the phone memory as that name because her first is Mary, which is annoying. She might be calling to borrow salt or whatever, but it's too risky. I cancel the call and then block the number.

The first stored call is the one Dad probably answered, so I call it back. It is indeed a tosspot reporter, who answers with his name, Alan, and the name of his newspaper, like I give a toss. 'You called here about my brother.'

I have to give Tom's name, as if the guy has been phoning the families of slaughtered people all morning. But once I do, his voice lights up. I cut him off before he can start asking questions.

'My brother's wife was in court today. She got bailed. She's going to plead guilty to involuntary manslaughter at the next hearing. Her name is Lucy Packham, and she killed Tom Packham in Cullerton, in Lancashire, and he might be buried in the woods. Now don't call again.'

There's no gag order stopping *me* from talking to the media.

Just in case a whole bunch of these fools have been calling, I check the next message. This caller gives her name, Claire, and a website called Savannah Crystal. And a promise that she can help me find Tom. Right. I load the website to find it's for a psychic. Savannah can apparently contact spiritual dimensions to help the grieving like me. For a price.

I call the number and when she answers, I say, 'You want to help me find my brother? Cut me out of all the build-up about connecting to him and sensing he's near water and in pain and all that other shit. Get a wheelbarrow, bring his body to my front door, and then I'll pay you. Until then, don't bloody call this number again.'

I head back in to see my father. One damn psychic and a reporter just this morning. I nipped those in the bud in time, but it's going to be an uphill slog to keep the parasites away from Dad. I need to be the one to tell him the truth, before he sees it on the bloody TV.

I put the cordless phone on the arm of his chair and kneel in front of him to block his view of the TV. He shifts a little so he can still see the screen past my head. I better get used to this position: if the pendulum is swinging into the murk, the shitty news I'm about to hit him with won't imprint in his mind, and I might have to bomb his world all over again tomorrow. And the day after.

There's no easy way to build up to it, so I dump it in one short sentence: 'Dad, Tom is dead and Lucy killed him.'

His reaction is a shock. Still with one eye on the TV, he giggles and says, 'Tom.'

It seems the murk is thick and black this morning, but I can't walk away now. 'Dad, Tom is dead. That's why he hasn't been round. He was killed by his wife, Lucy. *Fawlty Towers* woman. She hit him on the head. Do you understand?'

'He's at the shops. What happened to his head?'

I take his hand. This is starting to hurt me. 'She hit him and he's dead. Do you know what I'm saying?'

'It doesn't suit him, that new look. Is he alive? Call him.' He lifts the cordless and hands it to me. I swat it aside and reach up to grab his chin and turn his eyes away from the TV in the hope that that will make him concentrate. And then I stop as I realise something. Dad hadn't said *Is he alive?*

He said *Is it live?*

I turn my head to look at the TV, and what I see there makes me gasp.

Tom.

LUCY

Just like when I spoke to Leona for the first time in years, my nerves shed and soon I was on speakerphone with my mother, talking as if we were best friends who saw each other every day. I was, again, virtually dancing around the room. The fearfulness made an encore when my mother put my father on the phone with her, but within seconds a relaxed attitude returned. Usually

I preferred listening over talking when on the phone, but today I couldn't be silenced.

My theory to explain this was that previously, during a handful of Christmas and birthday phone calls years back, I had been trying to sell my life as a happy one, which had made me feel awkward and reserved and perhaps in fear of being unmasked. Now, there was no chance of any such subterfuge, nothing I could say or do would paint me in a darker light, and I had nothing to lose.

The irony wasn't lost on me that I had hidden away from my parents because I was embarrassed about my life, yet here I was, at the lowest ebb in my existence, back in touch with them, and loving it.

I talked about Tom, and my beautiful house, and my role as a German tutor, and all manner of things in between and all around, but I kept my distance from recent events as if they were a pack of wild animals waiting to pounce. But this was a subconscious action and in the very moment I realised I was doing it, that I was again wearing a mask, I abruptly stopped talking. It was mid-sentence, so my mother said, 'Lucy? What's wrong?'

'I killed my husband, mother. He tried to attack me, so I hit him with a rock and he drowned in the river. Please say something.'

It was my father who answered. 'We know. Leona told us when she called. But why don't you tell us the story?'

I realised that when Leona ended our call earlier, with a promise to call back at five, she must have planned to set this conversation up. She must have called my parents and told them exactly what I'd imparted to her, which was everything. The whole truth. It must have been a real overload for them, to receive contact from a woman they didn't know who then spun a wild tale about their daughter. But despite the shocking revelation...

They had called me.

They had no way of knowing if my killing of Tom had been accidental, especially if they'd read any of the acidic comments all over social media, or they'd spent half a nanosecond listening to Mary. I could be a hapless victim, or an ice-cold murderer, but...

They had called me.

This strange day was about to take another twist.

During our chat, my phone had interrupted three times to tell me of a call waiting. Each time, my solicitor. Each time, ignored. Nothing was going to spoil my reunion with my parents, and, besides, the CPS was unlikely to have decided to drop my case, so it would only be more bad news.

What I couldn't ignore, though, was a fist banging on the door.

The peephole showed me my solicitor, sweating and heaving with breathlessness. I told my mother I'd call later and hung up. When I opened the door, he virtually fell inside.

'Have you seen the news?' Even as he said it, he waved his phone under my nose. A video to watch. I took it and sat on the bed. He sat on the other end and tried not to have a heart attack. I would join him within seconds.

The video was a news report from Nottinghamshire. It claimed that a missing man from Yorkshire, one Tom Packham, was presumed dead, and the police had arrested someone close to him for murder – no mention of my name, but getting it would require no leap of logic. However, a local man out with his girlfriend thought he had spotted him. It had taken place that morning, just a few hours ago, in a town called Kimberley, a few miles north-west of Nottingham.

Here the report cut to mobile phone camera footage. It

showed a small roundabout surrounded by shops. The camera, bouncing in someone's hand as that person walked, closed in on a place called Vape World. A new voice, male, probably that of the camera owner, said, 'There, that guy. At the counter. I watched him go in.'

The camera was right up to the full-size window, displaying the interior of the store, although the glare of the sun off the glass made it hard to see. It was possible to make out a man at the serving counter with a store clerk. A ginger woman poked into the left side of the screen, pressing up against the window and cupping her hands around her eyes in order to see inside better.

'Get back, don't get seen,' the cameraman said. His hand shot into frame to haul her back.

'He's coming,' the woman said, and suddenly scuttled out of shot.

'Just stay behind me.'

The camera panned to the door, which opened moments later to discharge the man who'd been at the counter. He was tall, wearing a grimy blue tracksuit, clean-shaven and completely bald. He got one step outside, spotted his audience, and froze.

'My God,' I said, unsure if what I was seeing was real.

As the man looked at the camera, the picture paused and a split screen displayed that image next to another. Tom. I recognised it as a two-year-old picture from Tom's Facebook, taken by Tom himself outside the Crucible Theatre when he'd gone to watch a session of the snooker world championship. In that photo he didn't have his new thick beard and the hair was shorter, which made it easier to see the similarities between that image and the one of the bald man.

I couldn't believe it. I couldn't take my eyes off the bald man. It was Tom. Or was it?

The mobile phone footage continued. The man who resembled Tom turned sharply away from the camera, and it was this that convinced me of the truth. No surprise or puzzlement in his actions, but fear. He knew he'd been recognised.

The bald man started to walk briskly away, but the camera followed.

'You him?' the cameraman-phone holder said. 'Hey, pal, look round. You the missing guy from up Yorkshire?'

The man gave no reply except to increase his speed. As the phone holder called out again, and jogged to keep up, the picture jumped and wobbled. The female with him gave a warning to give it up and call the police, but her boyfriend ignored it.

The bald man started to run as he turned left into the small car park of Hama Medical Centre. The cameraman followed, but upon making the turn the world bounced and flipped and went black. A curse from the man was beeped out. He had dropped his phone.

He got it back in time to show the bald man alongside the medical centre and climbing onto a large, wheeled bin at the end of the passage.

'Hey, pal, everyone's looking for you. Stop.'

The bald man didn't stop though. From atop the bin, he leaped over a wooden fence behind it and vanished. The cameraman ran to the bin but didn't attempt to climb; he instead raised the phone to point it over. The bald man was shown running past a children's play park, into what I'd later learn was Stag Recreation Ground. The phone operator turned away and started to talk to his girlfriend, which was where the amateur video ended. The remainder of the news report gave some details about Tom and what people should do if they spotted him.

I was stunned. My solicitor grinned at me, but waited for my vocal reaction. 'It can't be him.'

'What if it is, Lucy? He could be alive. You might not have killed anyone. You only saw him fall in the river, and they never found a body. I think the shaved head and face are a good sign. He's trying to change his appearance. I've had plenty of clients who did the same thing when they went on the run, or because they're scared of police line-ups.'

It still wasn't sinking in. 'But why?'

'It might be exactly as you've said before. It could be revenge against you. The police are already starting a search of that area where Tom was seen, so clearly they're taking this video seriously. This is great for us now there's doubt he's dead.'

I got my wits back. 'The courts have got to drop the case, right?'

'The CPS have a loophole of sorts, called a discontinuance. It simply means they decide not to pursue the case. It's not an acquittal because they can reinstate the charges at any time. And they'll definitely go for the discontinuance because the police will need time to investigate this sighting. They can't have you in prison for a wrongful death conviction when Tom suddenly comes home. The discontinuance will end your restrictions. But also the media restrictions on publishing your name and picture. And your name won't have been cleared.'

I didn't care about the media. In the future, when my face was all over the newspapers, yes. Right now, no. 'If they find Tom's body, I'll gladly say I'm guilty. But if he's alive... I don't want a conviction waiting to pounce on me like a stalker. What can we do?'

'We tell the CPS to send you to prison,' he said with a grin.

'What?'

I was so perturbed he had to explain it twice. The case would discontinue while everyone waited for identification of the man in the video, but we would force the CPS's hand by changing my plea to not guilty and then exercising my right to apply to revive proceedings. That could compel my enemies to go ahead with my prosecution, but this time fighting me at trial. Too risky for them while Tom could be out there.

So there was a chance the CPS would offer no evidence in court. To me that conjured the image of a lawyer just sitting in his chair during trial, calling no witnesses, showing off no exhibits. But what it meant was a total dropping of the case. A formal acquittal of all charges, like a not guilty verdict. Case closed.

It could all go wrong, of course. If Tom turned up dead after all, or if the bald man was never identified and compelling new evidence put the gambling bug in the CPS, the double jeopardy rule – which prevents acquitted people from facing the same charges again – could be bypassed. I could find myself hurtling first class right back into the nightmare.

Later, when my solicitor went away to make some progress on the case, I found the same news report and rewatched the video. The bald man was Tom, I was sure. The downward curve of the edge of his lips. A blue tint to his chin and cheeks, suggesting that a beard had been recently shaved. And his left temple appeared to have a scar – the same spot where I'd struck Tom. I felt hate rising within me.

Before my solicitor left, I'd surprised him by saying I wanted to have a day in court.

'You want to go to trial?'

I did. But not as a defendant. 'I want to be there when Tom is punished for what he's done to me.'

27

MARY

I'm driving to run an important errand when I get a pair of phone calls. The first is my dad, who was asleep when I left the house. I put it on my car speakers.

'I fell, Mary. Fell. Kitchen. I can't get up.'

It pains me to think of my dad in the kitchen, struggling to get up, but I can't go back. I know it's heartless. 'I can't come now, Dad. I've got something important to do. Get to the cupboard for the footstool.'

'Why is the TV not working?'

'You can't use the TV, it's broken. The power surge, remember? Crawl to the cupboard for the stool. You can use that to get up. Listen, Dad, remember what I said about Tom? The police might think Tom is alive. They might come to the house. Don't answer the door or the phone. You need to not believe them. What I told you about Tom is true.'

'What did you tell me? What do you mean? Who's alive?'

This was my worry. After seeing Tom on the TV, I'd told my dad it couldn't be him. Tom was dead. I had to make sure Dad believed that because all this silliness about his son being spied in Nottingham might make things worse in the long run, given Dad's unpredictable memory.

That was proved just minutes after I'd convinced him Tom was dead, after he'd had a cry and kind of gotten used to the fact. A second news report that put Tom in Nottingham had overridden what I'd told him, and I'd had to go through it all again. Can you imagine that?

The last thing I needed today was not knowing which story Dad believed, so I had cut the plug off the TV, and warned him not to answer the door. The phone was a risk, but I couldn't leave him defenceless and he wasn't one for outgoing calls anyhow.

'Dad, you'll be okay. Use the stool to get up and then go have another sleep in your chair. Leave the phone alone. I'll be back tonight.'

'I've hurt my ankle again, Mary. Where are you?'

For a moment I churn over the idea of going back to him. But I can't. I can't. 'Too far away to get home in time. I'll try to fix the TV and the phone when I get back. Please try to get the stool. I'm sorry, but I can't come home right now.'

The next call is from Reavley, who immediately says, 'Have you seen the news?'

A bunch of times. I've also read comments on news websites and social media. Seems like everyone who believed Tom was dead has switched it up because of that stupid video of a bald man in Nottingham. Nobody's got a good reason why Tom would want to hide from the whole world, from his sister and Dad and all his buddies, but they're ignoring logic because, oh, they've got proof. Nottingham Man has a shaved head and he ran when recognised, and that's what you'd do if you wanted to pretend you were dead. Slam dunk.

Worst of all, Lucy's getting all sorts of sympathy. Some

people never even knew Tom was missing in the first place, but they've heard this story and they're on Lucy's side. Most are just whining how hard it must be for her, having her hubby run away and getting accused of killing him, but others are going further. They want Lucy to be compensated, as if she just spent thirty years locked up. They want an enquiry into police conduct and major heads to roll. I bet placards are being knocked up at this very minute.

Some moron on a blog wrote a piece called *Debt of Society*, which called for Lucy to be given free rein to commit crimes whose sentences would total what she might be given for murder – she could kill Tom, or she could do three robberies, or steal eighty cars, etc. He even cautioned her to hold back a couple of years in case something happened in the future, like she's saving points on a store card.

I've lost myself a little and Reavley has to yell my name to bring me back. 'Yes,' I say, still jumbled in the head. 'The news. Bald man. Saw it. Not Tom.'

I would like to hope it's my brother, but I can't stretch my imagination that far. I know he's dead. I know he's in the ravine or the woods. If he'd survived Lucy's attempt to end him, then shaved his head and beard, it means he wants to hide from the world, wants everyone – as Lucy once said – to think he's dead. Makes no sense why he'd do that, which means he didn't do that.

'It certainly looks a lot like him,' Reavley says. 'Enough so that her solicitor is going to push through a motion to get her case postponed pending investigation. And I think she might get it. Remember, we don't have concrete proof Tom's dead. Police went into that vape shop to try to find fingerprints, but the bald man didn't touch anything. They printed the door handle, but nothing usable on it matched Tom. There's no interior CCTV, but they're hoping to find more and track his route after he leaped over that fence. Maybe he dropped something important.'

Here I stare at my phone, thinking about what I have stored inside it. I'm silent so long that Reavley asks if I'm still there.

'Yes. I've seen the bloody news. I'm angry. It looks like you and me, Aaron. We're the only ones who know that Tom is buried out there in the woods.'

I said this to prompt a reaction, and I get it: a pause long enough to tell me exactly where he stands. When I accuse him of believing the news, he's careful with his response.

'We have to investigate this, Mary. I just called to let you know about what might happen to Lucy–'

'Don't bother, I can work it out. The CPS pussies will let her go because they don't want egg on their faces. But they don't know what I know, Aaron. I know my brother is dead because Lucy told me she'd killed him way before she told you. And she's smug about it.'

'What? When did she tell you this?'

I have to pull in to the side of the road to control my breathing in order to get my words together. 'I called her the other day when she was driving to the cottage with you. I recorded the conversation. You remember her taking a call?'

'When she was with me? You didn't call her. She did get a call, but that was from a phone company.'

It took me a moment to realise what must have happened. 'She lied to you, Aaron. I was the one who called her, but she didn't want you to know that. She just about admitted she'd killed Tom. She must have kept her answers vague because you were there. I overheard you say something about a lunatic on a motorbike. Remember?'

Judging by his silence, that's a hell yes. His next words are forceful: 'I want that recording, Mary. Where are you?'

'I'm not coming to you, I have something to do. I'll play it.'

Last time, I had sat in shock and listened to a recording of Lucy's voice, played by Reavley. Now our roles were reversed. I pulled up the recorded voice files on my phone and hit play.

Lucy's phone rang and was picked up. I spoke before she could.

MARY: I'm the smarter one in this thing, bitch. You realise that, don't you?

LUCY: No, actually it's Lucy Packham.

MARY: Tom hated you for a long time, did you know that? Your marriage was a sham.

LUCY: We've never had any problems. Tom and I have always been happy with what we had. Our connection has always been perfect.

MARY: I'm onto you. I was right from the start. Tom told me what you were like. I know everything. I'm better than you.

LUCY: Better? Ha ha. Okay, let's hear what you've got.

MARY: There's no time right now, not for you. You don't have time at all, because yours will soon be up. And I'll make sure of it. I'm going to see to it that you pay the price eventually.

LUCY: Oh wow. Okay, tell me your magnificent plans. In fact, just cut to the chase and tell me: what will this cost me in the long run?

MARY: It'll cost you everything. Don't you see the end is coming? You're an idiot. How long did you think you could get away with his murder? How long did you think you could simply pretend that my brother was ill, or had just popped out, or was asleep, or in the bath? Weeks? Months?

LUCY: Oh, a long, long time. And a long time to come.

MARY: You bitch. Crapping self, gonna end you.

LUCY: No, at the minute I'm happy. So why would I change things?

MARY: But I'll offer you a way out, right now, a one-time deal.

LUCY: I don't really care about any sort of deal.

MARY: Give yourself up. I'll help you say it was manslaughter. You'll get ten years locked up, maximum.

LUCY: Locked... *in* for ten years? You're dreaming. Ten years isn't happening. No amount of time will be happening, because I've got what I want already. And nothing you can offer will change that.

MARY: That's a mistake, that's what I think. You should think carefully. I think–

LUCY: Look, get it into your thick skull. I'm not interested. If I was, or Tom was, we would have shown interest in you from the start. But we never did. Don't contact us ever again, please.

I end the recording and say to Reavley, 'I didn't share this with anyone before because it doesn't make me look good. I'm threatening her. I also wondered if people might think Lucy's responses were because I was antagonising her. But this lark with the Nottingham Man means I have to show it.'

'It certainly sounds like you were harassing her, but that's understandable. And it won't mean anything if it eventually turns out that she did kill her husband. And her responses, while possibly a knee-jerk reaction to annoy you, and carefully worded so I wouldn't suspect anything about that phone call, certainly don't help her case. But listen to me, Mary. Two things. One, keep that to yourself for now, please. You can't publish that. You can't show anyone. Will you promise?'

Are my ears deceiving me? My recording had caught a psycho with her mask slipping, and he saw a 'knee-jerk reaction' to Lucy having her buttons pushed? 'Anything else from me, detective?'

'I need to know about all the contact you've had with Lucy since Tom disap–'

'You've had that. I told you everything.'

'That was informal, Mary. I mean a signed statement. And

things have happened since then, like that phone call neither of you told me about. I want an up-to-date statement from you, including everything you've said to Lucy since. Every word. Every threat. Your version of what happened. Can you do that? Now? Where are you?'

'Yes, but I'm not coming to the police station. I told you I've got an important job to do. Nothing to do with Lucy, so relax.'

'Nothing to do with Lucy? Do you solemnly swear?'

He says this with a little chuckle, obviously remembering my use of that term earlier. Even though he's not in the car to see, I give my answer the way my brother used to: hand in the air, eyes raised skyward. 'I solemnly swear I am not heading off to harass Lucy.'

'Good. As for the statement, there's no need for you to come into the station. I can send someone to your house to write it down–'

'No, I don't want to wait for that. Forget writing. I'll tape it. I'll record right onto this phone, right now, and send it to you. I'll come down later and sign some form or whatever to say it's the truth and my words and whatever. But what do I start with?'

He pauses to think, but eventually decides this idea is doable. 'Okay, record it on audio. I can get it transcribed. Start with when you first realised Tom was missing. The spark that told you something was wrong.'

After the call, I access the voice recorder again. I'm angry because it's not lost on me that Reavley carefully chose his words: *your version of what happened.* Seems the content of that taped conversation between Lucy and me hasn't hurt her credibility one jot, but mine has had a tyrannosaur bite taken out of it. Could this day get any worse? I take a deep breath, hit record, and begin:

'Everything spat out of Lucy's foul mouth is a lie. Take that bullshit, burn it, and bury the ashes. Don't believe her, not back then, not now, not in the future. I'll tell you the truth – not a *version* – of what happened. And it all starts with a nasty feeling that something is wrong...'

LUCY

There was a lot of social media activity about me and Tom. It's split as to whether people believe that man in the video was Tom. Those who accepted it were calling for all charges against me to be dropped, and compensated. Someone even suggested I should play myself in a film of my life.

But it was hard to focus on the positive comments when reading the acidic words of others. One of the wildest was a claim I'd set the whole thing up – that I paid a Tom lookalike to be sighted as part of a plan to kill a conviction. The bizarre theories should have been the sort most easily deflected, because few would believe them, yet the more outlandish, the more it hurt.

But the online world and the anonymity it offered allowed people to act in such ways, and in real life things might be different. So I decided to test the waters by heading out. I called a taxi and waited out on the road. Drivers and pedestrians passed me by the dozen and nobody pitched a hateful glare, or even one of recognition. No one came up to me, nobody shouted out.

My plight was my world, of course, and I was deep inside, seeing nothing else. I had overplayed its scale in terms of magnitude and importance. It wasn't exactly national or even front-page local news. Buoyed by this, I took the taxi home.

Home, though, was the epicentre of my world and another matter entirely. As the taxi drove slowly past my house, faces appeared at windows and a man got out of a nearby car. He wasn't a local, I knew, but he clearly recognised me. And when he pulled out his phone, I knew he was a reporter.

The house itself was still a crime scene, with a single police car and a forensics van parked outside. My own vehicle was gone though. Perhaps now in a workshop, being analysed for blood and other evidence. I saw no police or scientists, but figured they were inside the house.

I told the driver to go past, drive on, get me out of here. It was clear I had no business or welcome here, and wasn't allowed anyway. I don't know why I'd come. All I'd done was upset myself again. He asked if I was okay, but did not enquire about the police presence. Courtesy or ignorance, I didn't know. But I was thankful.

I needed to get out of the city. I wanted to see trees and fields, and feel the wind, so I would just drive to blow away the cobwebs, to exist for a time in a world without my life. But there was something else I needed to do first. I asked the driver to let me out somewhere quiet and wait. And when he did, I stood under a tree and made a call.

Although I'd sent her a thank-you text, I hadn't spoken to Leona since she'd hung up on me prior to contacting my parents, and I desperately wanted to. But this call wasn't to her.

It was to Mary.

We seemed to have developed this little game where the person who answered a call from the other would say nothing at first. I didn't expect this today because I was on an unknown number, and Mary obliged me. But not because she didn't know it was me. It was because somehow she did.

'This is a false dawn.'

So, she didn't believe the sighting of Tom in Nottingham was real. Which meant she still believed he was dead. I hadn't expected to gain a new friend from this call, but that was a shock.

'He's not dead, Mary. It was as I said all along. Tom left me. You and me of all people would know that that man in the video was Tom.'

'Use your brain. Tom decided to go into hiding and never see his father or me or his friends ever again. He can't spend money. He can't work. He can't be seen.'

She hadn't mentioned me in that list. 'Use your brain, Mary. He can't see those people, or anyone else, if he wants the world to think he's dead.'

'And why would he do that?' she spat in disdain, as if I'd claimed Tom had moved to the moon.

'He wants me to be blamed for it.'

Mary said, 'If Tom was alive, I'd have no trouble believing that. You crushed his skull with a rock.'

How did she know that? Somehow, she had heard the content of my confession to the police. But how much of it? 'And do you know why?' I wasn't sure I would truly answer that question if she pressed for an explanation.

She didn't. 'Aaron now knows about your phone call to me when you were driving with him to the cottage.'

So she knew about my confession, probably from Reavley, and now it seemed the detective knew about the vicious phone call I'd pretended was from a broadband cold caller. But I tried to ignore any thoughts of problems this might present in the future. 'Do you remember when I threw salt in Tom's eyes by accident?'

'I'm not sure that was an accident. You nearly blinded him. Is there a point somewhere here?'

'But that's exactly my point, Mary. Tom pretended he'd gone blind. For a whole day, he had me believing he couldn't see. He went to the hospital. He tried to get me to call work and quit for him. He wanted me to buy him a guide dog. He tried to punish me.'

From the way she gave a witch-like cackle, I knew she'd figured out my point. And sure enough: 'You stupid bitch. I know Tom played a joke to make you regret throwing the salt. If you think I'll believe that Tom would pretend to be dead to score a point, you're stupid. And if you think he'd put himself out like this, and make everyone worry, just to teach you a lesson, then you're even more dangerously insane than I thought.'

I heard a car door open and slam, and the sound of the wind. Then footsteps on metal, rather like the walkway across the river at our cottage. I pictured her climbing iron steps. Mary said nothing, but I could hear her breathing change. The rage in her was building and I totally understood why: she still believed she'd lost her brother to murder, and his killer was trying to sell an outrageous defence. If she didn't like that, she was going to loathe what I said next.

'I hate him for this...'

'You hated him before this. That's why you killed him. It's a good job his cat ran away, or you would have killed that, too.'

Now, suddenly, my earlier dislike of that claim filled in the gaps. Zuzu had run away, but I hadn't told anyone. I hadn't mentioned it at all, anywhere.

'You killed Zuzu,' I said. 'You couldn't have known he was gone, unless you had something to do with it. And that was Tom's cat.'

I slammed the phone down. I had called her with hopes of mellowing the storm between us. But now I swore I would make her pay.

As I was walking back to the taxi, my solicitor called and said, 'DI Reavley wants to talk to you. He wasn't happy that you left the hotel.'

'I can leave if I want. He's got no right. What does he want?'

'Your permission to call you. I told him you got a new pay-as-you-go phone. Do you want to talk to him? He has a question for you.'

I gave my permission and Reavley was given the number. I returned to my quiet spot near a tree on the pavement and waited. It wasn't long before a withheld number rang. Reavley got straight to the point.

'I want the truth from you, Lucy. Here, on the phone. I don't want to drag you into a police station for interview.'

'I'm not sure you could, Reavley. And if you did, maybe I'd state for the record that you passed my confession on to Mary.'

He said nothing for a moment, which I reckoned meant a sudden worry about the trouble I could cause him. But he needn't be concerned. I might not like the man, but he was smart and dedicated, and I wasn't going to weaken the police service by costing him his job. 'Ask your question, DI Reavley.'

I knew what was coming. I'd heard it said, hinted at, theorised ever since that damned video of the bald man had appeared. There had been many motives proposed by those who put me in league with the bald man, and the clear frontrunner was the good ol' life insurance scam. No one seemed to know or care that murder of a policyholder by the nominee – and I had been set to plead guilty to Tom's killing – meant I wouldn't get a penny. I was locked and loaded and ready to hit Reavley with a round of fire.

'Have you got any other burner phones? We know about the five bought in Bradford. And there's this one you're on right now. Do you use any others, Lucy?'

I was puzzled. 'No. No other phones. Why?'

'The truth. Please. Do you solemnly swear?'

I couldn't put my finger on why, but Reavley's use of my husband's old honesty promise annoyed me. I hung up on him.

The phone rang again. Withheld number again. I planned to ignore Reavley after today, but I wasn't yet done reprimanding him. I wanted one more strike. I answered with, 'You forced me into buying this new phone because you seized mine. No, I don't have any others. You know about them all.'

'Lucy? How's things? Possible murder conviction notwithstanding.'

I nearly fell on my face. It wasn't Reavley. It was a voice I would never forget, never mistake, and thought I'd never hear again.

It was Tom.

PART III

28

TOM

Lucy. There she was, beyond the peephole, my girl, all alone. No point hiding, was there? She'd come all this way because she knew. Because I'd brought her here. And if a platoon of cops were waiting somewhere to pounce, so be it because I had no way out of this second-floor office except by the rickety old spiral fire exit she just came up.

So I opened the big iron door and took a step back and just gave a shrug, kind of to say, *You got me, you win, your move.* In the peephole; angry – now that anger got swapped for a quivering lip. I turned and went through the dusty shell of the main office, past a door to an empty storeroom containing my meagre clothing, and into a shitty little kitchen with a tiny worktop. On it were all the tools I needed to survive. Kettle, microwave, tin opener, one cup, one plate, one spoon.

There was a tacky foldaway table in there and I took the seat that put my back to the door, to my wife. Was I giving her a free hit? Deserved it. And she had form, ha ha. No hit came. My wife slid past me and took the opposite chair. I was nervous, weirdly.

How many times had I slept with this woman or argued with her or had a good old laugh? Ah, but this was the first time I'd ever gotten her arrested for murdering me.

Her eyes never left me. They were intense and wide. Think: you've just watched an alien spacecraft land in your backyard. Mine were on the table. Think: you've just come face to face with someone whose life you ruined. I was also a bit embarrassed because I was wearing the same tracksuit I'd had on in that video. I only had three, mind. But what was I worried about? Bad impressions? Looking unattractive?

She didn't say a word until I finally looked up. I did it slow, movie-like, for tension. Or maybe it was to get a longer look at her tits. 'You're really going to make me ask, aren't you?'

I shrugged again. 'It's a long story. Perhaps questions would be better. Easier.'

'For you. And why would my comfort matter, right?'

'I didn't want you to get hurt.'

She almost spat at me. 'I see only one way that would happen. I fall asleep, wake up in thirty years' time in my own bed, after my life sentence for murder. But maybe you could make that happen. You're good at performing miracles.'

I fixed her eyes with mine. No more kid gloves. 'I was young. I grew up. I grew out of you.'

I realised that I'd missed her. And wanted her, weirdly. In fact, no, that wasn't weird at all. She was attractive, wearing the business suit with the skirt that I'd bought her for filming those learn German videos she puts on the internet. But she'd banned sex for a week one time because I'd embarrassed her in a shop. Making her a hated killer destined for prison? Two-weeker, that.

But the line about growing out of her? True. The only remaining thing that attracted me to her was that most basic hot-blooded male desire.

I expected a slap, or the quivering lip. But she took a deep breath and let it out slowly. 'I knew that, I guess. You spent a lot of evenings away, working late or playing with that silly monster truck. And so this was your reason for setting me up for murder? Because we grew apart?'

I shook my head. 'But we'll get to the big answer soon. Not yet.'

She said, 'Of course. But if not reason for setting me up, it's reason not to care what happens to me?'

I nodded. 'But I do feel bad. I mean, if there was another way... I thought about backing out many times.'

'Many times? So it was planned for a long time. Seven months is my guess. Since last November.'

I wish I'd had a glass of water so I could spit it out in shock. 'It seems we're still connected enough that you can read my mind.'

'No. Last November was when you said you fancied growing a big beard and your hair. If I could read your mind, I would have known your evil plan and would have... done something. I would have known why you got me to cancel your snooker membership and your pension and get your car valued, and all those other things that the police would call circumstantial evidence. None of it means much by itself, but when all put together on the table, quite damning against me.'

'You've done your research. But I'm not sure evil is the right word.'

'I did research, you're right. I spent a lot of time alone in an empty room to think and then spent hours in another room down the hall talking about it with a team of researchers from South Yorkshire Police. And how about this word instead: wicked, or sinful, or malevolent?'

Her eyes seemed to have lost some colour. I remembered what she'd done to me with a rock. Knew I had to take care not to get this girl inflamed. I fell back on my old safety net of shrugging when the right answer was dodging me.

She said, 'You also had to show the world that our marriage was failing. Our argument in the pub the night before it all happened? The arguments in the street over the last half year or so? All the worries to your friends that I was unhinged? The texts about my threatening you, sent to your sister?'

'I had to make it look like you were ready to flip.'

'And now all that the police needed was evidence of something that might have pushed me over the edge. My antidepressants. You accidentally on purpose forgot to hand in the repeat prescription.'

I'd had enough of those eyes burning a hole in me. I got up and offered tea. A big fat no from her, obviously, and good job because I only had one cup. I'd just finished a tea, but I needed to get away from that table. I had to fill the kettle from a bottle because the water was off but the electric was on. Getting a cup and powdered tea and some sugar and waiting for the water to boil all burned a bit of time. Let me shake off some nerves.

She didn't even watch me do it, weirdly. She faced forward as if still seeing me in that chair. Like a zombie.

And it didn't work in the end. I had to slide right back into her fiery line of sight when I sat. It felt worse. Was she even blinking? I forgot what we'd been talking about.

'Antidepressants?' she said.

Oh yeah. I sipped my horse crap tea. 'It would look bad on you if you'd been off your meds for a week or so. Make the coppers think you more likely to go ape. But I did buy you a big bottle of gin, to make up for it.'

'Which I drank a quarter of over a week, and then the rest on the night you faked your own death. The insulin in the bin, you left that for the police to find, knowing I'd deny it was me. You left them the blood in the bathroom sink, too. And you told me a silly story about cutting yourself on a tap, knowing I'd pass that story on and it would sound pathetic.'

She blinked, thank hell. No cyborg, then. Just flesh-and-blood Lucy, still my wife. It eased my tension a jot. 'Well, the blood on the floor was for the cops. I knew they could find it with Luminol or whatever they use. Wasn't sure about the sink. And yeah about the story. You can't cut yourself on those taps in the cottage. I tried, to make sure. I used a razor blade. Oh, and blood on your clothes. I flicked it there when your back was turned. You missed the stain on the blouse, I hear.'

She took out a tissue to wipe her eyes. She was holding back the emotion. I felt bad for her. Maybe. She still hadn't asked why I'd done this to her. But it wasn't time for that answer yet. 'My turn. How did you work out that I wasn't dead?'

When I'd called her earlier, the conversation had been brief. Told her I was alive, which was a bit silly since I was talking on the phone. Said I wanted to see her. Gave her my address. Told her not to call the cops or I'd be gone when she got here, and not to try calling the phone because it would be dead.

She agreed to come, but hardly said a thing other than that. No shock that I was alive. No questions, either. Saving them for when she got here. She said she'd come and that was that. End of call. I knew then that she had suspected I might be alive, and not just because some dick spotted me out at the shops.

She got right back to cyborg stare. 'The sighting of you in Nottingham, mostly. But that only confirmed my suspicions. You made a mistake.'

'What mistake?' I said it nice and sweet, like I really wanted to know. But I was ready to shoot her down because I didn't make mistakes.

'You messed up with your vape. It was found in your backpack. Which was on your back when you jumped in the river.'

I didn't follow where she was leading, but I ignored it for a second. All the arguments recently, they'd been part of the plan, faked, and I hadn't been angry with my wife for weeks, couldn't remember the last time or what caused it. Until now, and this. 'I didn't jump, did I? You cracked me with a rock.'

'You tried to rape me.'

'No, no, no, that was all fake. It was to give the cops a motive. You were supposed to knock me off the walkway and over the waterfall.'

She gave a weak laugh. 'I must have read an older draft of the script.'

'I gave you a chance. Lucy. I sat back on my knees, right between your legs, and I ran my hands through my hair. A long pause there. That was your opportunity. All you had to do was kick me, and over I would have gone. But you didn't. So, I figured it was because you were looking at me. So I even flipped you over. I did everything I could to get you to do something. And oh did you. But I didn't expect to get my brains bashed out with a rock.'

'Next time you put your hands on a woman without her consent, expect that. Especially one likely to go ape without her medication.'

I gave a slight bow, admitting her point. 'Did you want me dead?'

For the first time, I saw worry in those volcano eyes. Holy shit, she *had* wanted me dead. Had? Still did, no doubt. When she bashed me with that rock, she actually tried to kill me. But why was I surprised?

I felt bad for her, put on the spot with that question, so I wouldn't make her answer it. I changed the subject by bringing up something that was niggling me. 'You said I messed up with my vape. Let's hear this mistake I made.'

'You put it in your pocket before you attacked me. A dead

man floating downstream somehow managed to get that vape from his pocket and into the bag.'

'Shit, that was bad. I shouldn't have taken it out of the bag before we left the cottage. But it wasn't a mistake. I was hoping no one would notice. I don't make mistakes.'

She was supposed to be impressed. A bit disheartened. Didn't happen. 'Oh, you did. Your phone call to me. That was a biiig mistake.'

Biiig? I doubt it, O Smarmy One. 'You sure, babe? Burner phone, used once, and I microwaved it. Remember I showed you that trick?'

It hadn't actually been a trick, truth be told. Months back, Lucy had moaned at me because I'd had pals round to watch a monster machine show on TV and we'd left empty food containers and lager cans all over the living room. She was bringing a handful of this crap to the kitchen bin and I stuck her phone in the microwave to score a point. I wanted her to drop all that stuff as she ran to save her phone, so I could complain about *her* mess.

I hadn't realised how quick the microwave would kill a phone though. She didn't get a chance to run. The instant I pressed the button, there was a flash. No more working phone. I was embarrassed and didn't want to admit I'd messed up. So I acted like I was punishing her for moaning. Not my finest hour.

That sense of hurt pride I'd felt back then? Felt it right now, too. But Lucy gave a grin that told me my big ego was about to get another whack.

'Oh, Tom, I'm not talking about tracing your phone. The phone you called me on was new and you shouldn't have had the number. Only my solicitor and a police officer and my family knew about that number. And one other person that I called on it. I think it's time for the big answer.'

While I was thinking how to respond to this, I sensed

movement from the doorway behind me. Lucy was right: *now* it was time for some truths.

'I guess that's my cue to enter stage left,' Mary said as she stepped into the room, carrying Zuzu, my cat.

MARY

I drop Tom's moggy, which darts under the table. Lucy picks it up, but the thing only allows her a brief cuddle before wriggling free and fleeing under Tom's chair. Like anyone else connected to Tom, it tolerated her because of him, but those days are history.

'So you stole my cat,' Lucy says with barely a glance at me. Just enough to register I really am here. Then her eyes are back on Tom, and she's got some serious hate eddying in there. But she's still sitting here, no cops around, and that still gives me a chance to turn things around. To Tom she says, 'You could dump me, and abandon your father and friends and your whole life, but not a cat?'

'It's not like that,' is his answer. 'It's boring here.'

Her head must be a boiling stew of incomprehension and rage, but she manages a little grin of disbelief at my brother's stupid answer. 'This is about the life insurance. Who recruited who?'

'Joint thing,' I say as I put a hand on Tom's shoulder. He scoots out of the chair and I take his place. It's strange to sit right across from Lucy. But I've got a job to do. 'It wasn't really like that. Words exchanged over time. Ideas here and there. All of a sudden there was a plan.'

'But you're the mastermind.'

'I couldn't trust this fool to run things,' I snap. 'I told him not to take that vape out of the bag. But that wasn't the only mistake he made. I managed to find a way he could get a stash of insulin pens. Very clever. Very secret. Very untraceable. Then this bozo buys a digital device to attach to it right off Amazon and has it sent to his office under his name.'

'Of course. The insulin dumped in the bin. How could I forget that little twist?'

I glare at Tom. 'And I warned him, many times, don't do her on the waterfall walkway. Now the insurance company will jump all over their dangerous activity clause.'

'It doesn't matter if I was skydiving, does it? She tried to bloody crush my skull, that's why I fell in.'

'I wonder how hard you tried. What, do you still love her or something?'

I say this to put him on the spot, make him answer right in front of her, and to see her reaction to it. But his reply's not what I expect. 'It's not that easy, Mary. We had a lot of years together. You wouldn't understand.'

'She tried to kill you, and then came up with a cover story about you running away. Aren't you thinking this through? Body or not, she should have mourned you and there should have been a funeral. But she was happy to leave you for the fish to eat. And to leave Dad lost.'

He shrugs, a habit of his that really grates on me. I turn back to Lucy. 'But even with those mistakes, Lucy, we could have gotten through this. Then the village idiot here decides to take a stroll to the shop, and now here we are.'

'I needed vape liquid,' Tom moans. 'And that man who recognised me could have had the decency to wait until I got bread. There's still no bread.'

I smile at Lucy. 'See what I'm dealing with? If he'd had his way, the cops would have found something rather stupid under the bed and the whole thing would have been ruined. But as it is, his foolishness has given us a big problem.'

Lucy gives a smile back. It's fake, she's just playing along, because I see worry and anger underneath the surface. Not fear. Oh, can it be she thinks she's got some slice of control here? A piece of sarcasm clears that up:

'Perhaps Tom could stagger into a police station and say he was kidnapped by gypsies and forced to work on a fairground.'

Sarky mare. 'Oh, it's not over yet.'

'No, but soon,' she says, which is a jot puzzling. Was that a threat? 'So now I understand it fully. Tom goes missing and everything points to me as having killed him. The law won't allow me to collect the life insurance payout. That money would then be allocated according to his will. But again I'm the sole beneficiary, because you and his father were removed. I know I'm right in thinking you put him up to that, although it's a puzzle why. Tom's estate would be dispersed by the courts. All sorts of distant family members would make a claim.'

I clap her, nice and slow and sarcastic. 'You know your laws. Having my name removed was all part of it though. The first thing the cops look at when someone's been murdered is who benefits, so I couldn't be a contingent beneficiary. I had to be as distanced as possible from any money paid out because Tom was dead. At no point could anyone be allowed to think I knew I could benefit from his death. The best way was to appear to leave it to chance, meaning the courts. Siblings are next in line after spouses. I'm the sister who lives close to him, sees him all the time, takes care of his father. No court is giving that money to some distant cousin. I get my half of everything, including the house.'

Now she claps me, the cheeky bint. 'The house. I hadn't even thought about that. All told, a nice payday. But all of that depended on my being convicted of his murder. What if that hadn't happened? You didn't exactly leave a smoking gun for the police to find. Without major evidence saying otherwise, Tom's death might have been ruled an accident.'

'But it wasn't.'

'True. Here we are. So, I get convicted of killing Tom, all his assets are sold, including my house, all the money is bagged up, and the government hands it to you. Tom has to spend the rest of his life in hiding, but he's got half a million to do it with.'

Tom gives a snorting laugh that makes me want to smash his face in. Lucy seems not to notice. She says, 'So, I know the plan. I know why. But we're missing a bit that I'm really intrigued to know. The bit in the middle where Tom managed to get from a raging river to this rotten old office. How?'

She's staring at me, but I lean back and look at Tom. 'Your wife just asked you a question. Don't keep her waiting.'

29

TOM

The bitch-slap hurt like hell. Not as much as crashing my ankle against concrete. But there's no use blaming stone. Damn bitch Lucy.

A woozy head made it harder to avoid the fallen fence post in the water just past the end of the clearing. In shallow times, it poked out and was good for crossing, but today it was submerged under three feet of water. The key was to hug the legs to the chest and float right on over, which was easily doable with my Helly Hanson Sport life jacket under my coat. But, woozy head. Twenty miles an hour, easily, ankle straight into it. Damn bitch.

No matter how bloated the brook, there was no floating down into the ravine. It was like a series of steps in places, with twenty little waterfalls where it was steepest. Probably more suited to a quad than a canoe. I had to climb down the majority of the way. No fun there because... well, think ice bucket challenge.

At the bottom, a pool, so here I could front crawl and get up some speed before being carried by the current. The view was great from down here in places where there were no trees. High cliff on the right. Pair of fat long hills on the left. No time to admire it though. The ravine floor was a bunch of humps, so there were places where the water carried me freely and spots where I had to dodge rocks and watch I didn't smash my knees on the earth.

A mile or so in was a fork in the brook snaking towards me out of the crease between the fat hills. The chosen spot was just before this. In a long run of small trees and big bushes. Had to be before the fork. Cops had to wonder which route I'd taken. Both hit the River Darwen, a mile or whatever apart, but it would make the cops work twice as hard. I aimed for two rocks up ahead that stuck up high and sharp, like stalagmites.

It was a deep part of the water, so the flow was fast, but I had a good eye and fine muscles. No problem. Straight between them, a hand planted on each. Then I could get my shoes on the ground five feet below. I could feel what I needed down there.

Between these two rocks was where the bag would go. Jammed in there, nice and tight, with part of it sticking out the water.

The bag was soaked, but cling film was wrapped around a five-inch section of one strap. Under that, a nice dry section. Change of plan here because of Lucy and her big overreaction. By now I knew she must have hit me with a rock because there was blood in my hair. So no need to reopen my finger cut. Just wiped my head on that dry bit of strap. For the cops. Job done.

I nearly forgot my vape. It was in my pocket. Quite amazingly, it still worked even though soaked. One last cloud of water vapour into the air, then I locked it up as evidence in the bag and dove under the water.

On the riverbed was another backpack. It was a chore to lift. Two big rocks used to keep it sunken. Had to stand around in the freezing water until I'd emptied a chunky one out. Then I could climb out. The other big rock got lobbed into the river. What else was in the bag? A plastic vacuum bag with my gear in. Jeans, long-sleeved T-shirt, baseball cap and sunglasses. And a new vape.

No damn shoes.

All my soaked gear and the wet backpack got stuffed in a large plastic carrier bag and off I set. It was a trek through the trees and out onto open flat ground and along the track between the fat hills. This way wasn't often used. Big stretches it got really muddy, especially right now since the rain had only stopped earlier that morning. But what did a bit of mud matter, what with my shoes being soaked? Quiet weekend stroll. I saw no one.

Beyond the hills was a village and I had to be careful here. I had to go off the track, through more trees. Feet were killing me by this point. Eventually I got to a road running through the woods, where I had to run out of cover and look left and right, because I'd lost my way. There, to the right, few hundred metres. Back in the trees, I headed that way.

It was a lay-by. 55-plate Honda Jazz, bought for cash last night, and not much of it. I waited until the coast was clear, hopped in the back seat. I dumped my bag on the floor.

'Lay down,' Mary said.

'You forgot my shoes.'

'They wouldn't fit in the bag.'

They would have fit if she hadn't used two rocks to weigh the bag down. Cerebral girl, but I was the practical one. Anyway, I lay down across that back seat. There was a blanket. Really? Overkill. Maybe the owner left it.

She turned to look at me. Then gave a big old cat grin. 'Please tell me Lucy gave you that lovely head gash.'

'Yeah. I think she grabbed a rock.'

'Perfect. So you made a move on her?'

'Yeah, I had to, didn't I?'

I'd told my sis that I reckoned I could rile Lucy up enough, just words. But no, Mary wanted to make sure, so it was her idea for me to pretend I was going to sexually assault my own wife. I was well not up for that, but fighting my sister is like dangling from a high ledge. You can only hold on so long.

Jesus, now that I thought about it, I was pretty disgusted by what I'd done. But it got the job done. And she'd clocked me with a rock. I wasn't entirely convinced Mary's idea had been all about guarantees though. On the day I'd met Lucy, when showing her around a flat, we'd swapped phone numbers, and Mary had been there and had watched it happen. And the first thing she said when we left was, 'I hope you don't plan to call that number. She's too old for you. I don't like her.' I'm not sure there had been a nice word about Lucy from Mary's lips, ever.

Now, I see my sister grin as she stares at my head wound. 'That's brilliant. Love it. She might have actually tried to kill you. For real. It would be perfect if she called the cops and straight out said she's just killed her hubby. We'd be laughing.'

'Yeah, I'll laugh over a Pot Noodle while in my sleeping bag tonight.'

'You left the blood in the sink?'

'Yes, I did everything.'

'The insulin in the bin?'

'Everything. Calm down.'

'No bag of lime or a saw or bin liners in the pantry?'

'Nope. You're the boss.'

She glared at me. 'And you didn't leave a blood-soaked knife under the damn bed?'

'Calm down, I said. I did everything right.'

'Lay down and let's get going. Under the blanket.'

She started driving. Turns here and there, as we headed out of the middle of nowhere. I had to rerun my entire morning for her. And she interrupted with questions, wanting every detail: what I had said, what Lucy had said, where we'd stood, what we'd done before heading out. She asked again if I'd planted the blood and the insulin, and again needed confirmation I hadn't secreted a bloodied knife under the bed or the tools of body disposal in the pantry. But even then she wasn't convinced.

'You didn't sleep with her, did you?'

Oh, I'd been warned about that. No sex in the few days leading up to the big moment. 'No.'

'Are you sure? You were cosied up last night.'

Definitely don't shag her Saturday night, she'd been adamant about that.

'No. I told you. I know the plan.'

'But I know you males. So you didn't wake up hard this morning? Didn't get turned on by seeing her naked and decide one little romp won't hurt?'

And definitely, *definitely* don't get frisky Sunday morning. She had this horror that the coppers would find out, Lord knows how, and wouldn't believe Mary's story about the marriage failing.

'I didn't. And I don't like my sister mentioning my hard dick. If I mention pink elephants, I can't help but put a picture in my head. No more talk of my hard dick.'

It was meant to be a joke, but she didn't laugh. She got right back to the interrogation, this time not on the past but the future. She tested me on the rules, the do's and don'ts of life as a dead man locked in an old office.

Some future. Think: fugitive. No more hanging out with my pals. No more monster machine shows, although I thought that one might be doable. Big crowds, anonymous. Maybe a face mask. No more sex, although Mary had mentioned prostitutes. I had to say no, didn't I? You don't tell your sister you want a whore, even if she brought it up. We'd give it a month and see how I felt.

'I smell McDonald's.'

'Get lost, Tom.'

'No cameras on the drive-through.'

'Willing to bet a million pounds on that? Just keep down. We'll eat later. Now, what do you do if someone tries to break into the office late at night?'

An hour that felt like a week later the motorway was gone and we were taking some turns again. When we drove over a kerb and onto grass, I knew we'd arrived. The car stopped.

I sat up. The street we were on was pretty hidden, a remote dead end. One side was the high back wall of a food factory. The other was a long terrace of three-storey homes redeveloped for commercial use. All the old homeowners moved out because a paedophile got housed there, so said a rumour.

The end property belonged to a dentist's, which was active but shut on a Sunday. But they'd bought only the ground and first floor, so the office space at the top was empty and for rent. And locked off. We were parked up on the grass against the gable end wall because the only way into that top floor was by a spiral fire exit to a high iron door. I'd had to bust the lock on that and it was held shut by Velcro.

The fire exit itself was a death-trap. It wobbled and rumbled as we climbed and dust rained down where the wall bolts were grinding against the brick and working themselves free. But I needed to leave the thing in that condition. It put off prospective renters.

'Let's see if any slimy squatters are low enough to have decided to call that cesspit their new home.'

Mary didn't laugh at my joke.

The coast was clear, but we sat in the car until Mary decided the coast was clear. And when we went, she made me take the blanket. Blanket, baseball cap, sunglasses. Jesus, that made me more conspicuous. Someone was going to think the old paedophile was being sneaked back.

Three rooms, sort of. One main office, kitchen, storeroom. No bathroom because that was downstairs, where I couldn't go. When I'd moaned about having to live here, Mary had harped on about her silly death-row dick. *Richard doesn't moan. Richard's stuck in a cell all day. Richard is forced to eat crap food.* Yeah, well Richard didn't have to shit in a plastic bag.

On a previous visit, this time in a suit, I brought some supplies, like a microwave and kettle and a sleeping bag. Mary had added something. I dumped two bags of gear from the car boot and picked up a boxed set of hair clippers.

'I thought I was going blond?'

'No,' my sister said, and that was that. Shortly after, she sat me down to cut my hair. She ran the clippers, no attachment, down the centre of the top of my head. Hair fell in my lap. Followed by the clippers. 'That's in case you try to do it your way. Now finish it. And don't forget the beard.'

My fingers found a valley through my hair right to the skin. Great. Bald it was, then. And I caught the wound on the side of my head a bunch of times, too. I got a good look at that once all the hair was gone. Damn bitch Lucy had caught me a good one. I said goodbye to the beard, too, but that thing could get lost forever. I had developed a habit of plucking at it until my cheeks hurt.

We spent half an hour running through the plan yet again, and then she went home. She needed to be at home when the news broke, just in case the cops came to see her. 'Enjoy your sofa and TV,' I told her as she left.

We had a pair of pay-as-you-go phones to keep in contact. Hers came from a store a few months ago. Mine we got off Amazon, using Dad's name and bank account so nobody could trace it to her, and then to me. It was a Binatone M250, and Christ would it have suited my dad. Big buttons, good only for texting and calling. Mary insisted on a phone with no internet, because apparently I couldn't be trusted not to mess up the whole plan by going on Facebook and watching the uproar as everyone realised I was dead.

So, no Google, no TV, no radio. Jigsaw puzzles, books, drawing pad, and the one that really annoyed me because I didn't know if it was a joke or just a stupid attempt to please me – a toy monster truck. Yeah, that would fill the void.

The afternoon dragged. Richard was probably chatting to a pal or a guard. I did a jigsaw. In the early evening, while listening to a bunch of idiots racing around outside on their motorbikes, I got restless. There was a monster truck show tonight, Animal was there, and I was going to miss it. We should have done this thing tomorrow morning. I smoked my vape so much it hurt my throat. Would it hurt to pop outside for a bit of sun?

I didn't. I finished the jigsaw. I ate two bananas. And then Mary called.

'No word yet. Nothing on social media.'

None of my friends had posted anything, but if they hadn't tried to contact me on the phone I'd left back at the cottage, then why would they suspect anything? I was off holidaying with the missus.

One friend was the landlord of the Serengeti pub, but that guy's most recent Facebook post, an hour ago, advertised a singer for next Saturday. Given the location of his pub, and his clout in the village, he would have heard about cop cars.

'Doesn't mean no cop cars went there. They could be past his pub in seconds. He doesn't live at the front window.'

No posts from any of my neighbours in Sheffield, either. So no cop cars had gone to my house.

'Well, I doubt she'd go home tonight without me anyway. I bet she's waiting to see if I come back alive.'

'And why would she do that? Are you all loved up? Are you sure you tried the rape?'

'I did. You saw the gash in my head. It's only been seven or so hours. I don't think she'd go straight to the cops. She'll wait and see if I turn up later.'

Nothing on the social media of either South Yorkshire Police or Lancashire Constabulary. There were lists of missing people.

'How about the Most Wanted list?'

She didn't find that funny. Aloud she wondered what the hell Lucy was doing.

'Hopefully, she didn't commit suicide at the thought of losing me.'

Apparently that wasn't funny either.

'You need to stay right there while I do this,' Mary said after careful thought. 'Don't bloody move. I'm going to go meet your trucker pals.'

'What are you going to do?'

'I don't like this. Something's wrong. I'd better go...'

MARY

'...up to the cottage and see what was what. Hopefully, you'd be a blubbering wreck by the river, with your phone dialling 999.

'So imagine my shock when I arrived at the cottage and you weren't blubbering at all. You were calm and composed and had a story about Tom being out. My jaw almost hit the ground. You thought you'd killed him by knocking him into the river, but instead of gushing with guilt and telling the police, here you were, with a made-up cover story. I thought, surely it can't be true. Is this woman, his wife, his killer, actually going to pretend he's not dead? Is she really going to try to pretend he's still alive? For years and years? My God, what weirdness. Tom tries to fake his own death, and you think you've killed him and go right ahead trying to cover it up. No thriller author would get away with something so far-fetched. As Tom said to me, it was exquisite.'

Lucy looks a little embarrassed. But she needn't be, really, because she was close to pulling it off.

'On Sunday I did wonder if you actually believed your own story. After all, Tom hadn't been dead when you knocked him into the river. Perhaps you thought he'd climbed out of the water and the reason he was missing was, as you said, that he was pissed and didn't want to return. But the next day, when his car was gone, I knew your plan. You'd gotten rid of it. You did that because you knew he was dead. I must say, I was impressed by how strong you were, your fortitude, and how you performed in front of the police. But I also knew the missing car meant game, set and match to me. Getting someone else to dispose of that BMW was the biggest mistake you made, and I loved that twist. My plan couldn't have gone any better if you'd actually been in on it.'

I stop here to allow Lucy to speak. I want her withered and lost and desperate before I make my move on her. She gets up and approaches Tom. He tenses as if expecting a whack, but I'm calm. Of the two of us, he's the minor player, and if someone deserves her wrath it's me.

Sure enough, no whack. She snatches his cup of tea, pours it down the sink and gets herself some water. Dry throat. Good. She sits again. 'Why have neither of you asked why I didn't go along with your plan? Why I didn't just phone the police and say it was an accident?'

She wants to tell us and I don't need to ask. So I don't. I just wait.

'I couldn't go to prison,' Lucy says, and then her face seems to darken with anger. 'You say I was strong? I say you have no idea what you're talking about. With this bastard gone, I was at my wits' end, my lowest ebb, worse than I ever felt in my life, even back when I was being beaten by my husband in Germany. I cried constantly. In my statement, every time I said I bathed, ate, exercised, watched TV, all of that was a lie. I did none of those things. I didn't have the will or the energy to. If I had gone to prison, I would have killed myself. But I wanted to live. I have a good friend and parents. We might not have the closest relationship in the world, but they'll get hurt if I go to prison, and I didn't want to do that to them. I was a wreck and you bastards did that to me.'

I don't reply, and neither does Tom. No reply I can muster seems worthy. Meaning I can't risk saying something cheeky in case I firebomb my chances of fixing what's wrong here. Lucy takes a moment and calms down.

'Exquisite, you say? But my actions still made you panic. I could have upset your perfect plan, and you needed to do something. Going straight to the blood upstairs. Finding the insulin bottle in the bin. Suddenly claiming to the police that Tom loved me. Your instantaneous assumption that I'd killed Tom makes sense now. But I wonder: would you have been so quick to condemn me if there had been no plan? I say yes.'

'Oh, I hated saying all that stuff about Tom loving you. It burned my throat. But we needed the marriage to appear to be sweetness and light, so the police would think it unlikely that Tom would leave. I admit I panicked and felt a need to rush once I knew you were going to hide the killing. Couldn't have Tom hanging around for weeks while everyone thought he was still alive. Couldn't delay that money. Couldn't risk your actually getting away with pretending Tom had run away. And as for your question... I say no. I knew Tom was falling out of love with you.' Here I glance at him. 'Or so I thought until today.'

'So you make mistakes too,' Lucy says.

'I don't make mistakes. If we discount my failure to put on a show of asking Tom's friends if they'd heard from him. But I had that covered anyway.'

'You thought you had *everything* worked out. Maybe you did, but not now. Now you have a big problem, and that's why you brought me here.'

She's opened the door for me. In I go: 'You can help us fix that big problem, and for that you'll get half the money. Well over five hundred thousand pounds. You could start a new life. You did it before.'

She laughs. 'What do you suggest? I continue to let the police think I killed Tom? Wait, I could treat my prison sentence like a job. Five hundred thousand pounds for, say, five years. A hundred thousand pounds a year. The prison governor won't even make that. I'll be the highest paid person in the prison. It sounds great. I applaud your plan.'

She's not applauding though. She's looking at me like I'm some dumb animal in a circus show, performing for her entertainment. But I have to keep calm.

I say, 'You mentioned no smoking gun. There was a reason we didn't leave overwhelming evidence against you, Lucy. This fool man of yours wanted to plant a bloodied knife and a bag of lime and bin liners for the police to find, but that would have been overkill. We couldn't leave such evidence because you would have realised it was a set-up. That would have changed things. You had to believe you had caused Tom's death. The evidence against you had to be a series of circumstantial pieces of information, which would look bad for you when taken as a whole.'

'Did that include my wedding ring? You stole it, didn't you? To make it look as if I knew I was free of Tom forever.'

I shook my head. 'No. I truly believed you'd thrown it away. If you didn't, then you have a mystery with that one. Anyway, the plan was that all those strange coincidences might make you think *Sod's Law*, but you couldn't be allowed to think *set-up*. And it didn't really matter if that evidence wasn't enough to convict you of murder.

'You see, in a wrongful death claim in civil court, the evidence required is much less. It's not a burden of proof. It's a burden of probability. All the judge would have to do is decide you *probably* killed Tom. A conviction would still cut you off from his money. So you see, the plan was perfect after all, and still can be.'

'Except you tried your hardest to make sure I was arrested and convicted of murder.'

'And you're surprised by this? You were supposed to go crying to the police that you'd accidentally knocked your hubby into the river. Instead, you tried to hide it. You didn't care about giving Tom a proper burial, or making sure his sister and father had answers. You thought only of yourself. So I decided you had to pay the price.'

'You said the plan was perfect and still can be…'

I choose my next words carefully so I can take a sideways swipe at her. 'All I have to do is suddenly reverse my opinion that you're a slimy cockroach of an excuse for a woman.'

'Ah, I understand. Suddenly the jealous, vicious, foul-mouthed sister decides to deliver a victim statement that praises me. With that and a not guilty plea, there's a chance I don't get convicted for murder. And if that happens, you take me to civil court, where there's a better chance the courts say I killed Tom. I avoid prison and we're all rich. But all of this requires that I leave here today and nobody knows that Tom is alive. It's why you've gone more than five seconds without calling me the Devil's name. You need me to say that Tom wasn't the bald man in the video.'

Touché on firing back with insults. 'When you hit Tom with the rock, you split his lip. Or you gave him a home-made tattoo on his face the night before. Or he broke his ankle. Something you can use to say you know for sure Tom isn't that man. Tom is dead, by accident.'

'There's a problem with your plan. It's already dead and you don't know it, nothing I can do will help.'

Lucy gets up and walks over to Tom, and kisses his cheek. 'Goodbye, Tom.' She tries to pick up the cat by his feet, but it skips behind Tom's legs. She gives it up. I'm still just watching as she heads for the door, loaded with disbelief. Is this real? She's about to walk out on me?

Tom and I look at each other. When he shrugs, I know it's really happening, and even if he's willing to call it a day and a life, I'm not.

When I get to the kitchen doorway, Lucy's already across the office and has the fire exit open. Beyond her, I hear the old thing creaking in the wind.

'Hey. Stop right there, you bitch,' I yell. 'You don't just get to leave. You're doing this for us whether you like it or not.'

She turns to face me and she's got that grin again. I've never hated it so much. 'Mary, Tom, there's no *this* to do. DI Reavley asked if I had another hidden phone. Then I realised why. The police have the phone Tom dropped over the fence when he ran. Tom was hiding, supposedly dead. Why would he need a phone? Who would call Tom, or be called by him? Perhaps there was a number stored in that phone. If the police trace that new number, I wonder where it will lead them.'

I might have forgiven the bitch laughing the way she did as

she stepped out of the door. I might have forgiven her telling the cops where I am.

Not both.

I crash into her out on the fire exit landing, sending her hard into the far rail just inches from the steps. The whole construction vibrates and shifts and both side handrails wrench their moorings right out of the crumbling brickwork. I feel the massive jerk forward as the thick central post tears partly from its ground plate, and then a sudden stop as it keeps a grip. The steel tower leans away from the building.

And then I hear a yell from Tom. Following behind me, he steps into thin air as the landing vanishes beneath him. He feebly grabs for the handrail, slips away from it, and tumbles. Most of this event is explained to me later, but with my own eyes I see my brother hit the short grass thirty feet below with a thud.

Lucy scrambles past me, yelling his name, and leans over the handrail. I forget Tom for a moment as all my rage and blame zeroes in on her. Again I throw myself into her. The structure vibrates with a deafening rumble.

It's not the only sound. I can hear shouts, and pounding feet, and sirens. Lucifer has brought the cops into the game after all.

'You bitch,' I yell as I throw an arm between Lucy's legs, raising her skirt all the way to her hips. I slam an arm into her upper back as I hoist, and she tumbles over the rail. But she locks both hands around the metal bar, somersaults, and her back slams into the metal landing apron. She screams. It's enchanting music.

The impact shudders the central post, causing it to tear again in the ground plate, and the entire tower topples another few feet before jerking to a halt. The landing is angled like a ramp and my feet slip. I land hard on my knees and slip into the steel balusters with a grunt of pain.

'Lucy,' I hear Tom moan from below. His worry for his bitch

wife, and not his stricken sister, drives a spike of seething hurt right through my mind.

I launch myself towards her, pushing off the balusters and clamping both sets of fingers around the handrail, right by where the bitch holds on for dear life. Frozen in place, with both hands occupied, I've got just one option. I drop my face into the back of one of her hands and sink my teeth in like the wild animal I have become.

Again, that fine melody, and away she tumbles with bloody knuckles. But, below, I see Tom leap towards where she'll crumple and break, gambling his stupid flesh to cushion her fall and earn a chance at a moment between her thighs down the line. The impact is hard, but a thud is all I hear from the bitch. Not the break of bones. Tom lays still, but she's on her back, staring up, eyes clear. And, one more time, free as a bird.

All around I see cops converging on us, yelling. That's not music.

Roaring like a stabbed bear, I grab the handrail and shake it, all my power, bolstered by mania, and damn if I'm not too strong for my own good. A shriek of metal announces the central post's divorce from its ground plate. After that, it's all about prayer as I clutch the handrail and join the tower in an irresistible hurtle towards the ground.

30

LUCY

I met with DI Reavley in the lobby of the Mercure Bowdon Hotel, Manchester. I had an hour spare before I needed to head to my destination. I had spoken to him twice in the three days since the events at the empty office where Tom hid out. The first had been in an ambulance. Tom and Mary had ridden to hospital separately, also with police escorts.

My hip was getting better, but I was still on crutches. Every blast of pain propelled my mind back to that evening, back to Tom, who had hurled himself beneath me as I fell from the fire exit. I'd landed sideways across his upper body; my legs and hip had hit the hard grass, but his chest had provided a cushion for the rest of me. I'd broken his spine, so I couldn't bear to imagine what damage I would have sustained without him.

But I was without sympathy. He'd put me in that position in the first place. I did, though, feel a modicum of gratitude. The memory of the fall and the shock of all I'd learned in that old office meant my mind had had no time to dwell on silly things like the eternity of deep space. Since that night, I hadn't been assailed by the Infinity Dream and had slept peacefully, with the help of painkillers. Knowing I didn't have a prison cell in my future helped.

I also felt no sorrow for Mary. Cat-like, she had jumped clear of the fire exit just before it crashed down, suffering only a twisted ankle upon landing. She probably wished for more. By the time I was discharged the next morning, Mary had already been through the first of many interviews at a police station. Brother and sister had been charged with a list of crimes and denied bail. Both had been interrogated by a lady called Susan Metcalfe, and that very same officer had yesterday sent me a box of chocolates and a get-well soon card.

She was the detective sergeant who had interviewed me.

When Reavley saw me struggle into the lobby, he rushed over to help. By the time we'd gotten back to the sofa, a pair of young men had taken it. The sight of his flashed police ID, rather than my crutches, got them to depart.

Now that all the furore had died down, Reavley's presence was a reminder that I hadn't thanked him for his immaculate timing that night. There had been no time for praise during the ambulance ride because I'd been too eager to learn how he and Nottinghamshire police managed to materialise in the nick of time.

Searching the commercial properties listed with Tom's estate agency had been a painstaking process. With none standing out, the police had had to start at the top of the list and work down. With no certainty Tom was alive, or that he'd even pick such a place as his hideaway, this hadn't been a priority task. By the time I'd been arrested for his killing, only four offices had been visited – reluctantly. The sighting of the 'bald man' had given the police a focal point, but unfortunately the database had listed no offices to let or buy in Nottingham.

However, just a couple of hours before Tom called me,

someone went back to the list. Somehow, this police staff hadn't known that Nottingham was a red flag; even worse, he hadn't used the computer from Tom's office, which contained the live database, but instead searched the older copy of the file found on the personal laptop seized from our home. But an error that could have spelled doom turned out to be a stroke of luck.

While going down the Microsoft Word list of addresses, he had opened the estate agency's website in order to see pictures of the properties. And then he found an anomaly, which he thankfully mentioned to a superior. No website entry for one of the establishments on the list. At some point after Tom had made the copy file, a small office at 6 Queen Lane, Kimberley, Nottingham had been removed from the live database.

In interview, Tom had admitted personally removing the entry from the live files so nobody could view the property, and that he'd told his business partner the owners had cancelled the listing. Peter had been cleared of any knowledge or involvement.

The police had already been staking the office out for half an hour when I arrived. That, Reavley had told me, had made a few of his team angry – it looked like I was in league with Tom after all. If Tom had been there, and watching, and he'd seen the police, he could have vanished again. So nobody approached me as I parked and climbed a dangerous fire exit. They watched me go in, and then they prepared for a raid. But not yet. They were waiting for confirmation of the presence of an additional accomplice.

I had been right in my assumption that Tom had been in contact with someone using the phone he had dropped when spotted out. There had been calls between it and only one other number – the phone Reavley had asked me about – and the movements of this unregistered mobile had been traced.

It was close to Cullerton on Sunday morning when he disappeared and journeyed to Kimberley in Nottingham later that day. It had also spent time in Sheffield, close to my house, hence Reavley's theory I might be the owner. But close to my house also meant close to those of the dozens, maybe hundreds of people Tom knew.

To find out who, the police had inputted the car registration numbers of all his known friends and acquaintances into the Automatic Number Plate Recognition system, to see whose vehicles had been in the red flag locations at the right times. What could have been a lengthy process was cut by some luck.

Because she hadn't had the funds to pay for petrol a few days ago, Mary's vehicle had been registered on a petrol forecourt database of offenders. That was at a Shell garage at Roadchef Tibshelf between junctions 28 and 29 of the M1 northbound on Tuesday. This had been when she came to intercept Reavley and me at Tom's estate agency and it was suspected she'd been returning from Nottingham. From seeing Tom.

Because she was on the database, she was flagged as a possible non-payer every time her car was clocked by a garage camera anywhere in Britain. And she had been clocked today, her name flashing up when detectives put her registration number in the ANPR system. In Kimberley.

But Reavley had had his suspicions about Tom's sister for a while. 'Something started to niggle me about her,' he'd told me in the ambulance three days ago. 'She gave a lengthy statement and there wasn't much about how she missed Tom. She never spoke about what Tom was like, his childhood, the fun they had together, and I would have expected that as she grasped on to positive memories. She didn't show an eagerness to know if our proof of life inquiries had found evidence that Tom was still active. In my experience people desire that snippet of promise given by knowing a bank card was used or emails were read.

'From the very outset, and all along, she never displayed the hope I see in so many. They latch on to every clue someone could be alive and are in denial of everything else, sometimes even after a body has been found and identified. For Mary, it was the opposite. Tom was dead from the get-go and any evidence to the contrary was swept under the carpet.'

I had seen this absence of hope and expectation in Mary, but had failed to read it correctly. I believed Tom was dead and had assumed Mary was equally certain of the same. I now know her behaviour was down to the concrete knowledge that her brother was alive and well.

Reavley had continued: 'Also, she was past tense every time. Sometimes she would even pause before saying *Tom was* instead of *Tom is*, as if she was taking time to think. I've never seen that. People like to use present tense because it takes away that sense of finality. Even those who firmly believe in the *was* might make a slip here and there. Not Mary. Past tense, every single time. It just reeked of... planned.'

That wasn't something I had noticed.

'Most telling for me, though,' he said, 'was when I told her my reservations that Tom had gone in the brook, because I doubted a body could have washed as far as the River Darwen. Even if she didn't wonder if this meant he might not be dead, I expected her at least to reiterate her claim that you were lying and Tom's body must have been disposed of another way, perhaps buried in the woods. But Mary had never shown a real desire to personally search for Tom, and didn't insist on the police renewing their efforts in light of our failure to find a body in the water. Instead, she tried to convince me the river was still possible'

'She already had my guilty plea,' I had said. 'Her plan had worked. The last thing she wanted was for someone to start doubting my story and cause a problem or a delay in getting me convicted.'

Now, I laid my crutch on the floor. There were two cups of

tea on his arm of the chair and he passed one. Too much sugar, but at least he'd remembered that I didn't drink coffee. Reavley hadn't been on anyone's side throughout this, I now knew. He had played Mary just as much as he had manipulated me. It still felt a little weird to experience the man behind the mask. I had to shut down paranoia that he still had doubts about my role in this bizarre series of events.

Despite the evidence against her, Mary had been maintaining a lie that she'd known nothing about Tom's plan to commit insurance fraud; based on the sighting of him in Nottingham, she had gone searching and found him, right before the police turned up. She was denying that she'd spoken to me at the office and claiming I'd arrived, found her there, and immediately engulfed her in violence.

Her version painted her as just an innocent, loving sister who'd stumbled upon a scam engineered by Tom and his evil wife. Even Tom had gone along with this, at first, and they'd had no time to confer so it must have been a prearranged story. The police were having none of it, and the day after they had concrete proof of Mary's involvement. From Tom himself.

Reavley had visited me as I was preparing to leave hospital that morning and told me that Tom, who was in a room on the same floor, had agreed to confess to everything. And he would do it on tape.

But only to me.

At first I hadn't been sure I wanted to do it, but within five minutes of agreeing, I had been sitting by Tom's bed. He tried to apologise and engage me in a conversation, but I showed him the recorder and told him to start talking. He asked if there was a chance we could rekindle our marriage after he'd left prison – he was facing six to eight years, according to a nurse who'd googled fraud sentences – but I told him to start confessing, or I would leave and he'd never see me again.

So he did. And what he said was shocking. He started with, 'Your wedding ring. Mary did steal it. She saw it on the bathroom windowsill after you'd cleaned up my blood. Mary knew it would look bad for you if it was missing, but that's not why she took it. It was to send to the Death-Row Dick.'

The morning after Mary's arrest, police had raided her father's house and seized items, including a laptop computer that had turned into a goldmine. Once the police added Tom's statement to the evidence, a clear picture of the entire plot had emerged, and Reavley had confronted Mary with what he knew. It had become apparent that her relationship with a man on death row in America was not something to joke about.

Various internet searches had been made on her laptop. House prices and street plans of various places in Madison County, Franklin County, Greene County, all part of Pennsylvania, USA. These locations surrounded State Correctional Institute Greene, a supermax prison housing roughly a hundred and sixty death-row inmates, one of them Richard Chester. She'd also researched flight prices, hotels, restaurants, and various other things that suggested she was planning a trip to see her pen-pal boyfriend. Or more.

Police also found a desk drawer with some goodies. In an envelope they found a flash drive and handwritten letters from Richard. Hundreds of them over the years. The flash drive contained Mary's letters to Richard written on Microsoft Word. At face value, nothing untoward was put to pen, but then the detectives found a notebook with most of the pages missing. Pen impressions on the top sheet suggested that Mary edited her letters on computer but wrote the final drafts by hand on scented, flower-patterned paper.

It was in the back of that notepad that they found a cryptography key, and realised they'd hit paydirt.

Mary and Richard employed a code in order to speak freely

in their correspondence. One quote by Richard mentioned that *heroin* had taken all of his *honey-money*; much later, a plea for Mary to try to get him some lovely *honey-money* wouldn't catch the eye of the prison guards who sifted through the letters, but it was obvious to Reavley's team that the death-row inmate had been asking for drugs.

Developed over years in order to slip under the radar, this code had been used to formulate a bizarre plan, with a wildly optimistic ending that would see the doting pair living together as a married couple, happily ever after.

Richard Chester was convicted of two counts of first-degree murder, possession of an instrument of crime – a large knife – criminal conspiracy, and rape. He was given two death sentences for the killings and forty years for the rape.

I was shocked. I had never researched Mary's beau, having accepted that her version of his crimes was the truth. It was far from it.

Richard broke into a house to confront a drug dealer who robbed his girlfriend, that much was true. But he didn't kill the man in self-defence. He killed him while asleep, moved into the next room in the house and stabbed to death another sleeping male. Then he raped the second man's girlfriend, right there next to the bloodied corpse.

Finally, he attempted to bury all three bodies in the back garden – one still alive – but was apprehended when police showed up with an arrest warrant for the drug dealer and saw him in the act of dragging a victim into a hole. It was clear from the letters between the would-be lovers that Mary was not confused or mesmerised by any lies from Richard. He told her none. She knew every detail of the who and the how and the why. He thought of himself as having done no more than 'take the law into my own hands' and Mary agreed, remarking that the world needed more 'superheroes like you'.

According to Tom, 'it was all about the Death-Row Dick'. Richard's appeals had been filed, fought, and rejected, and he was destined to die in prison. Then, last year, a rumour had spread that a prosecution witness at his trial had lied, prompting Richard to seek a new battle to overturn his conviction. But he was no longer entitled to assistance of counsel and would need money for a lawyer.

Tom said Mary was 'bloody crying her eyes out for him, desperate to help, but... hmm... where could she get hundreds of thousands of pounds?

'Well, she'd just turn to her slave dog, wouldn't she? Me. She started taking my money here and there, and she wasted all of it, and all her own, on sending that fool things all the way over in America. Things he could sell, like your wedding ring. And law books and stuff, or whatever he needed. A grenade up the arse is what he needs. She even wanted me to sell my business and I had to fob her off by saying Peter and I had an agreement that we couldn't sell our shares unless we both did. Told her I'd set that up to stop you hounding me for money. Sorry, babe. But it was the only way to stop Mary forcing me to sell my business just to pay for Death-Row Dick.

'And you know her ultimate plan? To move over there to be near him. Just so she can visit more easily, she reckons. But I know she's lonely, and as Dad's dementia got worse, he became more distant, less... human to her, if that makes sense. She needed someone to take his place, and Death-Row Dick was all she had. I know she's been fooled by his blabber that he'll be getting out soon. Killed two people, raped one, tried to bury all three, sure, off you go. And I saw one of the letters she wrote him. I had to post it, so I opened it. Ready for this? They're getting married. Believe that? And she'll stay faithful to him. He's locked up in Pennsylvania and there's no conjugal visits. If he does somehow pull a magic trick and get his conviction quashed, it'll take years to do all the motions and filing and whatever, but she'll wait for him. She's got nothing else.

'And if the cops can't believe she's really that obsessed, wait till they see her bedroom at Dad's house. Keeps it locked, but I picked the lock one day when she was out. Wish I bloody hadn't. It's like a shrine to Jesus or a film star, except it's that murdering bastard. I think she likes the thrill of knowing one of God's worst is hers to control. That she's the only human alive he would never hurt. Or some bullshit like that.

'And how did I fit into her plans? She wanted me over there with her. Believe that? Two of us, setting up a new life. I'd live with her until Richard got out, apparently. Call that ten thousand years. She made it sound sweet and lovely, but I wasn't fooled. She just wanted someone she knew close by, because she'd be in a strange country all alone. I knew I'd just be her little pet dog.

'I mean, she's treated me like shit all my life, even calls me a pet dog at times, and that was when I had a job and friends and could go out in the daylight. Imagine what it would be like over there, where I can't work, can't drive, can't do anything because I'm supposed to be dead. I'd do her bidding here and there, but mostly I'd stay locked away out of sight like the Man in the Iron Mask. Got rid of that spider, Tom? Okay, back in the cellar you go. I know exactly what her plan was, believe me. And I'm glad it all failed, Lucy, I really am, because I wouldn't want to be thousands of miles away from you...'

But Tom didn't know as much as he claimed. The long-term plan had had a twist he couldn't have expected. In one coded letter, Richard had said he was not happy with the danger involved in having Tom 'out there'. Richard was worried that Tom would make a mistake and unravel everything. It would only take one little misdemeanour, or one little accident, or one little anything else that got police interest in Tom.

He'd flag as an illegal alien and the police would call their UK counterparts just in case he was a fugitive. And when they discovered that instead of a cell with his name on it, there was a headstone, the entire carefully-laid plans of Mary and Richard would crumble.

So Richard came up with a new plan, which Mary happily agreed to. Happily. Of curious note regarding all the internet searches she'd made for hotels and flights and houses, etcetera – none had been for two people. Just Mary. But this didn't mean Tom was being cut out of the plan. Far from it. He was actually a major part of the changes, albeit not in a way he ever would have approved of.

In one letter, Mary had asked Richard if he had the clout, even in prison, to arrange for her 'pet dog' to be 'educated' when she arrived in America. Her pet dog, the police now knew – more from Tom's confession than any code – was the very man himself.

Mary had planned to kill her brother.

I had been shocked at learning that Mary and her boyfriend planned to kill Tom. But all of this had been three days ago. Now Mary was on remand at Peterborough prison, complaining that she got a cell for fraud and I got bailed for murder. But she was a flight risk, having already made plans to leave the country.

So why had Reavley insisted on seeing me today?

In a letter to Mary that was not so much carefully coded as rambling incoherently, Richard seemed to be talking of getting a transfer to an English prison, which could never happen. There was reference to their phone calls, where some details might have been worked out, but Reavley's team did not have access to any recordings that might exist. Even so, the police now suspected what to look for, and once-confusing data scattered throughout recent mail started to make a little more sense.

Enough so that Reavley had called SCI Greene all the way

over in Pennsylvania. There, a prison guard confirmed that Richard had been talking to inmates with knowledge of the UK. Mary's computer showed she had been looking at four women's prisons close to Sheffield. And there had been mention of 'the thing' taking place after 'the trial'.

But not Richard's new trial. Mine, for Tom's killing.

Mary had planned to have me murdered in prison.

'We could be wrong,' Reavley said when I put my head in my hands following his revelation. He started to talk about his information coming from snippets of letters and guesswork and... I ignored his attempts to make me feel better. Because I knew he was right about Mary.

I remembered a confrontation we'd had a few days ago, when we were caught at traffic lights. In response to my joke about Richard, she had said ...*when you're in prison, his contacts will bury you...* and then she'd looked shocked at her own words. At the time, I had assumed this shock was because she felt she'd overstepped a line. Now, it was clear she'd been worried that this unbidden threat, if recalled by witnesses following my murder, could condemn her.

I got up and checked my watch. Reavley rose too, and said, 'I wondered why you chose this place to meet. It's close to the airport. Flying somewhere?'

I didn't really want to give a long explanation, but felt I owed it to him. I settled for something a little cryptic and it brought a smile to my face. 'I'm off to collect a bag of jelly babies I won.'

'Nice,' he said. 'I understand.'

I wondered if he suspected my reasons for getting out of the country had nothing to do with relaxation. I was no longer a killer, and although it had been discussed there were no plans to charge me with obstruction of justice, but the cleanliness of my soul was in debate. After all, I'd *believed* I had killed Tom, hadn't I? And I had tried to cover it up with lies, caring not for the stress and pain of the police and Tom's family and friends. One tacky online newspaper called me a 'cyborg with the heart of an ice-wrapped stone', and a home with broken windows and graffitied walls proved this wasn't a lone opinion. Two weeks overseas wouldn't erase the black opinion of me that the whole country seemed to share, but hopefully some other story would be gossip by the time I returned.

Did I think such treatment was unfair? I had found it tough to perform any kind of self-analysis without agreeing with that diagnosis. You never know what you're capable of, and who you really are, until that path is laid before you.

Reavley gave the impression he wanted to say something else, and I doubted it was to ask for the strange answer to be explained. I'd gotten used to that look from him, so pushed for it.

'Lucy, I'm telling you this only because it's a sliver of... I won't call it good news. But maybe it will make you feel a little better. In one of her letters, Mary mentioned your life insurance. And something along the lines of *her dog turned his nose up at the grub*. We think that might mean–'

I cut him off: 'That the original plan was for Tom to kill me to collect money. And he refused. Perhaps it shows I still meant something to him, at least back then. But it's not good news and it's not bad. It's nothing. Maybe he gave up his own life as he knew it to save mine. Maybe he was scared of prison. One's good, one's bad, but I don't care either way. I'm in the middle. I feel nothing.'

He walked me to the exit. There, facing each other for our last-ever goodbye, I felt I needed something to say. 'What a twisted mess.' It was the only way I could think to describe this whole series of events.

'Bit of patience and perseverance was all it took,' Reavley replied, harking back to knotted cables in Tom's office. I had found mirth in that moment back in the office. I wasn't sure another smile was due my way for a long time though. I needed to be patient. I needed to persevere. Hopefully Hawaii would make a change in me.

I tried to smooth my slit right eyebrow. Reavley said, 'I hear that's a trend.'

'Not for me. I told Tom that I did it myself by accident in anger, and swore him not to tell anyone. And he didn't. He respected me for telling him a dark secret. But it was a lie. It was back in Germany...'

I paused as I felt a lump in my throat. Knowing I was broaching a difficult subject, Reavley told me I didn't have to explain. But I did. I wanted to.

'The last time my ex-husband attacked me, he tried to kill me. Because of that, I tried to kill myself and ended up in a psychiatric hospital. You know why he tried to murder me? Because a roast potato wasn't crispy. I said I didn't have my eye on it. He said I can have my eye on it now. The potato was still on the fork when he tried to stab me in the eye. You're only the second person in the world I've told that story to. I think that means I trust you, Detective Reavley.'

He leaned close and I let him. He touched one of the four almost invisible scars separating my eyebrows.

Reavley stuck out his hand and I shook it. 'I hope you get to enjoy the future, Lucy. You've had a lot of pain. But this is the next stage of your life. Things will...'

He seemed to be searching for the correct word. I knew one that fit the bill perfectly.

'Change, Aaron. Things will change.'

THE END

ACKNOWLEDGEMENTS

You, the reader, parted with your hard-earned/found/counter-feited/stolen money for this novel, and for that you get the lion's share of the thanks. I typed the words, but getting them in some kind of decent shape and into your hands was all down to the hard work of the brilliant Bloodhound Books team, especially Betsy Reavley, Fred Freeman, Ian Skewis, Tara Lyons and Heather Fitt. The only way to get readers coming back for more is to deliver a good story*, and I hope we did that.

I also want to thank some beta readers who gave up their time help: Amanda J. Finlayson, Lynda Checkley, Sally-Jo Wicket, Deanne Groocock.

There's other ways. A woman enters a library and asks, 'Have you got any books about paranoia?' The librarian says... [punchline coming soon.]

Printed in Great Britain
by Amazon